Rebel

A BALLSY BOYS PRODUCTION 1

K.M. NEUHOLD
NORA PHOENIX

Rebel (Ballsy Boys Book One)

K.M. Neuhold and Nora Phoenix

Copyright ©2018 K.M. Neuhold and Nora Phoenix

Cover design: K.M. Neuhold and Nora Phoenix

Editing: Rebecca J. Cartee at Editing by Rebecca

All rights reserved. No part of this story may be used, reproduced, or transmitted in any form by any means without the written permission of the copyright holder, except in case of brief quotations and embodied within critical reviews and articles.

This is a work of fiction. Names, characters, places, and incidents either are the products of the author's imagination or are used fictitiously. Any resemblance to actual persons, living or dead, businesses, companies, events, or locales is entirely coincidental. The use of any real company and/or product names is for literary effect only. All other trademarks and copyrights are the property of their respective owners.

This book contains sexually explicit material which is suitable only for mature readers.

PROLOGUE

Break-up artist for hire:

WHY GO through the hassle and mess of breaking up with someone when you can pay me to do it for you?

You can choose the method or just let me worry about the dirty details, and you can focus on picking your next lady or lad.

Don't stay stuck in a bad relationship a minute longer. Email me now!

$100 up-front via PayPal or Venmo. The cost might be higher if your specific request is extremely out of the ordinary.

1

TROY

My stiff muscles twitch and spasm, letting me know I slept in one spot way too long last night. Which can only mean one thing... Someone broke my rule and slept over.

I close my eyes and say a silent prayer for patience, before rolling over to figure out who the fuck I took to bed last night, and what gave him the dumbass idea he could break my rules and spend the night?

Beside me is a cute little twink I'm sure I had a blast fucking last night. And the taste of garbage tequila in my mouth lets me know why I can't remember a damn thing.

"Hey," I rasp, giving his shoulder a little shake. "Um..." *Fuck, I don't have the first clue what his name is.* "Dude, get up."

He grumbles and rubs his face. When his eyes blink open, his expression goes from sleepy and annoyed to sultry. "Good morning, stud. You want another round and then we can talk about breakfast?"

"No, man. You've gotta go."

His eyes harden and his lips pucker into a full-on bitch fit face. "*Sorry*," he spits out sarcastically.

I settle back and watch as he gets dressed in a huff and then stomps out of my apartment without a backward glance.

I'm not always so dickish, but there's an art to severing ties with someone. Not everyone needs to be dumped the same. Some need a gentle hand, others to be tricked into thinking it was their idea, and some people need to be told to fuck right off afterward.

Maybe I know too much about cutting someone out and not enough about getting anyone to stick around.

I sit up and attempt to roll the tension out of my shoulders. When that doesn't work, I reach for my laptop. While it starts up, I get comfortable beneath the cool sheets. I reach down and give my semi-hard cock a lazy stroke.

My screen comes to life, and I click immediately on my favorite site, saved to the favorites bar. Ballsy Boys, the best damn gay porn site in existence.

A little shiver goes through me as the crystal blue, virtual eyes of Rebel meet mine. I was hooked on Rebel from first sight. His broad shoulders and stubble-covered jaw got my dick hard with nothing more than a glance.

When he fucks, he gets this passionately tortured expression that drives me fucking insane. I could get caught up for hours watching his toned ass flex as he thrusts into a greedy hole. And his moans, oh, his moans are otherworldly.

My stomach jumps with excitement when I spot a newly uploaded video labeled *Rebel Tries Fleshjacking*.

Be still my beating heart.

I click on it, and Rebel's shy smile fills the screen. I've wondered if this is really the way Rebel is or if this is just a character. And if this is a character, who is he really? I know Rebel isn't his real name, but what do his friends and real-life lovers call him? Does he fuck the same off-camera as he does on, or is that an act too?

"So, tell me Rebel, have you ever used a Fleshjack before?" an off-screen voice asks as Rebel holds up the box to the camera to show off for the company that paid for the publicity.

"No, I've never had trouble finding a willing partner," Rebel banters.

"Are you excited to see how it feels?"

"Yeah, I've heard it feels better than the real thing. If that's the case, maybe I'll give up getting out of bed altogether." He winks at the camera, and my cock thickens under my unhurried playing.

Rebel answers a few more questions, but I tune out the chatter and focus on his full lips, wishing like hell I could feel them wrapped around my cock.

Maybe Ballsy Boys is hiring; that would pay for the rest of my degree. Then I'd get paid and get the chance at fucking or getting fucked by Rebel. Not a bad idea.

It's a throw-away notion. I can't see doing porn myself, and who knows how it could affect my future prospects in video game development. In many ways, these days, being a game designer is a public persona, and with all the judgment and political correctness, it's easier to avoid a misstep as epic as fucking on camera. Personally, I don't think there's anything wrong with doing porn, but unfortunately the world doesn't always see it that way.

Rebel lays back with the Fleshjack in one hand and his hardening cock in the other. I match his strokes, my eyes roaming over his body the same way I wish my tongue could. What I wouldn't give to taste every inch of his tan flesh or run my fingers through the dusting of hair on his chest and stomach.

He slicks his cock with lube, a sticky sloshing clearly audible. Then the camera pans in for a close up as he attempts to position his tip at the now slippery entrance of the toy.

My ass twitches, imaging Rebel lining up his cock to fuck me. I reach between my legs with my free hand and tease my middle finger around my fluttering hole. On screen, Rebel's broad, purplish head enters the toy with even more obscenely wet slurping sounds.

"Ooooh. Wow." Rebel gasps, his hand stilling.

The veins on his thick cock throb, and his balls are already pulled tight. My mouth waters imagining the musky taste on my tongue as I'd suck and lick his full, heavy balls.

My own cock aches, a clear sting of pre-cum rolls down along the little V where the head meets my shaft. I gather it with my thumb and rub it around the head, shuddering with restraint. I could come in seconds flat if I just fucked into my fist hard and fast. But I want to draw it out. I want it to build until I'm sure I'll go insane if I don't come.

Rebel strokes himself with the Fleshjack in a long, smooth motion. His hips twitch, and his breathing is heavy. He lets out desperate little moans that grab onto my balls and don't let go. That's what I fucking love about Rebel. You don't feel like he's hamming it up for the camera. It feels like every gasp and moan is just for you.

"Fuck, this is really good. It's so fucking tight. Holy fuck."

I can see the tremble in Rebel's muscles that lets me know he's close, so I speed up my own tugs, adding a little twist at the head.

"Oh fuck, fuck. I want to come so bad."

"Yeah, come," I encourage through the screen.

Rebel lets out a long, low moan, whips the toy off, and grips himself with his other hand. I gasp out my own impending pleasure as I put my feet flat on my bed and thrust into the tunnel of my fist.

I close my eyes and just listen to every strangled groan as Rebel is wracked by his orgasm. I imagine him kneeling over me, thick ropes of cum spurting from his cock onto my stomach, his head thrown back and his muscles taut.

The tight ring of my ass clamps down around my finger shoved inside, and heat rushes from my center and out through my cock. Every hot spurt drains the tension I'd been feeling when I woke up.

I open my eyes just a slit as aftershocks ripple through me. Rebel's expression isn't far off mine as he plays with the cooling cum on his skin and uses his eyes to flirt with the camera just a few seconds longer.

"*Thanks for cumming*," he says and then winks again before the screen goes blank.

Fuckin A', I love my Ballsy Boys.

I let out a long breath and close my laptop. Then I reach for a crumpled shirt beside the bed and use it to mop up my release. I chuck the soiled shirt in the direction of my hamper and grab a joint out of the little box beside my bed. I light it and inhale the acrid smoke into my lungs, holding it until my head starts to swim a little and my lungs and throat burn.

Somewhere in my apartment, I can hear the alarm notification on my phone chiming.

"Oh, fuck."

I'm going to be late to my morning class if I don't get my ass out the door. I take a few more hits before stubbing out my joint and placing it back in my stash box. Then I roll out of bed and throw on a pair of worn in jeans and a red henley. I run my fingers through my hair, likely making a worse mess of it, but fuck it.

I find my phone under my couch, and then I'm out the door, only a few minutes late. So basically, I'm crushing it this morning.

2

REBEL

The downstairs neighbors are at it again, so I plug my headphones in to listen to some Fall Out Boy while I'm reading a fascinating book on script writing. I swear to god, if I'm eighty years old, I do not want to be spending my life fighting with my significant other.

Fred and Grace are super nice to me, but apparently, they've gotten to the point where they can't stand each other anymore. All I hear from them is bitching and fighting, and at that age, it's not pretty.

My mood improves slightly now that I'm able to drown them out, but happy is still a ways off. The fact that Tom hasn't replied to my last text may or may not have something to do with my mood.

If you send a guy a dick pic, the least he can do is reply with a thumbs up or something. Especially if it's such a nice dick, like mine.

I've seen my fair share of cocks in my line of work, trust me, and mine compares rather favorably, if I do say so myself. It's a good eight inches, but more importantly, it's thick and perfectly curved upward. Seriously, when I'm hard, it's a fucking work of art.

It's one of the reasons why I'm in the top ten of the most popular Ballsy Boys. What can I say? Everyone loves watching me fuck. Or get fucked.

I'm vers, so it doesn't make any difference to me. I give as good as I take, and I'm especially popular for threesomes. One cock, two cocks, fucking me on both ends, all fine with me.

We get quite the number of applications from guys who think they're Ballsy Boys material, but Bear, my boss, is highly selective. People think being a porn star is awesome, but the reality is that it's damn hard work. Sure, you get paid to fuck, or get fucked, but it's a lot more than that.

You have to have chemistry with people, be easy going, sexy. You need at least some acting skills, because trust me, after you've been fucked for three hours, the last thing you want to do is look ecstatic. But it's the job, so we moan and act and come on command. Well, we try anyway. Some of us are better at it than others.

I glare at my phone. Why isn't Tom answering my text? Do I text him again? God, no, I'm not that desperate. Right?

It's not like we're dating for real.

We met a few weeks back at Bottoms Up, the local gay bar slash club. I don't do a lot of hook-ups, because I usually get enough sex on the job, but he had a great smile and a fan-fucking-tastic ass, so we had a quickie in the bathroom. We exchanged numbers, texted back and forth, had a mutually satisfying phone sex jerk-off, and hung out a few times.

He doesn't know what I do, obviously.

If men don't recognize me, I'm not telling them. It's none of their fucking business, especially since I'm not looking for anything serious anyways.

Hell, even if I wanted to, I couldn't. Not with this job. The only thing that seems to work is to find someone in the business and be willing to share.

No one wants to date a porn star, no matter how much they seem to be okay with it at first. After, like, five failed relationships, I should know.

I'm not saying they were all super serious, but all five of them broke things off with me over me doing porn. I guess technically, in three cases, I ended it, because I didn't want to give in to an ultimatum of having to stop shooting porn. I don't do well with demands like that.

But if Tom doesn't know who I am and what I do, why the fuck is he ignoring me?

I almost drop the phone when it suddenly rings. Bossman is calling.

"Hey, Bear," I say.

"I have a new kid that needs to be broken in, you up for it?"

Bear doesn't do pleasantries, which I can appreciate. He's extremely nice, but professional. "Sure. When and what were you thinking?"

"Brewer had to cancel a shoot 'cause he has the flu, so any chance you could do today? I'd already booked all the equipment and crew, and the new kid is available."

"No problem. What's the angle?"

"He's a cute little twink. He's got that whole innocent look that goes perfectly with your sultry sexiness. Go for sweet, honest attraction. Shouldn't be hard, the kid is highly fuckable. Lots of foreplay, kissing. And make him suck you, 'cause I need to know if he can deepthroat. If not, we'll need to teach him."

Sounds like a perfect shoot, getting paid to basically

make out with a cute twink. "If he needs lessons, let Brewer show him. Nobody sucks cock like him."

Bear laughed. "Fuck, yeah."

"So I'm strictly topping? Do I need to prep?"

If I know I'm bottoming, I always adapt my diet a little. Makes the prep a lot easier. Not that that would be an option on such short notice, but I would prep as best as I could, obviously.

Bear makes a noncommittal sound. "Pixie's not interested in topping, which is good, 'cause I'm a tad low on pure bottoms. Depending on how he does, I might let him rim you, but nothing more than that."

I grin. "Pixie? Who the fuck picked that name?"

"I did. I swear to god, it's the perfect name for him. Wait till you see him. He's a little imp, all boyish and cute."

"What time?"

"Would noon work?"

I hum my affirmation.

"Thanks, Rebel. I owe you one," Bear says.

"You mean the little twink wasn't your gift to me?" I joke.

Bear is still laughing as he hangs up.

My mood has radically improved. There's nothing like the idea of breaking in a cute twink to brighten my day.

∽

BEAR WASN'T LYING. Pixie, or whatever the fuck his real name is, is the cutest thing. Slender but toned body, angular face with a strong jaw, gorgeous misty eyes underneath dark eyebrows, and plump lips that will look damn perfect around my cock. Yummy.

"Hi," I say. "I'm Rebel."

I swear, a blush creeps up his rosy cheeks. Where in the world did Bear find this adorable imp?

"I know. I mean, I've seen your videos. You're... I know who you are."

This is why Bear likes to pair me up with newbies. Some of the more experienced guys can be real asses, but I have endless patience with nerves and shyness.

I wink. "Good. Which one was your favorite?"

He'll probably say the threesome with me, Brewer, and Prez, who left Ballsy Boys a few weeks back. Brewer and I have great chemistry, and Prez is this massive muscled bear who fucked the shit out of us both. My ass hurt for days after that one, but damn, it turned out great. It was the single most popular video on the site the last few months.

"The one with you and Johan."

I raise my eyebrows and shoot a quick look over my shoulder to see if Bear is listening in. The shoot with Johan was unique, because Bear wanted to do something else and went for a highly romantic angle. It was all slow, soft, lots of kissing and languid fucking. A surprising choice that gives me an indication of Pixie's preferences.

Bear nods to signal he's heard it. Good. This will help him come up with good scripts to use Pixie well.

"Bear has gone over today's script with you, right?"

He nods.

"And you prepped according to his instructions?"

More nodding. He'd better be wearing a plug, because we won't have time for prepping and stretching. And with my dick, you need prep for real.

"We'll start with the interview. Try to relax. I'll take the lead, so keep your eyes on me and simply have a conversation with me, okay?"

He bites his lip. God, the kid is nervous.

"They can edit anything out, so don't worry too much about saying something stupid. Follow my lead, and you'll be fine."

Ten minutes later, we're parked on a comfortable couch, both wearing boxer-briefs. Usually, the pre-scene interviews are done naked, but with newbies, Bear likes to start more conservatively, ease them and the viewers in. Fine with me. The kid looks totally adorable in tight, red Tommy Hilfigers.

Bear sits cross-legged on a chair across from us. He always asks a few questions, the various cameras recording multiple shots of us at the same time. He nods at me to signal we've started.

"Rebel, we've found you another newbie to break in!" Bear says with a laugh.

I smile, first at him, then at Pixie, as I let my eyes slowly roam his body. "You did right by me, Bear. He's damn cute."

Pixie blushes, lowers his eyes.

I chuckle. "Look at that adorable blush." I look straight into the camera. "Can you imagine how he'll look when he's well-fucked? His cheeks all rosy and heated, those lips puffy and swollen from kissing and sucking, his gorgeous hair all messy."

Bear laughs. "You like him, huh?"

I let my eyes trail down Pixie's body again. "Damn right, I do. Can't wait to get started."

Pixie looks at me from between those long eyelashes and sends me a hint of a smile.

"I like breaking in newbies," I say conversationally, while trailing a finger over Pixie's shoulder. He shudders. "They're so eager to please and so honest in their reactions. I mean, seriously, this one blushes... How totally fucking cute is that?"

"What are you gonna do with him?" Bear asks.

"I like to start with mapping his body. Find out what makes him shiver, what makes him moan... Is he a nipple guy who goes all weak when I play with his nipples? Or maybe he's real sensitive around his ears... I wanna suck his earlobe and find out."

Pixie shivers again, that delightful blush still staining his cheeks.

"I'm definitely gonna spend a lot of time kissing him, because, hello, have you seen those lips? They're gonna look real nice wrapped around my cock, too..."

I reckon Pixie has had enough time now to get his first question. "But maybe Pixie has some ideas of what he wants to do as well?"

I hear him take a deep breath, and then he lifts his eyes to meet mine. "I prepared well for this, you know," he says softly.

I lean a little forward. "You did?"

"I watched every video of you at least twice. All in the name of research, of course."

He's got a sense of humor. Thank fuck. "Mmm, I can appreciate that. What did you learn about me?"

He lifts his arm, lets his hand land on my biceps. His touch is soft, almost sweet. "Everyone always raves about your cock."

I grin. "I've been told it's one of my best assets."

His lips curve into a sexy smile. "Oh, it's damn near perfect, don't get me wrong, but personally, I'm partial to your hands."

"My hands?" My surprise isn't faked. I have no idea where he's going with this.

He lets his hand journey down my arm, then reaches for my hand and raises it. "You have beautiful hands. Long.

Graceful. I can't wait to feel them on me, to watch you touch me."

Hot damn, the kid's got game with words. Serious game.

I don't have to look at Bear for permission. He lets us do whatever the fuck we want, as long as we stick to the general script.

"Come here, you little imp. Let's see if reality matches your dreams."

He lets himself be maneuvered on my lap, his back against my chest, his butt pressing against my dick. Mmm, I like.

He leans his head back against my shoulder, reaches backward with his hands to curl them around my head. His neck and back arch in a way that makes my cock pay attention. He's gonna look so damn sexy when I fuck him.

I splay both my hands on his chest, covering his nipples. "Look at my hands, sexy. I think they look good on you, don't you?"

I rub his nipples with my thumbs, and he lets out the cutest little moan. My tongue comes out to play, licking his neck, then his ear. A little nibble on his ear lobe drags another moan from those perfect lips.

"Where exactly did you picture my hands, when you imagined us playing?"

"Everywhere. God, I want you to touch me everywhere."

There's an eagerness in his voice that feels real. Interesting. Either he's got a case of hero worship going on, which has happened before, or he really loves to be fucked. I can work with both. But before we move things along, we need a bit more conversation.

"Now that I've got you exactly where I wanted—though we're both still a little overdressed for the occasion—I'm dying to know what makes a cute thing like you tick. What are you into, Pixie-boy?"

Pixie subtly twists his bubble butt into my cock and turns his head sideways to look at me. "I love sex. I swear to god, I love everything about it. My parents honestly couldn't care less about me, so I've been on my own for a long time. I was a virgin, had never even kissed a boy till my senior year of high school. That changed after my first hook-up. This big, furry papa bear fucked me, and I was hooked. Figured if I liked being fucked so much, I might as well make a career out of it."

It doesn't happen to me often that I'm speechless, but I did not see that one coming. Pixie transformed from shy and innocent into a sultry little sex-beast right before my eyes. He's sending me a come-hither look that sorely tempts me to drag his boxers down and fuck him without any foreplay.

From the corner of my eye, I catch Bear subtly rearranging himself. Good to know I'm not the only one who's being turned on here. Shit, breaking Pixie in is going to be way more fun than I imagined.

We banter for a few more minutes, then seamlessly transition into kissing. The little shit kisses like he's getting graded for it. We rub and grind into each other, my cock happily leaking pre-cum.

My hand dips inside Pixie's underwear, and I squeeze that perfect bubble butt. Hot damn, his skin is so soft and his cheeks so plump. Can't wait to bury my cock inside him.

As I dip into his crack, my fingers touch the slightly flared end of a butt plug sticking out of his hole, and I sigh inwardly with relief. Thank fuck for newbies who can follow instructions.

"Cut," Bear announces.

I break off the kiss and slap Pixie on his butt. "You're doing good, baby boy."

I get up off the couch and stretch my limbs a little while Pixie awkwardly climbs to his feet as well.

Bear steps close. "How are you holding up, Pixie?"

The confident, sexy twink disappears, and he blushes again. Sure, it takes some getting used to being naked on set —in our case, almost naked since we're still wearing underwear—especially when everyone else but your partner is dressed.

Bear is wearing his usual ripped jeans and tight shirt. The guy is a bona fide silver fox, his long black hair interspersed with silver streaks, pulled back into a ponytail. I can only pray to whatever god is listening that I'll have a body like that when I'm forty, because holy fuck, the guy is hot. Not my type at all, but fucking sexy nevertheless.

"I'm good... Yeah, it's good. Rebel's...nice," Pixie stammers.

"Nice? What a fucking blow to his ego," Bear says, slapping me on my ass.

"Hey," I protest. "Hands off the merchandise, boss. Or I'll sue you for sexual harassment."

Joey, the first cameraman, laughs. "You and that dick of yours are a sexual harassment in itself. Fuckin' hell, Rebel, you're giving us all an inferiority complex here."

I flip him the bird and turn to Pixie. "Time for the next phase. We're gonna start in the same position we were in, but then we're gonna move into you sucking me off, okay? Take it slow, no rush. The goal isn't to get me off, but to make it look sexy. Try to make sounds, because viewers love to hear us, but don't get too over-the-top moany."

"Says the guy whose nickname is the Moaner," Joey says.

"Dude, my moans are a form of art. People have made

my moans into a ringtone. You wish you were that good at moaning...or at fucking, for that matter."

It's Joey's turn to flip me off, and I smile. The atmosphere on set is always relaxed, which is another reason why I love what I do.

"If I'm getting too close, I'll tap you out," I tell Pixie. "That's your signal to slow down, okay? Anytime you wanna transition into rimming me, that's fine. Joey will be really close with the camera to get a good close up shot, but don't look into the camera. Focus on what you're doing or on my eyes."

Pixie looks at me with a serious expression, nods.

"Time to lose the plug," I say gently.

"Where...?" He must realize the stupidity of that question at the same time he asks it, because he blushes again. God, I hope he never loses that innocence, because it's fucking endearing.

"Lie down. I'll do it," I say.

I don't make a big fuss out of it, and everyone pretends to look elsewhere, so seconds later, the butt plug plops free. I dispose of it quickly and wipe my hands on a towel. We always have plenty of those laying around.

Pixie pulls his boxers back up, which is good because we'll need that for scene continuity. I lay back on the couch, pull Pixie on top of me, and start kissing him again. It's interesting how he completely relaxes as soon as we get going again. I'm pretty sure he doesn't even notice the camera that's right in our faces.

I make quick work of both our boxers. Ah, that's so much better with my cock rubbing against his soft skin without anything between us.

After about a minute of wet kissing, and me teasing his hole with my finger, he raises those misty eyes at me and says in a hoarse voice, "Can I please suck you off? I've been dreaming about having your cock in my mouth..."

I don't think I've ever been asked so nicely, and I happily give permission.

Note to Bear: the kid can deepthroat and does not need lessons. At all. He's got my blood pumping within minutes, and I have serious skills when it comes to denying myself an orgasm.

The most amazing thing is that he's so happy doing it, like he's seriously over the moon at being allowed to suck cock. Where the fuck do I find me someone like that?

Another note to Bear: the little imp can rim like a pro, too. He digs in like my ass is a buffet, and he hasn't eaten in weeks. Can we, like, clone him or something?

Bear calls for a break again, and after some stern admonishments to Pixie to please signal when he's about to come, we move on to the fucking part of the scene. Bear and I have a quick discussion, but decide against me sucking him off.

Pixie looks like he's not far from blowing, and he doesn't have any experience with edging yet. If I give him a blowjob, he's bound to blow his wad. Fucking it is. It's not like I mind burying my cock into that delicious bubble butt.

He's prepped well, thank fuck, and I sink home in a few careful thrusts. His eager little moans and squirms are a total turn on.

I know there's an ongoing betting pool who can hold out the longest while fucking. Tank currently holds the record at almost three hours, and I've been hell-bent on breaking it —but it won't happen today. Not with this minx who takes my cock like it's nothing.

I last an hour and a half, with Bear getting pretty much

all the positions he'd asked me to do. Pixie is hella flexible and happily lets me fuck him into a whimpering mess.

He comes after fifteen minutes of fucking, but he remembered to signal he was about to blow, so they'll edit that one out. His second orgasm sneaks up on him right after I come all over his abdomen and chest. Joey was close with the camera anyway, so he caught it. Thank fuck for that.

All in all, it's been a pretty good shoot, and Bear looks happy. He throws me a towel when I get up, so I can wipe myself off. "Nice job, Rebel. You had great chemistry."

I nod. "He's good. Eager."

Pixie shyly steps closer, patting his face with a towel. "You did good, little imp," I tell him.

His face breaks open into a big smile. "Thank you."

"Who do you think would be a good fit for him?" Bear asks me. "I was thinking Campy?"

I nod. "Yeah. Brewer would work, too. Not Tank. That guy can fuck for hours, and our boy here doesn't have the stamina for that just yet."

Bear grins. "I agree. Tank is not for beginners."

I hit the showers with a quiet Pixie beside me and get dressed quickly after. When I check my phone, there's a new text message. It seems Tom has deemed me worthy of another date.

Hoo-fucking-ray.

3

TROY

My morning classes passed slowly. I knew studying video game design was going to be a lot of technical classes about coding and computer science, and I'm all for that. But some of the professors could really work on their monotone delivery.

My calendar on my phone reminds me that I've got an appointment with my advisor in twenty minutes, which is more than enough time to hoof it over to the faculty office building. On my way, I make a quick pit stop at Randall Hall dorms to break up with some poor sap named Greg whose boyfriend is sick of him. What can I say? It's a cool hundred bucks, and I'm really good at dumping people. I'm marketing my skillset.

"Troy Kline?" I'm greeted when I enter my advisor's office only five minutes past our scheduled meeting time.

"Yeah, that's me." The pleasant buzz of an orgasm and half a joint have long since worn off, leaving me uneasy about the reason why this meeting was requested.

"Troy, glad you were able to stop by to chat this afternoon. I noticed you haven't paid off the balance for this semester yet, and I wanted to see if you needed financial aid information?"

My gut twists, and I sink down in the chair opposite my adviser, Mary.

"I told you, I don't like the idea of ending school with a huge debt. How long do I have to pay the balance for this semester?"

"It's due April seventeenth. If you don't pay by then, you'll be dropped from your classes."

"I'll figure it out," I assure her.

I've always found a way to pay each semester, one way or another. Last semester is when the idea of posting the ad to break-up with people for money came to me. And that got me through. I'm sure I'll find a way to pay this semester, too.

"If you change your mind, I'll be happy to go over options for loans with you."

"Thanks."

I fling my backpack over my shoulder and exit the office without a backward glance.

What the fuck am I going to do?

I have a few grand in my account from my side gig, but I was counting on that for living expenses. I'm going to have to pray a lot of people need someone to do the dirty work of dumping someone for them this semester if I'm going to squeak by.

I slump down beside a gnarled tree on the quad and bury my face in my hands.

"I've gotta dump this chick, but I hate the drama, you know?" some dude says from off to my left. "I know there'll be water works and questions about *why* things aren't working. It's my hell."

I laugh to myself and shake my head. Breaking up is easy; it's keeping someone around that's the trick. I couldn't keep my parents from ditching me, couldn't find a foster family to keep me, and by the time I figured out what my dick was for, there wasn't a chance in hell I was giving any man the chance to leave me.

"It'd be cool if you could pay someone to break up with her for you," the dude's friend jokes and they both laugh.

I shove to my feet and run my hands through my unruly hair again before spinning to face the men with my best friendly smile.

"Excuse me, but it sounds like you have a problem I can help with."

The two men share a confused look.

"We're not trying to buy drugs," one of them says, looking me up and down.

I'm not a drug dealer, fuck you very much. I bite back that retort and force myself to chuckle like I appreciate the humor of the misunderstanding. Sure, I'm a little rough around the edges with my messy hair and constant stubble. My jeans have holes and combat boots are a staple in my wardrobe. I don't look like anyone's idea of high class, but I don't sell drugs... I do them on occasion, but I don't sell them.

"No, I offer a...service. I'll let your girl down gently for the low price of a hundred bucks. The break-up is taken care of for you without the hassle."

"No shit?"

"No shit," I confirm. "Just give me her name, a picture would be good, and where I can find her. If there's anything specific you want me to say I can do that, but otherwise I can just feel out the situation once I'm there."

"Yeah, hell yeah." The guy smiles and reaches for his cell phone. "I can Venmo you the money, right?"

"Of course," I agree and give him my information.

I breathe a small sigh of relief. I'll work the money issue out; I always do. Most importantly, I need to keep my eye on the prize.

Being bounced from foster home to foster home, the one constant was that they were all more than happy to toss me a video game console and encourage me to stay out of their way. I came to love the increasing complexity of games over time. I loved solving the puzzles in *Resident Evil*, I was intrigued with the deep storyline in *The Last of Us*, and I even appreciated the artistry of *Journey*.

And by the time I was sixteen, I knew without a shadow of a doubt that I wanted to create games. I wanted to learn all the behind the scenes drama, the blood, sweat, and tears that created the world I wanted to wrap myself in. There's no way in hell I'm going to let a few thousand bucks stand between me and my dream.

I saunter across campus, basking in the buzz of energy that always accompanies the beginning of a semester. Everyone is still fired up and sure this is going to be their best year yet. They excitedly grab their friends and discuss future plans for weekend parties and student jobs that will change their life.

A small tinge of jealousy hits me in the chest. I have plenty of enthusiasm for my future, parties and otherwise, but what I don't have is friends to share it with.

I have a good reason for keeping people at a distance, and the fact that I'm so self-aware must mean I'm emotionally healthy, right? But that doesn't stop me from being lonely from time to time. Don't get me wrong, there are people I chill with from time to time, but no one I'd call to bail me out of jail.

I shake off my melancholy as I bound up the steps to my Ancient History lecture.

When I get back to my apartment after my afternoon classes, I find five responses to my Reddit post. *Cha-Ching.* Four of the replies request standard "Don't hurt him/her, just let them know it's over between us", and I message each back for details and to let them know where to send their payments. But the fifth message catches my attention.

Tom: I need you to dump this guy I've been seeing, and I need it to be humiliating. There's a song and dance and a costume that I'll pay you an extra hundred bucks for. But I need this guy to feel like an idiot.

Sounds to me like I'm the one who's going to feel like an idiot. But for two hundred bucks, I'll be the biggest idiot in the world.

Troy: Done. Just need a name and address and you'll need to send me the $200 up front.

4

TROY

I grumble to myself as I pull on a fucking banana suit. When Tom explained to me exactly what he wanted, I told him it would be three hundred instead of two, thinking he'd change his mind. But he was happy to fork it over, and now I'm dressed as a banana, getting ready to show up at some dude's place to tell him he's dumped. You'd think there'd be an easier way to make money. Unfortunately, a minimum wage student job isn't going to cut it.

I check the address Tom sent me, and I head out to break some poor schmuck's heart. I earn a number of strange looks as I walk the few blocks in my banana suit.

When I reach the correct apartment building, I'm lucky enough to catch someone on their way out so I don't have to buzz to get in. I make my way up to the third floor and find the apartment number Tom gave me. I take a deep breath, steeling myself for what an ass I'm about to make of myself, and then I raise my hand to knock. Seconds later, the door swings open, and I suck in a surprised breath.

My stomach swoops, and my cock immediately starts to plump as I find myself looking into the unmistakable baby blues of none other than Ballsy Boy Rebel. Fuck, he's even sexier in person.

His mane of sandy hair is wild and begging to be used as a handle for cock sucking. His pouty lips are tempting and bitable. And fuck me, his broad shoulders and well-toned arms are sorely lacking passionate claw marks. I can't say I'd noticed his hands before, but after the latest video with the new twink, I can't help but latch onto his long, slender fingers that Pixie waxed poetic about.

A lazy, flirty smile spreads over my lips before my brain kicks in and reminds me that I'm in a goddamn banana suit.

Fuck my life.

"Uh, can I help you?" Rebel asks, his forehead creased in confusion.

"This is fucking embarrassing," I lament, glancing down at the bright yellow costume I'm wearing. "Here's the thing, Tom sent me here to break up with you. There's this dumb song and dance that makes the costume a lot more relevant. But holy shit, you're Rebel, and who the hell dumps a porn star?"

Rebel's face falls. "What an asshole," he mutters to himself. "Thanks for letting me know."

He starts to close the door, but on impulse, my hand flies out to stop it. "Rebel, I'm really sorry. Were you together a long time?" *Why the fuck am I even asking that?*

"No, I hardly knew the guy. Which is why the theatrics seem particularly dickish."

I nod as if I understand what he's going through, when in reality, the only thing my brain can seem to grasp on to is the fact that I'm standing within touching distance of Rebel. It's not every day that an opportunity like this falls right into a person's lap, and there's no way I can let this pass without at least *trying* to fulfill one of my ultimate fantasies. Worst case scenario: he turns me down. But, *best case scenario...* Hell yeah, I'm going for it.

"Yeah," I agree. "You know, if you really wanted to stick it to him I could suck you off."

A slow smile spreads across those tempting lips, and his gaze flits over my costume again with amusement. In two point five seconds, he went from vulnerable guy to porn star Rebel.

"And how exactly would a blowjob from a banana stick it to Tom?"

"Dude, it's a blowjob. Work with me here," I press, my voice dropping low and flirty as I send a prayer to the god of perfect porn star cocks to let me have a taste.

"Sure, why the fuck not?"

Holy fuck, yes!

I can't believe my luck as I step into my favorite porn star's home...still dressed as a mother fucking banana.

"I'm going to lose the banana suit if that's okay?"

Rebel snorts a laugh and then shakes his head like he can't believe what's happening right now either.

"As much as I was looking forward to fucking around with a banana, you're welcome to lose the costume if you prefer."

"Thanks."

I don't waste any time tearing the costume off and leaving it in a pile by his front door. Rebel's eyes roam over me with an appreciative gleam as I stand in front of him in nothing but a thin white undershirt and a pair of black boxer briefs, already tenting in the front with my arousal.

He licks his lips and smirks when our eyes meet again. "I didn't think it was possible, but you're actually cuter out of the banana suit."

"Shut the fuck up and whip out that legendary cock."

Rebel's eyebrows raise, but he doesn't argue as he reaches for the zipper on his jeans and slowly tugs it down. The sound of the metal teeth unlocking to give me access to the very cock I've jerked off a hundred times imagining sends a shiver down my spine. Rebel reaches into the confines of his jeans, and his erection bobs free.

"Fucking hell," I murmur as I drop to my knees to worship at the altar of the god of perfect porn cocks, who hath bestowed upon me this bounty. Now that I'm up close and personal, I grant myself a few seconds to just admire. It's rare to see a cock as perfect as this. I've seen all kinds of cocks: fat, skinny, red, purplish, curved to the left, cut, uncut... You name it, and I've probably had it in my mouth. I yank Rebel's jeans and underwear down around his ankles and take a second to appreciate the view.

Rebel's cock is heavy in my hand, girthy, and flushed reddish pink. He's cut with a rough circumcision scar just below the head. He has pronounced, throbbing veins that I want to memorize with my tongue. And his balls, fuck, they're even better in person than on screen. Some balls hang too low and flop around when you fuck, but not Rebel's. He has heavy balls, resting high and proud.

It's kind of a trippy thought to realize for the first time I'm in the presence of a man who's probably been with more people than I have. It definitely makes me want to pull out all the stops to impress him.

"You're clean and shit, right?"

"Of course," Rebel says, looking down at me with fire in his eyes.

"Thank god, I hate having to suck on rubber."

My mouth waters as I flick my tongue out for my first

taste of Rebel's salty, warm skin. Rebel lets out a quiet gasp that sets my blood boiling.

I wrap my fist around the base of his cock and bounce it a few times against my tongue until I taste a burst of tangy pre-cum and draw another heavy breath from Rebel's lungs. I wrap my lips around the broad head and tongue the slit as I suck.

"You're a tease."

I release the head with a popping noise and grin up at Rebel. "Not a tease, just getting warmed up. I figure you've been sucked off by the best; I need to make a good showing here."

"Not really a wrong way to suck cock," Rebel assures me.

"But there's undoubtedly a right way," I quip before tightening my grip and giving him a long, firm stroke. "By the way, I don't mind it rough, so feel free to grab my hair, fuck my mouth, whatever moves you."

And then I open wide and wrap my lips around the steel rod of a cock that's beckoning me.

Fuck, he's big.

My lips are stretched tight around his weighty girth, his cock heavy on my tongue. I can only imagine how good it would feel pounding my ass. I suck in a lung full of oxygen through my nose, not sure when I'll have the chance for another full breath, and then I grab Rebel by the hips and pull him all the way into the back of my throat.

"So good," Rebel grunts, and his fingers tangle in my hair, holding me still with his cock buried down my throat.

When his grip eases a fraction, I'm able to pull back and suck in another lung full of air before taking him deep again. My hands begin to roam over the vast expanse of Rebel's smooth and tempting skin as his fist in my hair guides the speed of my mouth taking him deep over and over. My eyes water, and my jaw aches, and I love every fucking second of it.

Rebel spreads his legs as I trail one hand up the inside of his thigh and between his legs. I palm his full balls, rolling and tugging them.

"Christ, that's good," Rebel gasps.

I'd grin in satisfaction, but my mouth is pretty full so I moan in appreciation instead.

Everything about sucking Rebel's cock is better than I ever imagined. I want to spend the rest of my life with it rammed down my throat. I don't need to eat or drink or fucking breathe—I just need to choke on Rebel's cock.

His grip on my hair tightens, and his hips start to flex, fucking my throat in long, fast thrusts. My cock jerks and throbs in the confines of my boxer briefs, my balls already tight and aching for relief.

Another salty burst hits my tongue. I slide the hand that's on his balls back and tease the rim of his hole with my middle finger.

"Fuck yeah, finger my ass."

Without hesitation, I push my finger inside. Rebel roars out a moan, and his whole body stills before his cock begins to pulse against my tongue, and my mouth floods with his thick, salty cum. I suck down every drop he gives me, and then I lick his cock clean, not wanting to waste a drop.

"So, how'd I measure up?" I ask eagerly.

Rebel sags against the wall and chuckles. "Are you looking for a points breakdown?" he teases.

"Fuck yeah, I feel like I just competed in the blowjob Olympics. I need to hear the judges' comments."

"Excellent technique, some of the best deepthroating I've ever had, and an impressive dismount. A solid nine point eight."

"Nine point eight?" I repeat with indignation.

"Always have to leave room for improvement," Rebel explains with a wink. "Now, do you want me to suck you?"

"Actually, ever since that video with the new twink, I've been dying to know what your hands feel like," I admit.

"A handjob it is," Rebel agrees, kicking his jeans away and stepping forward. He pulls down my underwear without further need for conversation.

I should fuck around with porn stars more often. They know how to get right down to business.

"You have a nice cock, too," Rebel comments as he wraps his hand around the base of my cock in a firm grip.

Blowing him got me worked up enough that this won't take long. I clutch the front of Rebel's shirt as he sucks and licks my neck, his hand tugging with slow purpose. On each upward stroke, he adds a twist at the end, making me gasp and pant.

I cant my hips, my head falling back on a raspy moan. Rebel jerks me harder, reading all my non-verbal cues. Fuck, he's good.

My skin heats, and my balls draw up tight as I gasp out some incoherent mixture of prayers and curses, my seed spilling over Rebel's fist. I sag against him as my legs turn to Jell-O and my brain to mush.

Holy hot damn, I think I'm spoiled for regular men.

5

REBEL

He's cute. Strike that. He's gorgeous. Absolutely fucking gorgeous. His eyes stand out the most—he's got this intense look in a pair of golden eyes that drill into you, like he's seeing much more than what you're showing him.

His hair was sort of styled when he arrived, but after I held his head while fucking his mouth, he's got the whole just-out-of-bed look going, and it fits him like a too-small condom on a ten-inch cock.

I wipe my hand off on my shirt, then pull it over my head to throw it on the floor. I'll put it in the hamper later. It's not like banana boy here has never seen me naked.

And fuck, I just now realize I don't even know his name. Holy mother of all awkwardness. Dammit, I fuck guys for a living. I'm way cooler than this.

"Were you planning on telling me your name anytime soon or would you prefer me to call you banana boy?"

He grins. "Troy. My name is Troy. Nice to meet you...Hendrix."

Oh, god, I forgot. Tom gave him my real name, which

few people have. Dammit. Living under an alias is a lot harder than it seems.

"Yeah, well, would you mind calling me Rebel? I try to keep my personal name, you know, personal, and since you already know what I do for a living…"

He shrugs. "Sure. I probably would have anyway, since that's how I think of you."

"You think of me that often, do you?"

This guy does not blush. Instead, he sends me a cocky grin. "Let's just say I've seen all your videos more than once."

When I started in this business, I would get weirded out when people would say shit like that. Because when people say they've seen all my videos, they mean they've jacked off or masturbated—I have a lot of female fans as well—while watching me. That was a little unnerving at first, to be honest.

Now, I'm used to it. Men and women come up to me all the time to tell me they love me, and I appreciate it from all genders, equal opportunity guy that I am.

Troy stretches and his shirt rides up to gift me a peek at his stomach. Nope, haven't had my fill yet of this guy.

As if he can read my mind, Troy says, "You wanna hang out for a bit? I've got some great weed."

"Sure, why the hell not."

Weed is not something I allow myself to enjoy often. Drugs don't mix well with this business. You gotta keep your body in great shape and your head clear and in the game. But I've got nothing else planned for today, and despite the fabulous blowjob I just received, I'm still pissed at Tom.

I cannot believe that motherfucker dumped me like that. Sending someone in a banana costume. Fucking asshole. I have no doubt he discovered what I do, because that's the only reason I can come up with for him wanting to humiliate me like this. But fucking hell, what a dick move on his part. Can I pick 'em or what?

I guess that puts the score at six ex-boyfriends, though in my mind Tom hadn't made it to boyfriend status yet. Shit, he dumped me before we even got there—and fucking paid someone to do it for him. A little pick me up sounds damn good right about now.

"Do you think we could move it farther inside than the hallway?" Troy asks.

I laugh. "You want to move...inside?"

He doesn't miss a beat. "Say the word, man, and I'll be inside in a jiffy."

"In a jiffy? Fuck, I hope you last longer than that. Besides, who says you'll ever get a go at this fabulous ass?"

He pretends to be confused. "I thought we were talking about your living room?"

"Sure we were. Come on in." I make my way to my living room, which looks kinda messy, but not like a total pig sty. "You want something to drink?"

"You got any soda? Alcohol and weed don't mix well for me."

"Coke or Sprite?"

"Coke. Thanks."

I grab us both a Coke from the fridge, while he makes himself comfortable on my Ikea couch. I love Ikea. Aside from the fact it's highly affordable, their couches have washable covers. You wanna know how handy that is after a quickie?

I bring a small glass jar as well to use for our cigarettes. When I walk in, Troy is busy making two nice, fat joints. I set our drinks on the coffee table—also sponsored by Ikea, thank you very much—and plop down on the couch next to Troy.

Wordlessly, we light up, and I sigh with pleasure as the first buzz hits. Mmm, perfect. A hot guy and a thick joint.

"So, what do you do?" I ask after a minute or two.

Troy snorts. "I'm smoking a joint and hanging out with Rebel from Ballsy Boys."

Maybe it's the weed, but I find that extremely funny, and a not exactly attractive giggle escapes from my lips. "No, you shithead, what do you do? In life, I mean. Or for a living. Whatever. In general."

"Jesus, you're articulate when you're high."

"Don't forget dumped. I'm high, sexually satisfied after that amazing blowjob you gave me, but still dumped."

"Come on, don't tell me you're seriously regretting that fuck who broke up with you. Who the hell breaks up with Rebel?"

I sigh, suddenly less happy. "My guess is he found out about my job. They all do, you know, and it's always an issue."

"I don't care," Troy says with nonchalant confidence.

"Can I be rude and point out that you're not my boyfriend? Slightly different perspective."

Troy shrugs. "Hypothetically speaking, if I were your boyfriend, I still wouldn't care."

I raise my eyebrows. "You'd be okay with your boyfriend fucking other men?"

"Why the fuck not? First of all, it's your job, right? It's not like you're cheating. You're doing what you get paid to do, same as everyone else, only more fun. Second, people need to lighten the fuck up with the whole boyfriend thing. It's not like dating means you're getting married and having babies. Whatever happened to hanging out and simply having fun together without all that pressure of ever after?"

I take another deep drag of my joint. "Exactly. That whole thing with dickhead Tom was supposed to be that: fun. We met at Bottoms Up, for fuck's sake. No one meets their happy ever after guy at Bottoms Up. All I wanted was to hang out, have some fun, share the occasional fuck. But noooo, he had to go all angsty on me and break up using a guy in a banana costume! No offense."

"None taken. It was a dick move."

I let out a distinctly unmanly giggle. "Dick... That's so funny, because his dick was really unimpressive."

Troy smiles. "Small?" he guesses.

"Normal, but a tad crooked...and his technique sucked. Having the equipment is one thing, but knowing how to use it is way more important."

Troy laughs. "Could it be that you're just a little spoiled? You do this for a living, you know. It's like comparing a serious gamer to a mobile gamer."

I shrug. "Maybe, but I've fucked newbies that were way better than him. Damn, I'd ten times rather fuck a Fleshjack...or a banana boy."

Thinking about fucking makes me hard again, or maybe it's the weed? I sigh with contentment and let myself fall sideways with my head on Troy's shoulder.

"I like you, Troy," I say. "You give great head."

"Fuck, you're a lightweight, dude. One joint and you get all cuddly and shit on me. Well, at least you're a happy druggie."

I look at him from underneath my eyelashes. "Happy and horny. Wanna give me another blowjob?"

6

REBEL

I do a quick look around the studio to make sure everything is set up correctly. Bear hired a new assistant, and while the kid scores high on the cute factor, he hasn't fully mastered all the details of his job yet. Especially with a more complicated shoot like today, details matter.

Like the fact that this is supposed to be a bedroom, and yet there's an office calendar on the wall. I walk over to take it off the wall and shove it under the king size bed, where the cameras won't pick it up.

"Good catch," Joey comments.

"Yeah, but we need something else there to avoid looking at an empty nail. Lemme check in the props room. And don't let Campy jump on the bed, for fuck's sake, 'cause he's gonna mess it up, and it looks perfect now."

"I'm gonna fuck up what?" Campy asks, walking in dressed in a dark blue pinstripe suit. My mouth drops open slightly. He's this tanned, cute-as-fuck guy with puppy eyes who's usually dressed in ripped jeans and shirt, but this makes him actually look...adult.

I whistle between my teeth. "Looking sharp, man. Turn around."

Campy grins, twirls easily.

"Nice. You look almost respectable."

"Almost, huh?"

"There's still the fact that you look like you just got fucked," Joey quips. I swear, for a straight guy, he can make damn witty jokes.

Campy flips him the bird, then turns to face me again. "Do you think this tie goes with the suit?" he points toward a baby blue tie with a pattern of white and dark blue diagonal stripes.

I frown. "How the fuck would I know? I've never worn a suit in my life, man. What's the alternative?"

Campy digs into the pocket of his suit jacket and comes out with a soft pink tie. He holds it up next to the other one. "I like the pink one better, actually," I say, squinting to see it better. "It contrasts more."

"See? That's why I ask you shit like this. You have an eye for this stuff, man."

I shrug. I'm not so sure I agree with him, but I have to admit I love hanging out in the studio during a shoot. Bear asked me to coach another newbie in his first major shoot, an inked up bad ass who calls himself Heart. He's done an intro shoot with me and another low-key one with Brewer, but this is a big one. Bear is directing, so he asked me to coach Heart specifically.

Speaking of the bad boy, here he is now. Heart's wearing jeans that ride so low you can see most of his bright blue boxers and that will drop right to his ankles if he so much as sneezes. He's got a white T-shirt that he's got draped around his neck like a scarf. His ears are decorated with loud bling and an expensive pair of sunglasses is shoved back in his dark hair.

Heart's, like, seriously the coolest guy I've ever met in terms of style, but right now he looks like a fucking gangsta. Which is exactly the idea, considering the script.

He shoots me a lazy grin. "What up, Rebel?"

We do an intricate hand-shake-slap thing that only he could pull off without looking like a total moron. "You ready, sexy?"

Heart is sex on a stick. I mean, all of us Ballsy Boys have something, I suppose. As Joey pointed out, Campy always looks like he has just been thoroughly fucked. Tank has this intense, dark vibe that makes every bottom in a fifty-mile radius want to bend over and take whatever he's dishing out. Brewer is a total fuckboy who clearly loves having sex. Pixie is new, but holy hell, that kid is up for anything. Me, I guess I do have this sultry vibe Bear's always waxing about.

But Heart, he's in a class by himself. He's pure sex, every pore of him radiating something that draws you in. Everyone, and I mean literally everyone, wants to either fuck him, get fucked by him, or watch him fuck. He's vers, like me, and I have to say I utterly, absolutely loved fucking the shit out of him and then getting back everything I'd served him.

"Good, you're here," Bear says, walking up to us. "Nice suit, Campy. Perfect. You, too, Heart. I dig the vibe. I need you to practice your lines with Rebel while we shoot the first scene with Campy, okay? Make sure you know them well."

Heart nods, all serious now.

"Come on, let's go to the locker room to practice," I say.

Heart follows me, holding a crumpled copy of what I assume is the script in his hand. "You nervous?" I ask.

"Yeah. Kinda. It's a big shoot."

I turn around once we've reached the locker room and

gesture at him to sit down on one of the benches. "No, it's not. It's five minutes of talking, and then you move on to the fucking. You know that part."

He grins as he lowers himself. "I think I got that covered."

"Tell me the story in your own words."

He takes a deep breath. "I'm a punk who got caught vandalizing an expensive car. The rich owner wants to call the cops on me, but I've been busted twice before, so it would be my third strike. I'm desperate to stay out of prison, so I offer him anything to not call the cops on me. He decides to let me pay in sex."

I nod. He's got a good grasp on the core of the scene. "Campy's our best actor. Don't let the laid-back vibe mislead you. He will be a different person, so be ready for that. Your job is to be bratty, mouthy, yet desperate. Campy, Jeremy in the script, has all the power, so keep that in mind. This is not a tender scene, no reciprocity. You're gonna get fucked hard and long in every hole."

There's a reason I'm blunt as can be. Heart's new, so he needs to know what's gonna happen. And I need to make sure he can take whatever Campy will dish out. Having your mouth fucked hard is not for everyone, but when Heart sucked me off, I noticed he didn't have much of a gag reflex, so that'll help.

"I'm good with the script, man," Heart says, taking away my worry over him.

We keep running lines until Bear walks in to signal he's ready for the next scene. They shoot it in two takes with two cameras filming at different angles. I'm proud of Heart when I see him ad lib a few times, perfectly within his character. Campy is fab as ever. Holy hell, that guy can act. I'm surprised he's still doing porn.

Bear calls a timeout before they move on to the first fucking scene. "What do you think they should start with?" he asks me.

I consider it before answering. "No kissing, 'cause it totally doesn't fit the scene. Jeremy is pissed off about his car, so it should be an angry fuck. Rough, demanding. Heart should be forced on his knees, Campy standing..."

As I'm talking, I suddenly have an idea. We could take this much further. The idea right now is to have Heart suck Campy off and then get fucked five ways till Sunday, but we could do more.

"Bear," I say, my voice excited and my eyes lighting up. "What if we expand on this? We start with this scene and have Heart suck him off and get fucked. But then Campy realizes he still has him by the balls, and he invites a friend over to share in the fun. We can make it really dirty, demeaning. We could even throw in a DP."

The corners of Bear's mouth pull up in a big smile. "That's fucking genius! We'll have to check if Heart is up for it, though. His contract states he's open to it, but since he's new, I wanna make sure he wants to do it."

I'm pretty sure he will be. This is one wild mofo we're talking about. I don't know him well, but from the snippets of his background I've heard, there's not a whole lot this guy hasn't done before. But I respect the shit out of Bear for asking to make sure, and it's one more reason why I dig my boss.

"If he's game, who do we ask?" Bear wants to know.

Our eyes meet, and our mouths break out in identical grins. "Tank."

Turns out I was right. Heart is game, especially when Bear informs him how much extra it would pay. Bear has a pay rate scale depending on the shit we're willing to do, and

DP is a fat bonus. It should be, because for most folks, it's hella uncomfortable. I don't have an issue with it, but I've become really good at prepping, and I know damn well who to do DP with and who not.

"Want me to try and see if Tank can come in?" I ask Bear.

"Yeah, that'd be great. I can start filming the first sex scene."

Five minutes later, I have Tank on the phone; he is more than willing to come in. He's dependable, no matter how un-sexy that sounds. He never cancels a shoot, never underperforms, does everything we ask him to and then some.

"What do I wear?" Tank asks, practical as ever.

Hmm. Good question, actually. He could wear a suit, too, but it won't jell with his vibe. It will look fake, especially when the suit comes off and you see the hot, tattooed body underneath. No business man ever looks like that. No, he has to be something else.

My mind races. I'm thinking high level crime boss. Smart. Mean. Menacing. Energy zings through my body as I come up with the perfect plot twist. Oh, this is gonna be so good.

"Do you have a leather jacket?" I ask. "Tight jeans, big belt?"

By the time Tank arrives, Campy and Heart have wrapped up the first scene with Campy coming all over Heart's face after a rough blowjob. Bear announces a thirty-minute break so everyone can relax a little, clean up, and hydrate.

Bear gives Tank a onceover, then turns to me. "I expected him in a suit."

I shake my head. "It wouldn't work. No one would believe Tank would have a job where he'd wear a suit. No, I was thinking we make him a criminal. Loan shark, maybe?

This Jeremy character is in debt to him and all of a sudden, he sees a way to appease this guy who's giving him a hard time about repaying his loans. He calls him, lets Heart service him as well."

Bear's eyes gleam. "Brilliant. I love it. Tank, you up for this?"

Tank nods. "Walk in the park. What am I called?"

"We'll call you Donny," Bear decides, and I snicker at his *Donny Darko* reference. "Yeah, I like that name. Yo, Campy!"

Campy walks over, still dressed in his suit. We shot the blow scene with him dressed, which is perfect because it stresses that whole demeaning vibe. Heart comes up, too. He must've washed his face, because I don't see any dried cum. No wonder, that stuff itches like a mother when it's dry. We all prefer to clean it off right away.

Bear explains in a few sentences what the idea is. Campy nods. "Sounds good."

"Heart?" Bear asks.

Heart smiles, then steps forward and extends his hand to Tank. "Hi. I'm Heart. Thought I'd introduce myself, seeing as how your dick is gonna be buried in me later on."

Tank shoots him one of his rare smiles, shakes his hand. "Tank. You done DP before?"

A flash of something clouds Heart's eyes before he pushes it away. "Yup. All good."

"Let Rebel prep you," Tank says. "He's good at that shit."

My eyes widen at Tank's unexpected praise. I've done a bunch of scenes with him, but this is the first time he's complimented me.

"We'll start with Jeremy fucking you," Bear decides. "He calls Donny while he's fucking you, and when Donny arrives, Jeremy has just come. Donny takes over, makes him suck him before pounding his ass. Then we move on to the

DP. We'll take breaks before each change of scene, okay? And I agree with Tank, Rebel. We'll take an hour break before the DP so you can prep Heart."

I watch as they shoot the scenes. Campy is perfect, as always. You wouldn't guess he's actually a really nice guy if you watch the total asshat he's portraying now. Still, he doesn't fuck nearly as hard as he can, though it looks rough. He knows Heart has a lot more to take, and I can tell he's being careful.

When Tank shows up and assumes his position after a short break, I'm mesmerized. Here's this big, intimidating guy, yet he's so graceful when he fucks. Even now, when he's pretending to be this badass, he's still beautiful. God, the way he fucks Heart's mouth, holding him by his hair first, then with a hand around his throat, it's so fucking hot.

When they move onto Tank fucking his ass, he slams Heart against the wall. A shudder dances down my spine. I have a weakness for wall sex. Call me stupid, but it's so damn sexy. In this case, it's perfect.

Tank kicks Heart's legs apart, makes him bend over, and then pounds the shit out of him. He's perfected the art of making it sound like he's fucking really hard, with his big balls slapping against flesh, while in reality, his strokes are smooth.

By the time Bear calls for a break, Heart looks tired. No wonder. He's given two blowjobs and has had his ass fucked for close to two hours now. I throw him a bathrobe. "Come on, sexy. Let's get you relaxed a bit and ready for your next shot."

We have a relaxation room, actually. It does double duty as a studio set as when we need a homier look, but there are couches and chairs so we can hang out a bit between scenes or shoots. Heart plops down on the couch, and I grab us both a water from the fridge.

"How are you holding up?" I ask, handing him the water. He guzzles it halfway down before answering me.

"It's fine. Bit tired."

"Sore," I state, knowing he has to be. "I know you are. It's normal."

He hesitates for a moment, then nods. "How long have you been doing this?"

"Porn? I started when I was twenty, so coming up six years. But I don't do as many shoots as I used to."

"You're tired of it?"

I shrug. "Not tired, exactly. More selective. I like scenes that are more than the standard wham-bam. Like what we're doing today. This is fun, exciting, and I know viewers will love it. You've got great chemistry with Campy and Tank, and it translates well to camera. You're a natural, kid."

Heart chews on a health bar, giving me a thoughtful look. "You got a boyfriend?"

I don't know why, but my thoughts immediately go to Troy. It's ridiculous, because we only hung out once and haven't even seen each other since then. I want to, though. He's damn sexy, relaxed, and he doesn't seem to have an issue with my job. Still, boyfriends is nowhere near what we are.

"No," I say. "Finding someone willing to accept you as is and who doesn't want to change you is hard in this business."

"It's hard in general," he says, and there's that flash of sadness again.

I always think of us porn stars as either dark or light. Pixie, for instance, is definitely on the light side, and so are

Campy and Brewer. Tank is firmly on the dark side, and it seems he's got company in Heart.

Me? I'm in between, like with everything else. I'm the middle guy, the compromise. Everyone's friend, but no one's everything. Good enough to fuck, but not enough to love.

We hang for a while, both lost in our thoughts, before I realize I have a job to do. "Let's get you prepped, sexy."

Heart's green eyes focus on me. "Hey, Rebel, would you mind not calling me that? I know you mean it well, but it reminds me of someone I really don't want to think about, if you catch my drift."

My heart wells up with softness. Definitely dark side for him. "Sure thing. Can I call you sweetie, then?"

He nods. "You think I'm sweet?"

For a second, I think he's joking. Despite his bad ass vibe, he's such a softie at heart. Doesn't he realize that himself? The insecurity on his face tells me he doesn't. I guess there's a difference between feeling sexy and feeling sweet.

I extend my hand, and when he grabs it, I pull him up from the couch close to me. I cup both his cheeks. "You're gorgeous, beautiful." I drop a quick, soft kiss on his lips. "Not pretty, like Campy, or hot like Tank, but gorgeous, breathtakingly beautiful. There's something about you that draws people in. But you've got a big heart as well. You're a good kid, sweetie. A real sweetheart. Don't let anyone tell you different."

His smile is grateful and sad at the same time. I don't know what happened to him, but I bet it wasn't good. Someone did a real number on him, and beneath that tough exterior and all the stunning tattoos beats a broken heart.

7

TROY

I still can't believe I sucked Ballsy Boys Rebel's cock.

What's more, it seemed like he'd be up for messing around again as long as I can keep things casual. Well, *hello*, casual is my middle fucking name.

I'm fucking flying this morning despite my lack of sleep and burning eyes. I couldn't sleep last night because I was hit with major inspiration. I'm talking a million-dollar idea for a game, and I couldn't let myself close my eyes until I had all the details hammered out and written down so I wouldn't forget them.

I duck into the coffee shop on the way to my morning class and groan at the long line of bleary-eyed students waiting for their own caffeine fix. I check the time on my phone and decide it'll be worth being a few minutes late to my first class if it means getting some coffee. Not to mention, I have a job I need to get out of the way. Why not kill two birds with one stone?

I shove my phone back into my pocket, resisting the urge to text Rebel. It's not like I *like* him. It's the novelty of the thing. How often do you have a porn star's phone number who you could text for a hook-up if you wanted? Not that I'm going to abuse it, but it's pretty fucking cool.

Maybe I'll hit the club this weekend and look for some fresh meat. I always enjoy a bossy little bottom or a bathroom blowjob. I'm young, hot, and I love to fuck, and I'm not going to apologize to anyone for that.

"Hey, Troy," a familiar voice pulls me from my thoughts, and I glance over my shoulder to see a dude who shares many of my classes. He's a computer programming major too, and I think his name is Nick? Nate? Something with an N, I'm pretty sure. Sad thing is, this is probably the guy I've talked to most in the past two years.

"Hey, man."

"Mason," another guy calls from across the room.

Mason, that's it.

"Semester starting okay?" I ask, because if we're going to be standing in line we might as well make small talk.

"Yeah." He smiles and glances nervously over to the guy who just called his name. "That's my boyfriend, Brad, so I'd better go."

"Oh?" I search my memory for any previous mention of Mason's apparent boyfriend...or the fact that Mason is gay. He must have mentioned it, right? Because he's admitting this now like I should know what he's talking about.

I'm surprised it didn't stick in my mind that Mason is gay, because he's actually cute as hell with a few little freckles on his nose and his light green eyes hidden behind thick rimmed glasses. His brown hair is a mess of curls on the top of his head, and his lips are all pink and welcoming. He's totally nerd cute to the max. But it's obvious he's serious about his boyfriend, so that must be why I file that information under *irrelevant* in my mind.

Mason hurries over to his boyfriend, who seems to have

some sort of bug up his ass since he's scowling and posturing before Mason even reaches him.

"Who the fuck is that?" Brad asks Mason loud enough for anyone in the coffee shop to hear, but I do my best to ignore it.

"A friend from some of my classes," Mason answers in a more hushed tone.

Brad snorts and something about the condescending sound makes my fists ball. I don't know this guy, but he's clearly a grade A asshole.

"I guess I shouldn't be worried anyway, not like anyone else would want to put up with your socially awkward ass. You know, it'd be nice if just once I could take you somewhere with my friends without you being weird and quiet," Brad complains.

"I'm sorry," Mason mumbles, and he sounds so resigned I start to wonder if I should go over there and say something to Brad about what a dickwad he's being.

"*Sorry*? Right. I don't know why I even bother with you. What's in it for me? Not sex, that's for sure. You're nothing but a pain in my ass, and I'm getting really tired of carrying your dead weight."

All right, that's it.

I step out of line and stalk over to the table Brad and Mason are sharing. With a toothy smile that's honestly more of a snarl, I slam my hands down on the table and lean close to Brad.

"Hey, fuckface, you might want to keep it down. I don't think the entire coffee shop wants to hear how little you think of your boyfriend. Who, by the way, is a smart, cute, friendly guy who can do a hundred times better than you."

Mason gasps, and Brad's jaw and shoulders tense. "And just who the fuck do you think you are?" Brad growls.

"I'm Mason's friend. And I'm the guy you're going to have to go through if you plan to keep talking to him that way."

Brad stands up, his chair scraping loudly on the tile floor, and the entire coffee shop goes deathly silent. I'm sure everyone is waiting to see if we're going to throw down with a fistfight. The fact that all eyes are on us seems to register with Brad because he looks around and lets out a long sigh and then laughs. His gaze falls on Mason who's full-on deer in the headlights.

"You're not worth it. It's been fun, but we're done."

Mason's face pales, and he watches silently as Brad strides out of the shop without a backward glance.

"Shit, I'm sorry. I didn't mean to... Fuck, he was just being so damn mean to you," I stammer a half-assed apology.

Mason bites his bottom lip and nods, his eyes full of sad resignation.

"Tell me what I can do to make this up to you?" I ask desperately.

Mason shakes his head and then stands, coffee in hand. "What class do you have this morning?" he asks.

The abrupt non-sequitur throws me off balance, and I almost call him out on it. But one look into his eyes show that Mason is desperately trying to keep it together.

"Algorithms and Data Studies," I answer without further comment on his douchebag boyfriend...or ex-boyfriend, as the case may be.

"Cool, me too," he says with a nod. "Get your coffee, so we aren't late."

The line has thinned out, so it only takes two minutes for me to order my coffee. When I catch the barista's name tag as she hands me my coffee, I plaster on a friendly smile and lean slightly over the counter so I don't embarrass her by saying it loud enough for others to hear. "Stephanie, I'm really sorry, but Jake wanted me to tell you it's over."

She looks shocked and then her face falls, and her eyes start to glisten with unshed tears. "He wants to break up?"

"He does. And if you ask me, you can do better than a jackass who can't even face you when he ends it."

Apparently, I'm just anti-cupid this morning.

∽

I PULL ON A FORM FITTING, royal blue t-shirt that I'm confident enough to say looks sexy as fuck on me. A touch of gel lets me achieve a just fucked look with my hair, and a quick glance in the mirror confirms that my ass looks edible. I'm officially ready to hit the club and score some helpless hottie.

I glance at my phone, and for a second, I consider texting Rebel to see what he gets up to on a Friday night. Probably something epic. Off-camera porn star orgy maybe? Or it's possible he leads a totally normal life when he's not fucking like it's a sport. Maybe Friday nights, Rebel is just Hendrix, sitting on the couch, binge watching his favorite show on Netflix. I wonder what his favorite show is. And I wonder what he looks like lounging on the couch in nothing but his underwear.

I can almost picture it. His lean muscles on display, long hair pulled back out of his face, hand casually down the front of a pair of plain colored boxers.

I shake off the thought and shove my phone into my pocket. I don't need to call Rebel. If he wants to hook up again, he can text or call me. And if he doesn't, there are a million other willing guys in the world waiting to spend one night with me, even if they don't know it yet.

I Uber it to Bottoms Up, the closest gay nightclub, and bypass the long line thanks to a close, personal relationship with the bouncer.

The heavy pulse of club music reverberates in my chest as I make my way up to the bar to get a drink.

"Hey, baby. Haven't seen you in here in a minute," the bartender—I'm pretty sure his name is Ryan—greets me with a flirty smirk.

I smile back but don't offer an explanation. He took it well when I gave him a gentle let down after we hooked up a few months ago, so I'm not going to insult him by giving him a lame excuse. I avoided the club on nights I knew he'd be here to make sure he wouldn't expect a repeat.

Not that I wouldn't enjoy a repeat every once in a while. It can be fun getting to know someone's body a bit. But few people are capable of fucking around with the same person on the regular without developing feelings. Ryan had been fun, and I wouldn't have minded a second time around, but he was also kind of sweet and starry-eyed, and that's dangerous.

"Can I get a rum and coke, please?"

"Sure thing."

Drink in hand, I turn and scan the crowd, checking for anyone who might catch my interest for the night.

And then I see someone who *really* catches my interest.

I try to fight the smile on my lips and fail while I sip my drink and will my heartbeat to stay calm.

I roll my shoulders back and add an extra swagger to my step as I approach the group of men so beautiful it should be illegal.

In my mind, I'm trying to decide how to play this. Should I stand in their general vicinity and wait for him to notice me? Or I could go the straightforward route and come right out and greet him? The decision is made for me within seconds as Rebel turns his head and our gazes lock. He smiles instantly, his baby blues lighting up in recognition.

"Hey, it's banana boy!" he shouts over the club music and my step falters.

My freaking porn star crush just called me banana boy in front of a bunch of other porn stars. This isn't real, right? This is one of those awkward naked in class dreams? Because I was *really* hoping I could pull off being cool for at least a few seconds.

"Banana boy?" the man beside Rebel asks.

Even in the flashing club lights, I recognize him instantly. Sexy, playful, fuckboy Brewer. He's mouthwatering with his messy brown hair and his ink-covered arms. He's the kind of guy you can tell from watching his scenes that he's truly having a good time.

"I can't believe I didn't tell you guys; this dude showed up at my place in a banana suit the other day," Rebel explains, and they all laugh.

Of course he's only going to tell the embarrassing part of the story, not the part where I sucked his dick...twice. In all honesty, I've imagined this moment many times, being surrounded by the entire Ballsy Boys crew, and never once did I envision they'd be chuckling at me...or that we'd all be fully clothed.

Since this didn't go how I'd been hoping, I start to slowly back away while some of my dignity is still intact. But I only make it a few feet before Rebel is grabbing my arm and tugging me against his side.

"Sorry, I didn't mean to embarrass you. I was just surprised to see you. And you have to admit, it was pretty funny that you were dressed as a banana when you came to my place," Rebel says close to my ear, his hot breath tickling my neck and making me shiver.

"You could've at least told them how good I am at sucking dick," I joke.

Rebel shrugs and then looks back toward all his friends. "I should also mention that this dude gives insane head."

"Better than me?" Brewer asks with mock indignation.

Rebel glances between me and Brewer with a look of contemplation. "Yeah, better than you. Sorry, man."

I know he's probably just being nice, but I still feel damn proud. I catch Tank rolling his eyes in Brewer's direction, and it occurs to me that of all the guys here, Tank and Brewer are the only two I've never seen in a scene together.

I notice Pixie off to one side talking to Campy, who seems somewhat less comfortable in the club than the other guys. And then I spot one of the newest Ballsy Boys, Heart. "Oh my god, you deserve a medal for the epic pounding you took in that new scene. DP from two guys as big as Tank and Campy, much respect man."

Heart looks startled by my praise, and I realize it might be bad form to fanboy all over porn stars. "Uh, thanks. Sorry, this is all pretty new. It's kinda weird to have someone talking about watching me get fucked."

"Sorry about that, didn't mean to make it weird."

"Not at all, it's actually pretty cool, and I'm glad you enjoyed it. You're right; Tank in particular is no joke."

"Aw, don't let this big bear fool you," Brewer coos, stepping up beside Tank and petting his chest. "You just have to know the right way to stroke him so he doesn't get all growly."

On cue, a low rumble erupts from Tank's chest, but by the deadly glare he's turning on Brewer, I don't think he's amused. "How many times do I have to tell you I'm not one of your fuck toys, so don't touch me?" Tank grits out, shouldering Brewer off him.

To my surprise, Brewer doesn't seem the least bit put off by Tank's reprisal. "Aw, my grumbly bear just needs a good snuggle, doesn't he?" Brewer nuzzles his head against Tank's massive, hairy bicep.

"Do you want to dance?" Rebel asks before I can see if Tank is actually going to crush Brewer with his fist or not.

"Sure."

8

REBEL

He's taller than me. It's a strange thought because at my five-foot-nine, I'm not that tall, but for some reason, I hadn't realized Troy is taller than me. Not by much, an inch maybe, but it's enough to make me feel...warm inside.

"I suck at dancing," Troy informs me as we take position amidst dozens of sweaty bodies, his mouth close to my ear, giving me shivers.

"That makes two of us. I only asked to get away from Tank and Brewer. I swear to god, those two drive me nuts. Brewer's biggest hobby is to ride Tank and get a rise out of him, and Tank would gladly serve Brewer's head on a platter."

Troy laughs, then grabs my neck and yanks me flush to his body. "We'll have to grind, then, instead of dance."

Now here's a plan I can get on board with.

I circle my arms around his waist, as he pulls me even closer, our bodies melting in a way that would get us arrested in half the countries in the world. Not this one, though. Not in this club. God, I love this place.

We sway to the music, every inch of our bodies pressed against each other. At first, our heads are apart, somewhat awkwardly, but then I surrender to this deep urge to put my cheek against his shoulder. The shirt he's wearing, which so perfectly brings out his eyes, is soft under my skin, and I can't resist scraping my stubble against it.

His body is perfect, if you ask me.

Confession: I have a biceps fetish. It's one of those weird, unexplainable tics everyone has, and this is mine. Every time I check a guy out, I look at his biceps first.

Well, maybe not first. You sorta take in the face and the whole appearance automatically, but it's the first thing I specifically look for. Other guys check out asses or six-packs, or they wanna make sure their man has a solid seven-inch cock, or whatever. Me, I dig solid, toned biceps.

Not the Arnold-Schwarzenegger-in-his-glory-days type, where the biceps are as thick as my thigh. But I hate skinny arms. I love a perfectly sculpted, well-developed set of muscles in the upper arm.

My first crush was on my neighbor kid—well, he was seventeen to my fourteen, so kind of a kid, still—and he'd been helping his dad in the junkyard all summer. He was tall, tanned from working outside, and he always wore these black tank tops. Wife beaters, they're called, which is a stupid-ass name for tops that looked so damn sexy on him I drooled every time I saw him. His arms were perfect. Absolute, sheer perfection. Ripped, but not bulky.

Just like Troy's. I've eyed them before, and they're right in my line of vision now, these perfect, strong arms. His muscles flex and ripple as he holds me tightly against him. So. Damn. Sexy.

My hands drop lower and lower, until I find his ass. His firm, fuckable ass. Mmmm. I was fucked hard yesterday by a guest star named Dick—and holy fuck, was he aptly named 'cause he was a major asshole—and I'm the mood to pound. What are the odds I could have a go at this sweet ass?

I squeeze softly, first his right cheek, then his left, and Troy lets out a delicious little growl right next to my ear. Encouraged, I subject him to the one true top-or-bottom-test I personally designed and have tested on fuck knows how many guys. I trail my finger down his crack, not even under his jeans, but right on top, and press gently when I reach his hole. Troy shudders, then involuntarily spreads his legs.

Bingo.

He's a bottom, or vers, like me. Probably the latter. But there's no fucking way he's a strict top. Tops don't spread their legs when you tap their hole. Tops don't moan into your ear like Troy is doing right now when you increase that pressure ever-so-slightly. And tops don't whisper "Please...oh, fucking hell, more..." with an urgency that makes it clear they really like what you're doing to them.

We're grinding against each other full force now, all pretense of dancing gone. Suddenly, he pulls me back by my hair and slams our mouths together. Fuck, yes. Controlled aggression? Such a fucking turn on.

He tastes minty fresh. And that's the last coherent thought I have before he starts fucking my mouth with his tongue, and holy fucking mother of everything, I like. I love. I need.

My head spins, and my cock is leaking, and dammit, I want to fuck him against a wall. Literally.

I rip my mouth off his and stare at him with narrowed eyes, both our chests heaving with desperate breaths after sucking each other out of oxygen. His eyes drop to my mouth, as if he is contemplating going for round two. I wouldn't object, but I have something else in mind. He's as hard as I am, so I'm pretty sure he's up for it.

I lean in and place my mouth to his ear. My teeth scrape the edge of his ear, and his hands grab my arms, digging in almost painfully. I find his earlobe and bite down gently. *Oh, somebody likes that.*

My breath teases his ear as I say, "I really, really, really want to fuck you. Preferably against a wall, but any surface will do. You game?"

He shivers. "Fuck, yes. If I say please, will you think me too easy?"

I smile. "There's no such thing as too easy. I dig guys who love sex."

I lean back again, and our eyes meet, sparks still flying. "Why against a wall?" he asks, slightly hoarse.

"Have you ever had wall sex?"

He shakes his head.

"You're in for a treat, then. Lemme show you, rather than explain."

For one second, he looks at me, but then he nods. "Here?"

"No. Too many people watching. I don't mind that when I'm working, but this is private. Wanna come home with me?"

"Yeah."

We walk off the dance floor, and I wave at the rest of the boys. I notice Tank and Brewer butting heads again and sigh. Fucking morons. Campy and Pixie see me and wave back, so I know they'll update the others.

We barely talk during the ride home, Troy opting to ride with me because apparently, he doesn't own a car. Mine isn't exactly a Porsche, but my Toyota is dependable. Not sexy, but this is one area of my life where I really don't give a shit as long as it works.

As soon as we're inside, I kick the door shut, and then I'm on him. No small talk, no polite offers of a drink. I need him. Now.

Judging by the way he attacks me right back, I guess he feels the same. Our mouths crash into each other, hot tongues dueling and seducing. God, I love that he dishes out as good as he receives. I let him fuck my mouth with his slick, sweet tongue, before I return the favor.

His hands pull on my shirt, and I step back so he can pull it off. I fumble with the buttons on his shirt, then decide I really don't have the patience for it and give a solid rip, sending them flying everywhere. Troy shoots me a look that's somewhere between wanting to kill me and wanting to be fucked desperately. The latter can be arranged.

My hands find his zipper, and seconds later, I've shoved down his jeans and underwear. I groan with appreciation at his leaking cock and make short work of my own clothes. I don't have time for slow stuff right now. My blood is pumping, my ears are roaring, and I have this desperate need to have him that won't be denied much longer.

Panting, we're staring at each other with hungry eyes, both naked now. "Wall or bedroom?" I ask.

Troy's mouth pulls up in a devious grin. "Wall. Show me."

Hell, yes. "Turn around, both hands against the wall."

I dig up a condom and lube from my wallet, suit myself up in seconds. When I look up, Troy is standing wide spread against the wall, his hands flat against the surface, and his ass sticking out at the perfect angle. He looks at me over his shoulder with impatient eyes.

I step in, squirt the last bit of lube on my fingers. We haven't talked sexual history and experience yet, but something tells me Troy is anything but an amateur at this. I nibble on his neck, which gives him goosebumps, and tap his hole with my right index finger. He pushes back in a clear invitation.

I press gently, but there's no need, because he bears down on me and sucks me in greedily. "Not your first rodeo, huh?" I breathe in his ear.

He lets out a moany laugh. "I love riding cowboys. Now hurry the fuck up."

I love a guy who's impatient. There are times when I like taking my time, but then there are moments like this where I'm not in the mood for foreplay. I just wanna sink into that absolutely perfect ass, and I couldn't be happier that he and I are on the same page.

I add a second finger, wriggle around a bit until he's loose, meanwhile scraping his ears and neck with my teeth. He keeps letting out little gasps and moans.

When he can take three fingers with ease, I know we're good. With guys I've never fucked before I'm always careful because of my size. I've had my ass ripped open a few times, and it fucking hurts for days.

"You good?" I double check.

"Hell, yeah. Gimme."

I line up, and he pushes back, letting me in with ease. Usually, I try to stay shallow at first, but something about his greedy ass makes me slide in slowly but surely until I bottom out.

"Oh, damn," he groans. "You're... Fuck."

"You good?" I ask again.

"Perfect. Now work that cock. I haven't been this full in a long time, and fuck, I need it."

The one downside to fucking for a living is that it can be hard for me to shut off my brain. I'm always aware of where the cameras are, of my moves, and especially of my partner. The kind of videos we make at Ballsy Boys, we try to find actors who take care of each other. That means being tuned in to someone else's subtle signals.

Right now, every signal Troy is emitting is screaming at me to please, for the love of everything holy, pound the motherfucking hell out of him. He impatiently pushes back, his ass wide open, his hands strong against the wall. He wants this, wants me.

And he's gonna get it. Every fucking inch. Every last drop.

I start out slowly, almost leisurely, until I get a feel for how our bodies fit. And holy fuck, they fit well. His ass grips me tightly, and when I bottom out, his globes have the perfect amount of jiggle. And those arms of his, the way his biceps tense when he holds strong against the wall. I could fucking worship his arms.

I pull out all the way and spread my legs a little farther until I'm perfectly positioned. My hands come round him, one arm on his chest, the other on his throat. "Brace," I simply say and then the fun starts for real.

I surge into him, and our combined moans echo through the hallway. Is there any sound more beautiful than the *shick* noise my cock makes when I slam into him? Maybe it's the wet slap of my full balls against his thighs. Or the little grunt he lets out when I do it again, only harder and deeper.

"Goddammit, you're so fucking big," he grunts, shamelessly pushing back against me. "So fucking thick. It's the best damn feeling ever."

I am in the mood to pound, and that's exactly what I do. I fucking ravish his ass, and he takes it, takes me.

My brain finally switches off as I break out in sweat everywhere. My heart is racing, and the all-too-familiar first tingles of my orgasm are teasing me. And for once, I don't have to hold back.

I wanna see him when he comes. Moreover, I want him to come all over me, while being buried as deep inside him as I can possibly get. I want to watch him unravel, feel his cum on me.

I pull out entirely. "Turn around," I tell him, my voice hoarse.

He obeys without hesitation, and it stirs something deep inside me, as if he knows I'll take care of him and bring him pleasure, too. His cheeks are flushed, and his body is as clammy as mine, with little droplets of sweat pearling on his forehead.

I hold my arms out. "Jump."

He frowns for a sec, then seems to get what I'm proposing, and a big grin splits his face open. He jumps up, and I catch him. He wraps his legs around my waist, and I carefully step toward the wall until he can lean his weight back against it, both hands on my shoulders.

With a satisfied sigh, I wriggle until my cock finds his hole again. This time, when I sink deep inside him, his eyes bulge a little. I know why, because this position is fucking perfect for us both. I'm deeper inside him than I was before, and I love the sensation of holding his weight as I fuck him.

But for him, it's even better. He's stuffed to the max with my cock, and with that upward curve I have, I'm dead aimed at his prostate. He's gonna explode all over me.

"You like?" I manage, increasing my rhythm.

"I fucking love," he moans. "Oh, please, harder. Deeper. Dammit, Rebel, make me come."

He's almost whining, and I smile. Damn, I love fucking.

Especially when someone is this tight, this fucking responsive, and so hella gorgeous.

I thrust hard, resulting in obscene noises that make my skin tingle and my balls pull up tight. I'm about to come so fucking hard.

Troy drops his right hand from my shoulder, seeking his cock. It's leaking against my stomach, a deliciously dirty sensation.

"Put your hand back."

He shoots me a dark look. "I need..."

"I know what you need. Trust me. Put your hand back."

He does what I tell him, but his eyes are still shooting daggers. I do know what he needs. Friction. And I'm about to give it to him, because I'm a minute away from blowing.

I take one more step toward the wall, crushing his body against mine on the front and against the wall on the back. My hands push back his thighs, opening him even wider for me, and I grind my body completely into his, our skin touching everywhere. His cock is now trapped between our bodies, and I start moving my body in circles to give him the friction he needs.

Hands-off orgasm? Best. Thing. Ever.

I'm fucking him into the wall, and he's loving it. He closes his eyes, his mouth dropping open as a constant stream of erotic sounds fall from his lips. I want to feel those words, eat them, and I take his mouth in a hot kiss, greedily drinking in his every moan and mewl.

His muscles spasm, and he bites my lip with force as he comes, spurting hot liquid between our bodies.

So. Fucking. Hot.

I keep kissing him, the faint taste of blood in my mouth —he must've nicked my lip—until he becomes liquid in my arms, completely limp.

Only then do I allow myself to come, and I let out a deep moan as my balls unload. My vision goes white for a sec as I fill the condom, all the tension leaving my body.

Ahhhhh. Fucking perfection.

9

TROY

I gingerly wipe my sore ass with a damp washcloth. I've never been fucked like that in my life. Rebel's massive size would've been enough on its own to inflict some pain. Add in the force of the pounding he gave me, and I'm going to be sitting a little crooked for the next few days.

Totally worth it.

I glance at myself in the mirror and smile. My hair is sticking up in every direction, and my eyelids have a satisfied, sleepy droop to them. Anyone taking one look at me would be able to tell I've just seen god, and it turns out the door to heaven is between a porn star's legs. *Who knew?*

I toss the washcloth in the clothes hamper near the shower and head back into Rebel's bedroom. He's spread out on his bed, looking sexier than any man has a right to. The moonlight filtering in through the curtains casts shadows across his skin. His long hair falls messy across his pillow, and the thin sheet rests low on his hips, the outline of his softening cock still clearly visible beneath it.

A little shiver runs up my spine. I can't believe my luck at randomly bumping into a freaking porn star. Hands down, this will be one of those experiences I remember when I'm ninety and on my death bed.

Rebel's eyes drift open, and he smiles at me.

"Do you have to take off right away or can you hang out for a few?"

"Um..."

I rub my hand along the back of my neck. I *should* leave. This is already uncharted territory for me. I don't usually do repeats. On the other hand, Rebel is kind of cool as hell even when we're not fucking. How often does that happen? In my experience, *never*.

"You don't want to stay?" he asks, the slightest hint of insecurity in his tone.

"No, it's not that. I just don't usually fool around with anyone more than once, sometimes twice at most. And it's kind of weird that I do actually want to hang out with you. I'm not really sure what to do with that."

"Dude, I know you know I'm a porn star. No Strings is my middle name."

"See, now I know your middle name, this is getting way too serious," I tease, and Rebel flings a pillow in my direction. I dodge out of the way, and without letting myself think too hard about it, I crawl into bed with him.

Rebel opens his arms, and I lay my head against his bicep. I'm surprised to find it feels kind of nice to...*cuddle*. Holy shit, I'm cuddling with a dude after we've boned. There is everything wrong with this situation. On the other hand—as Rebel pointed out—if a break-up artist and commitment-phobe like myself and a porn star can't do casual, then who can?

"Is it tacky to ask how you got into porn? It's not exactly a job you dream of when you're five, right?" I ask with a chuckle.

"That's true. When I was five, I wanted to be a space cowboy, so things have gone horribly awry," Rebel jokes, and we both laugh. "I guess doing porn is one of those things that just sort of happens when you're not paying attention. I needed money, and I like sex, so I figured it was a no-brainer. That was almost six years ago, and I've loved every damn minute of it so far."

"That makes sense. You're happy, though? You're not like a tragic Lifetime movie waiting to happen or anything?"

"Hell yeah. I get paid to get my dick sucked and to fuck. I'm pretty sure that's the life lottery right there. I'm not saying I'll be in porn forever, but I can't see leaving the industry completely, either. I guess I'm just seeing where life takes me."

"Mmm," I hum to show I'm still listening, too relaxed and comfortable to bother with forming another sentence. I know I should get up and go home. But Rebel's bed is so warm and comfortable, five more minutes won't hurt anything.

I BOLT awake in a bed that's too warm. My skin is damp with sweat, and I realize the cause is a furnace-hot body pressed close to me. My heart flutters frantically against my ribs as my sleep-fogged brain grapples for the context of a large man in bed with me. I blink around the room, forcing myself to take even breaths and then glance over my shoulder with caution to see whose bed I'm in.

"Fuck," I groan quietly, realizing I accidentally spent the night at Rebel's place.

"Waswrong?" Rebel mumbles against his pillow.

"Nothing, I'm just late for class," I lie as I ease out of bed and glance around the room for my clothes.

"On a Saturday?" he asks, his voice clearer this time.

"Uh...yeah."

"Do you want a ride?" He finally opens his eyes and watches as I pull on my boxer briefs followed by my jeans.

"Nah, I'll just get an Uber, thanks though. Last night was fun, so I'll see you around?"

"Yeah, I told you, I'm good with no strings, but I would like to hang out more."

"Cool." I nod and tug my shirt on and give Rebel one last smile before making a run for it.

It's a short ride back to my place from Rebel's, but for some reason, the empty quiet of my apartment this morning is unnerving. I grab my laptop bag and head over to the student union to try to get some work done.

I can't shake the disappointment in Rebel's expression when I bolted this morning. I must've been misinterpreting that, right? There's no way he cared that I cut and run as soon as I woke up. I'm sure he has tons of things to do today, friends to hang out with, grocery shopping. Fuck, I don't know, he's got a life, and I have no idea what it consists of. And I have work to do, too. I can't let a little fun with my porn star crush sidetrack me from my goals.

"Are you working on that project for Coding?" Mason asks from over my shoulder as I work on my laptop in the student lounge.

"No, this is a personal project. I had an idea for a game, so I thought I'd try to put some of my education to use and see what comes out."

"Oh?" Mason's eyebrows shoot up, and he leans closer with interest. "What's the game?"

I hesitate for a second before deciding Mason isn't the

type to snake my idea and fuck me over. "It's a play on all the dating games. It's a break-up game. The player creates an avatar and goes on dates with Non-Playable Characters and then has to dump them. You get points for creativity, tact, stuff like that."

Mason's eyes light up. "That's brilliant. That could make millions as a mobile game."

"Hopefully," I agree with a chuckle. "The problem is, I'm shit at the artistic part. If I take this much further than I already am, I'll end up having to bring someone else in."

"Oh, well, you know my minor is graphic design. The visual aspect and world design is actually my strong suit."

"No shit?"

Mason blushes and pushes his glasses farther up the bridge of his nose. "Yeah, I'd love to work with you on this...if you want to, that is."

"Absolutely." I pat the seat next to me. When Mason sits down, I start to explain what I've been working on so far and what I'm picturing moving forward.

I'm practically bouncing with excitement. I was enthusiastic about this project before, but now it seems like this could really happen, and that's cool as fuck.

"Hey listen, I feel like I should apologize again for the thing with your boyfriend."

"*Ex*-boyfriend," Mason corrects. "And it's fine. I mean, at first, it wasn't fine. It was...just so unexpected. I was planning to propose; I thought we were happy."

I nod sympathetically while trying not to cringe. He was going to *propose*? He thought that at barely past twenty, he'd been dating the man he would spend his entire life with? Jesus, that's another sixty years, at least. And to *that* fucking guy? Christ, Mason had terrible taste in men. I shudder internally but refrain from adding my two cents.

"I'm sorry, that really sucks."

I shift uncomfortably, trying to remember how normal humans usually behave in these situations. I should offer some sort of comfort, right? I awkwardly reach out and pat his shoulder.

"Thanks. Now that I'm away from the situation, I'm realizing how unhealthy it was, I guess. I shouldn't have let him talk to me the way he did."

I nod and let out a relieved breath. I'm glad he at least knows that wasn't normal. "He seemed like a dick."

Mason lets out a quiet laugh. "Yeah, I guess he was," he agrees. "He wasn't totally wrong though...about the boring in bed stuff and the socially awkward stuff."

"Oh." I put my laptop aside as I try to figure out how I'm supposed to respond. I can't imagine that's an easy thing to admit. Am I supposed to offer him advice? I can certainly give him a few pointers. "I know a bunch of porn stars. I could probably hook you up so you could brush up your skills."

Know is a clear overstatement, but I'm sure I could make it happen for Mason if he wants.

Not taking his eyes off his computer screen, Mason wrinkles his nose. "A porn star? Isn't that a bit skeevy?"

I snort a laugh.

"No offense, but maybe that's the problem. You're all repressed and shit. There's nothing wrong with porn or porn stars. Sex is natural and fun. There's nothing to feel weird about. Forget the porn stars, find someone to just fool around with for fun."

Mason shrugs silently. *Well, at least I tried.*

"Well, if you want to come out to the club with me this weekend, you're welcome. I always say the only way to get over one man is to get under another." Not that I would know what it takes to get over someone. That would mean being emotionally invested, which, as we've already established, is not in my wheelhouse.

Mason grimaces. "Probably not this weekend, but maybe in a few months or something. And I don't think I'll have sex with a porn star."

"Never say never," I chuckle.

Mason focuses on his laptop, and the conversation seems to be over. I'm glad we cleared the air so we can focus on this project, and maybe eventually, Mason will let me help him with the whole *awkward and bad in bed* thing.

10

REBEL

I wholeheartedly believe in the power of intuition. It would be hard not to, considering the upbringing I had. My mom especially embraces anything and everything alternative, from talking to trees to healing stones to dolphin therapy. It's all good with me, honestly, even though as a kid I would have appreciated a Tylenol every now and then instead of a healing massage or acupuncture.

One thing my mom stressed is that our subconscious knows things our mind can't rationalize yet. She taught me and my sister to take our intuition seriously, and it's one of the bits of advice I've always tried to follow.

And right now, my subconscious is screaming "Hell, no!" about the guy in front of me. Bear has asked me to sit in on an interview with a possible new Ballsy Boy, a six foot two guy who uses "King" as a moniker.

I'm pretty sure it's a not-too-subtle reference to his dick size, because the guy is packing a serious tool down there. Everyone who applies and is deemed a serious candidate by Bear is asked to send in a couple of nudes and a jerk-off video. Hey, we're a porn studio, so checking out the goods is kinda important.

I watched his video, which was a little unimaginative but impressive because of his size. That being said, size isn't everything in porn—as pure bottoms will be happy to point out. Sure, a ten-inch cock looks great on screen, but good luck finding bottoms willing to take that up their ass for two, three hours. They'll do it once and then kindly refuse the honor of a repeat performance.

Bear shoots King a friendly smile. "You indicated on your application that you're a strict top. Is that a hard limit for you, because we always prefer men who are vers?"

"Yeah, definitely. I don't take cock. I only dish it out." King leans back in his chair, his tight jeans outlining his definitely hard dick. "And let's be honest, with a dick like mine, bottoming would be a waste of my natural talents, right?"

"I'm vers," I say, perhaps a little snappier than necessary.

King sends me a condescending smile. "Sure, but from what I can tell, there's still a sizeable difference between me and you..."

I bite back the not-so-mature words on my tongue and instead go with, "Well, as any gay man will tell you, size alone is not enough. You gotta know how to use it."

King grins. "I've never had any complaints."

Somehow, I doubt that, but call me jaded. This is not a guy who knows how to bring pleasure. This is a guy who knows how to pleasure himself above all.

"That's nice to know," Bear says non-committedly. "If we were to give you a shot, which one of our Boys would you pick to do a first scene with?"

King rubs his chin with his right hand. "Well, your boy Brewer has a rep for being a master cocksucker, so I'd like to see him try and swallow me. But I wouldn't mind tapping that sweet Pixie's ass. That kid needs to be taken hard and deep by my monster cock until that tight little ass of his is overflowing with my cum."

If his goal was dirty talk, he's failing, 'cause it's more like creepy talk to me. I have to keep myself from shivering with a giant case of the heebie-jeebies. And using Pixie was a dumb move on his part; for some reason, Bear is protective of our little imp.

The smile Bear had plastered on his face until now falters. "You do realize that even as a top, there's some reciprocity required?" he asks, his tone distinctively cold. "We like to see our tops engage in blowjobs and rimming, for instance."

King's cocky attitude dims. "I'm not gay. I don't mind sticking it in someone's ass, especially not if they're as hot as that little twink, but I'm not doing any ass licking or shit like that."

Bear's face darkens even more. "Being gay or bi is kind of a requirement for this line of work," he says curtly.

King leans forward, his eyes suddenly cold. "Yeah? You may want to ask your boy Campy about that, 'cause he sure as shit ain't gay."

Campy? What the hell is this asshole talking about? I've done countless scenes with him, and he's been working for us for at least two years. How can he not be into men? He may not be gay, but if not, he's sure as shit bi. There's no way he's straight.

"Look, King, or whatever your real name is, I'm not discussing private issues with my boys with you. If you are unwilling to engage in mutual satisfactory sexual acts with other boys, you're not a good fit for our studio. It's as simple as that. If you're straight, I'd advise you to try your luck with one of the many, many straight porn studios in town. I'm sure one of them will hire you, considering your size and body type."

King opens his mouth as if he wants to say something, then shuts it again. I'm not surprised. Bear is generally pretty laid back, but every now and then, he gets this tone, this authoritative, deep voice that oozes dominance, and when he does, you just have to listen. It, like, reaches deep inside you or something.

The interview is done, and King leaves, shooting daggers with his eyes. "What the hell was he talking about with Campy?" Bear asks me as soon as the douchebag has left the building.

"I honestly don't know. Does it matter?"

Bear sighs. "Maybe."

"You think this guy has it out for him?"

"He could. The more he talked, the more my alarm bells were going off."

"Oh, yeah, he was a total sleazebag," I agree.

"Look, do you think you could ask Campy? Not to confront him, but just to check, out of concern? I can't really ask as his employer."

"Bear, if it turns out he's straight, are you gonna fire him?"

Bear shoots me a disapproving frown. "Of course not. What the hell do I care, as long as he performs well. I just want to know so we can protect him if need be."

That actually makes sense. Information is power and all that shit. "I'll ask him, but I'm pretty sure I know the answer."

We discuss some upcoming shoots, and by the time I leave the studio, it's close to dinner time. This King guy has left me highly irritated with his distaste for gay sex. Fucking asshole. Why the hell is he applying with us when he thinks gay sex is beneath him? Probably because he can't get a job with a straight studio, I reason. Maybe because he misbehaved or something? Contrary to what many people think, most well-paying studios are quite strict in who they hire. There's enough people willing to do porn to be selective, especially straight, vanilla porn. If you act like an asshole, they'll toss you out. It wouldn't surprise me if that's what happened with this dude.

And now I'm getting frustrated with myself for spending way too much time and energy on this guy. I need a little pick me up, preferably in the form of a serious good fuck. I'm not scheduled for another shoot till next week, so I have to find someone willing to have a little fun with.

I have my phone in my hand before I realize it. Troy picks up on the second ring.

"Hey," he says.

"Hey, yourself."

There's an awkward silence before I realize that I called him, meaning I'll have to initiate the conversation.

"You free tonight?" I ask.

"Why?"

"'Cause I had a crappy day, and I would love to end it on a high note. With you."

"Okay," he says slowly. "Doing what exactly?"

I frown a little. Did I misinterpret his earlier signals? I thought he was up for fooling around every now and then. Admittedly, he was a bit weird after sleeping over, but that was a week ago. Surely he's over that by now?

Still, I take the plunge. "Well, I figured I'd stop by with some food, Chinese maybe, and we could watch a movie or something. And after that, I'd very much like to fuck you, if that would be okay with you?"

Troy chuckles. "Well, you're certainly asking nicely. Plus, paying for dinner."

I smile, the tension in my stomach easing. "I figured that was the least I could do in return."

"So basically, you're paying for sex with Chinese food."

I laugh. "That's one way of looking at it."

I can hear the smile in his voice. "I don't know if that makes me a cheap lay or plain stupid. My guess is you get a whole lot more to get fucked than a Sesame chicken with white rice. But I'll meet you at your place in, say, an hour?"

"Hey, I'll add some fortune cookies to my offer, how's that?" I joke. He's coming over, which means great sex, which means my mood just rapidly improved. Plus, I'm so happy to be able to joke around about my job. Troy really doesn't have an issue with it, it seems.

Troy laughs. "Oh, why didn't you start with that? Dude, for fortune cookies, I'll even throw in a blowjob!"

11

TROY

My fingers fly over my computer keys as I work to finish my coding project at the last minute. I would've gotten it done weeks ago, but between frequent hook-ups with Rebel and working on my own game with Mason, some of my classwork has fallen a tad behind schedule.

The weird thing has been that it's not just the sex with Rebel that seems to be taking up a large chunk of time. It's random Tuesday nights when he wants me to come over and watch a movie with him. At first, I thought that was just code for fucking around. But it didn't take long to realize that when Rebel wants to fuck, he says that's what he's calling for. And when he says he wants to watch a movie, you'd better believe he's keeping his hands to himself, and we're watching a movie.

It's weird as hell, and I don't know what to make of it. It's also kind of nice. Not that I'll admit that out loud, even under threat of torture. But just knowing that it's true is enough to make me squirm.

I type out the last few lines of code and then shake out

the cramps in my hands. Holy hell, I need to remember not to leave shit like this till the last minute again.

I check the time and realize I need to get to class. I close my laptop and shove it into my messenger bag along with my notebooks that I take to class even though I *never* handwrite notes. Then I pull on some fresh clothes and head out the door.

I slip into my usual seat in the back of the classroom only a few minutes after the bell rings, so more or less the same time I usually make it. Mason shoots me a look I've come to expect each time I'm late for class. The strange thing is, I kind of like having someone I can count on for something. Even if the thing I'm counting on is for him to be annoyed at me.

I'm trying to listen to my monotone professor when an iMessage pops up from Rebel.

Rebel: I'm horny

Troy: Lol, stop the presses. I'm in class, dude.

Rebel: Oh shit lol, sorry.

Rebel: So I guess it would be rude of me to send you a pic of my epic erection right now?

Troy: It seems rude to your erection to not let the little guy out to play

Rebel: Little????

Troy: Lol, I misspoke, not little. My ass can attest to that. Now, let's see it

I wait with baited breath, unsure if he's actually going to send me a dick pic while I'm in class. It's a ballsy move, and Rebel's just the kind of guy who would do it.

Seconds later, an image pops up, and I have to stifle a laugh at the sheer audacity of it. Rebel wasn't wrong; this erection appears particularly epic, and I'm kind of bummed I'm in class and can't help him take full advantage of it.

"Dude, are you looking at porn in class?" Mason whispers.

"Technically? I'm not exactly sure," I answer with a chuckle.

Troy: Is it technically porn when you send me a dick pic?

Rebel: Dictionary definition yes because porn is any image or explicit description used for a sensual purpose (says Google). But in a colloquial sense, I'd say no because we don't usually consider dick pics porn, we consider them "sexting".

Troy: Is it weird that I'm even more turned on by how smart you sound right now than by your dick pic?

Rebel: Not to make this weird, and I know you're allergic to emotions and shit, but that really means a lot to me to hear you say.

Troy: Yup, you made it weird. Lol.

Rebel: Asshole

Troy: You like my asshole, dick.

Rebel: You like my dick

Troy: We seem to be at an impasse here. Maybe your dick and my asshole can work this out later.

Rebel: Count on it ;)

I close the chat window with one last longing look at the dick pic and once again try to focus on class.

∼

I LIFT my fist to the door and deliver a few quick raps. I glance down at the paper clutched in my other fist and cringe inwardly. I'm starting to wonder if I should've read the note the guy gave me ahead of time.

The door swings open, and I brace myself for whatever I'm about to face. "Karen?" I check.

"Yeah, why?"

"Ryan has a message for you. I'm really sorry, these are his words, not mine," I explain before lifting the paper up and reading from it. "Ten reasons I'm dumping your ass: One, you never go down on me..." I flinch as the words leave my lips. *Oh damn, yeah, I really should've read this beforehand.*

Karen gasps, and her face turns bright red.

"I don't think you need to hear the rest of this." I start to shove the paper into my pocket, but Karen stops me.

"No, tell me what it says," she demands.

With extreme reluctance, I pull the paper back out and continue reading. "Two, you've got a fat ass...not in a good way."

Her fists ball, and her eyes flash with rage.

"Three, I already fucked all your friends, so there's not much reason to hang around anymore."

I don't see her fist coming, but as it crunches against my nose. I can't even say I blame her. There's no doubt in my mind I would've punched me too, if the situations were reversed.

"Fuck," I yell, clutching my nose as blood pours through my fingers. The hateful list falls somewhere, and the door slams loudly in my face. I whip my shirt over my head and press it against my nose as I pull my phone out of my pocket.

That's when I realize there's no one I can call to take me to the hospital. My heart sinks at that thought. I probably have a broken nose, and I'm going to have to take an Uber to the hospital because I don't have any friends. *How pathetic am I?*

I awkwardly try to wipe off some of the blood on my

hand onto the t-shirt crumpled against my face. Then I pull out my phone and order a car. The driver gives me a dirty look when he notices I'm shirtless and bloody, but he doesn't say anything for which I am grateful.

It takes ages for us to get to the hospital, because this is LA, and traffic is basically the tenth circle of hell. The bleeding slows by the time I get out of the car, but I can already feel my face swelling. There's no doubt she broke my nose. I should have just handed her that mean-as-hell list and walked away.

Luckily, the emergency room is quiet tonight, so I only end up waiting with my t-shirt pressed to my face for about an hour before a nurse takes me to the back.

"I'm pretty sure my nose is broken. Do you need to take X-rays or something?"

"Actually, we don't usually X-ray for a broken nose. If there's been a recent trauma and the nose is swollen and bleeding, there's a good bet it's broken. So, what we'll do is put you under a mild anesthesia, and one of our surgeons will be in to set and splint it. Now, I understand you came in alone. Is there someone who will be able to pick you up? You won't be able to drive after the mild anesthetic."

"Um..." I cast around my mind fruitlessly, trying to come up with a solution. I could order another Uber, but I doubt any of them would appreciate my drugged-up ass.

Mason would be a good option, but I don't have his number. The only person I can think of who I sort of consider a friend and whose number I also have is Rebel. But he's not exactly the type of friend I need to be calling when I need a favor.

"Can I stay here and sleep it off?" I ask in desperation.

The nurse gives me a skeptical look. "We don't exactly have extra beds to offer up for outpatient procedures."

"Fuck," I sigh. Looks like I'm going to have to bite the bullet and call Rebel.

"Why don't you sit tight, make some calls if you need to, and the doctor will be in shortly to get you taken care of."

As soon as I'm alone, I call Rebel before I can chicken out.

"Hey, sexy," Rebel greets in a playful tone. "Already dying for my cock in your ass again?"

In spite of the shame and pain currently burying me, my dick manages to take interest, hardening against my leg at the memory of Rebel's erection stretching me wide and pounding me without mercy.

"Uh..." I clear my throat and try to conjure actual words and sentences. "This is really fucking embarrassing, but I need a favor, and I had literally no one else to call."

"Is everything okay?" His tone has done a rapid one-eighty and is now full of concern.

"Kind of. I'm at the hospital, and I need a ride home in like an hour or two."

"Oh my god, what happened? Is it serious? Which hospital?" Rebel asks, and I hear shuffling and keys jangling in the background. I tell him which hospital and that it's only a minor injury. "I'll be there in thirty minutes." And then the phone goes dead.

I shove my phone in my pocket and lay back in the stiff hospital bed. As embarrassing as it is that I had to call Rebel, it's kind of sweet that he was so willing to drop everything to come pick me up.

A few minutes later the nurse is back, with the doctor this time, and they're shooting me up with the good stuff. I have no idea how long it takes them to fix my nose, but I do know I'm not feeling any pain as they do. When it's over, there's a big ass splint on my nose, and the drugs are just starting to wear off a little.

"Heeeeey," I greet Rebel in a goofy, excited voice when I see him waiting for me. "You're really hot."

Rebel's already blindingly handsome face lights with a smile, and I almost have to shield my eyes from his perfection.

"They gave you some good drugs, huh?"

"Yeah, I can't feel my face," I agree.

"Okay, let me figure out what we need to do to get you squared away, and then I'll take you home."

"Kay," I mumble, slouching back on the bed where the nurse put me to wait until I could be discharged.

As the drugs continue to fade, and the quiet of the room starts to feel like an oppressive force, it hits me again how pathetic it was that I had to call a fuck buddy to pick me up from the hospital. Who knows what kind of plans Rebel had to cancel to come pick my sorry ass up. He probably thinks I'm a total loser with no friends, which is entirely accurate.

Rebel returns a few minutes later with a handful of paperwork. "You're all set. Let me help you."

He comes around to the side of the bed and helps me up. The nurse enters the room with a wheelchair seconds later and insists I ride it to the exit.

"Oh wait, doesn't he have a shirt?" Rebel asks the nurse.

"Got all bloody," I answer.

"Hold on, it's a little chilly out." Rebel takes his jacket and puts it over my shoulders. A strange warmth spreads out from my chest and to the tips of my fingers and toes. Those drugs must've been *really* good.

"It's not chilly; we live in LA," I argue half-heartedly.

Outside, Rebel opens the car door for me for some reason. It's nice, but weird as hell.

"So who punched you?" he asks as soon as he's in the driver seat.

"Some chick I was paid to dump. I deserved it."

Rebel makes an unhappy noise in the back of his throat that sends a little thrill through me.

Aside from the directions I give him to my place, Rebel and I don't talk on the way there. I expect him to pull up in front of my building and let me out, but he insists on finding a parking spot.

"I'm fine, you don't have to walk me in."

"You're drugged up and injured. I'm going to come in and make sure you're settled. I'll make you a nice cup of tea."

"I don't have tea."

"Really? Why don't you have tea? Isn't that a staple?"

"No, because I'm not British."

Rebel chuckles. "My mom always makes me tea when I'm not feeling well."

My heart gives a little squeeze at the fondness in his tone when he mentions his mother. I wonder what it's like to have someone in the world care about you that deeply. Someone who worries about your comfort and happiness. It seems like it would be nice…

But that's for other people, not for me. Maybe I was a warlord or an asshole in a past life. Maybe there's something ingrained in my DNA that makes me undesirable. Whatever the reason, I *am* unlovable. That's life, and there's no point dwelling on it.

"You really don't have to come up. I have a shitty little apartment. It's nothing like your place," I tell him. "Plus, I'm obviously not up for fooling around."

"I don't give a shit."

I scoff and shake my head but don't argue further. If we

keep hanging out without fucking around, what does that make us? Friends? Something else?

In my apartment, I cringe inwardly, imagining what Rebel must be thinking as he steps into the one room that holds my whole life. Usually when I have a guy in here, we're too busy getting naked for me to worry what they think of my living space. And, beyond that, I can't imagine I'd care what any of those randoms think anyway.

"If you don't have tea, how about I make you some soup or something?"

"Why are you doing this?" I eye him skeptically.

"What? Do you want something more substantial? I can make a sandwich."

"No, I mean why are you being so nice?"

Rebel's eyebrows furrow, and the corners of his lips tug down in a frown. There's a sharp sadness in his striking blue eyes that makes me want to shove him away or crawl into bed and hide for a week, anything to get away from the pity.

"We're friends, right?" Rebel asks.

"You've had your dick in both my mouth and my ass."

"So...best friends?"

I want to laugh, but the pain meds are starting to wear off, and my nose is starting to throb. "I'm not usually friends with guys I fuck around with," I explain for what I feel like is the hundredth time since meeting Rebel.

"Then who are you usually friends with?"

My mouth opens and closes like a dumbass fish. I'm not sure if he was *trying* to throw shade, but damn if he didn't get me. "I don't have friends," I finally admit with a little bite in my tone. I don't want friends, and I don't need friends.

"We're friends; deal with it. Now, soup?" He skirts around me into my kitchen, leaving me at a loss for words. "Why don't you lay down on the couch and find something for us to watch? I'll bring you some food, and we'll get a dose of the painkillers the ER prescribed into you, and you can sleep through the worst of the pain."

I almost ask again why he's doing this, but decide that whatever his motivation, it feels nice to be taken care of for a change. I settle onto the couch and put on the second season of *Stranger Things*.

It's not long before Rebel brings me a bowl of soup, a second dose of the painkillers, and a glass of water.

"Thank you."

"Don't mention it," Rebel waves me off and then sits down beside me on the couch. "Cool, I haven't watched the second season yet."

"I might fall asleep after I eat," I warn.

"That's fine, I can let myself out or crash on your couch. Don't worry about me."

We fall into comfortable silence as I finish the soup Rebel made me. And before long, my eyelids grow heavy. I feel a blanket being laid over me and then a quick kiss brushed against my forehead before I'm pulled under by sleep.

12

REBEL

I wake up in the pitch black, and it takes me a second to figure out where I am and what the strange sounds are that woke me up. Right. I'm at Troy's, and he's the one making weird noises. I can hear his groans drifting through the room, and they're not the happy ones indicating he's about to come. He's in pain.

He fell asleep on the couch yesterday, and after about an hour, I carried him to his bed. I didn't want him to wake up with even more pain in his body after spending a night on that uncomfortable looking couch.

I can now affirm that couch is indeed hella uncomfortable, because after a few hours of restless sleep on this thing, my back is killing me. Sweet fuck, he really could use a new couch. I'll have to introduce him to Ikea, maybe.

I feel around for a light switch, because I know there's a small lamp on the side table. Why the hell is it so fucking dark in here? I can't see a damn thing. Finally, my fingers touch the switch, and I turn the lamp on.

I'd better get him some more painkillers. I crawl off the couch, my stiff muscles loudly announcing their discomfort.

The painkillers are in the bathroom, and I make my way to Troy's bed with a glass of water and the package of meds.

Troy has his back toward me in the queen size bed, but I can see he's in pain. He's whimpering a little in a restless sleep, his body curled up into a ball. Poor guy. That was one angry woman to clock him in the face that hard.

I turn on the lamp next to him before I gently put my hand on his shoulder. "Hey, Troy... Babe, wake up."

His body freezes before he relaxes again. I guess he needed a sec to remember who I am or something. "What's wrong?" he asks, his voice thick with sleep.

"You're in pain. I've got the next dose of your painkillers for you."

He turns around with a big groan. "God, my head is killing me. Why the fuck did I take that job?"

I help him sit up, shooting him a look of sympathy. "Here," I say when he's somewhat sitting up straight—more like slumping against the headboard—and hand him the water and a pill.

"Are you drugging me so you can have your way with me?" he jokes before taking the pill and washing it down with the water.

I grin. "Sure thing, babe. 'Cause you haven't put out so far, and I really enjoy fucking a guy with a broken nose."

He sags against the pillows with a faint smile, then gingerly touches his nose and cringes. "Do you think it will leave a mark? My nose, I mean. Will it stay crooked?"

I carefully sit down on the bed beside him and brush a lock of hair from his forehead. "I don't know, but you'll still be gorgeous."

He sends me a watery smile. "You're good with words. Much better than me. I never know what to say. I suck at this whole friendship thing."

Even though he's in pain, I don't wanna lie to him. "Yeah, you kinda do. Not because of the words, because I don't need them, but because you're so defensive all the time. It's okay to hang out, fuck when we feel like it, and be friends, you know? Those things are not mutually exclusive, and it's not like I'm looking for anything serious either."

He blinks slowly. "I guess," he says.

"Wow. Your enthusiasm is overwhelming. Need I remind you that we're best friends, considering I've had my dick in your mouth and your ass, as you so eloquently put it before? I expected a little more enthusiasm, dude."

I figure the best thing to do is keep it light. I don't know why he's so freaked out about the whole friends and hanging out thing, but right now, I just wanna make sure he's okay. He's still looking mighty pale. Despite that, his lips curve into a smile.

"Best friends, huh?"

I nod. "Besties, man. I'm at your service."

His smile widens. "Did you know that endorphins really help against pain?"

I know exactly where he's going with this, but I wanna see him play this out. "Endorphins? Really? Aren't those released when you do something pleasurable, like...hugging? Are you saying you'd like a hug from me?"

"For someone who calls himself my best friend, you're pretty shitty at reading my needs, bro. I was not talking about hugging."

"Oh. You weren't trying to emotionally blackmail me into giving you a blowjob at four in the morning, were you? Because that's not something best friends do to each other, right?"

He pouts, his bottom lip going all droopy and sad. He looks so cute when he's put out that I take pity on him. The guy is in pain, after all. "Okay, okay, I'll do it. Sheesh. The things I do to stay in your good graces."

I shimmy myself onto the bed, dragging the covers down. He's only wearing boxers, so that makes it easy. Then his hand touches my hair, grabbing it, and I look up.

"Rebel, you don't have to…"

"I know."

"I mean it. I don't want you to feel—"

It's sweet that he's worried about me feeling pressured, but ain't nobody got time for this. I simply drag down his boxers and drop down on his cock, which is still mostly soft. That's probably because he didn't have enough time to consider what was about to happen.

It's not often that I get to start a blowjob on a soft cock. It may be a strange thing to think about when you're sucking someone off, but usually, guys are rock hard and dripping when I work on them. It's a wonderful sensation to feel Troy grow hard in my mouth.

I start with gently suckling on his crown, and my guess is he loves it, because both his hands thread into my hair to keep my head in place. As if I was planning on going anywhere. Still, I like how it feels, this little gesture of possessiveness.

There's a difference between sucking someone off on camera and doing it in private. On camera, the goal is usually to draw it out, because we want the scene to last a little. Sure, most porn stars can hold out for a while—yes, there are tricks for this that we teach each other—but we also don't go all out. We make it look sexy, first and foremost, but it's not necessarily what would make someone come the fastest.

In private, it's different. I've given blowjobs that were aimed at making someone come really fast because I wanted it over with and others where it was fun to play around a little.

Right now, it's four in the morning, I'm still tired, my back hurts from that fucking couch, and Troy looks like he could keel over any second. You wanna bet how fast I can make him come?

He's all hard now, moaning softly. I deep throat him with ease, putting my tongue to good use for a little extra pressure, and I swallow him down. His hips come off the mattress, and that discreet moan transitions into a low growl.

I keep up the pressure, only occasionally coming up for air. Troy is almost pulling on my hair now, moaning beautifully. And then he jerks and unloads in my throat, his body going slack right after. I lick him clean, and by the time I tuck him back into his boxers, he's half asleep already.

"Mmmm...wasreallygood," he murmurs.

"I do this for a living, remember?" I say half-joking, but he doesn't even respond. I draw the sheets back over him and sit up. Do I really have to sleep on that lumpy couch? I debate it for three seconds before deciding Troy is passed out and won't notice anyway, and then I curl up next to him. I'm asleep in under a minute, my mouth still full of his creamy taste.

13

REBEL

I wake up restless, even though it's my day off. I helped set up a complicated shoot yesterday, so I spent all day at the studio. Bear told me he doesn't want to see me the rest of the week. That means I find myself strangely bored on a Friday morning.

I could go to the gym. I usually go at least three times a week, and my latest workout was two days ago, but I really don't feel like it. I hauled around some heavy stuff yesterday, and my muscles are already somewhat sore.

A quick glance around my apartment confirms that it doesn't really need cleaning, and I'm caught up on laundry as well. Seriously, when did I become this boring, walking and talking commercial for urban middle class life? Well, aside from the fact that I make my money in porn, of course.

No, I don't want to do something useful today. I want to do something fun. I need to do something fun, if only to prove to myself I haven't fully transformed into this nine-to-five, responsible adult. Yikes.

Something fun. But what? And with whom? As soon as I think it, I know who I want to hang out with. I gotta come up with a good reason, though, because if I call him to ask him to hang out for a whole day, he won't do it. He'll balk, get suspicious. I don't know why he keeps doing that, but I know he does.

I need to figure out an excuse. What if I...? Yeah, that should work. I make a few quick calls and have the whole thing set up in under fifteen minutes. My boys really are the best, even when they have no idea why I'm doing this.

It's time for the final call. I laugh when I see the picture I chose for his name: a banana. He'll never get rid of that association.

"Hey," he answers, sounding rather sleepy.

"Good morning, sunshine. Were you awake yet or did I wake you up?"

He yawns loudly. "I was...somewhat awake."

"Well, time to rise and shine, banana boy. Me and some of the boys are hanging out today, and I figured you'd want to come."

He's quiet for a second, and then lets out a sexy laugh. "Will there be coming involved?"

"Holy fuck, you and your dirty mind. Not everything is about sex, you know?"

"You're asking me to hang out with a bunch of porn stars, but you want to keep it PG? So not gonna happen."

I sigh. He's actually right about that. Me and the boys have been known to get a little...handsy every now and then. "Okay, there will be coming, at least for you, okay?"

"You're bribing me with sex?"

"Dude, there are porn stars. Why would you need bribing?"

"All right, all right, all right," he says with laughter sprinkled all over his voice. "Where do I meet you?"

I had planned to pick him up, but maybe it's better this

way. Less of a commitment for him. "You know the Wonderland Arcade?"

"Are you kidding me? I used to live there as a kid. Only happy place I ever had."

He's quiet after that unexpected revelation, undoubtedly because he revealed a bit more than he intended to. I think the best strategy is to pretend I didn't pick up on it. "Awesome. We're meeting there at noon."

I almost hold my breath, knowing he's one second away from blowing me off.

"Okay, see you there," he says, and I exhale.

When I arrive slightly after noon—arriving exactly on time is pretty much impossible with the unpredictable traffic here—Troy is already there. Dressed in faded jean shorts, a tight-fitting white T-shirt, and a pair of beaten up Converse, he looks edible.

He's talking to Brewer and Campy, and as I walk up, Pixie and Heart arrive as well. Tank isn't coming, of course. He doesn't do much social stuff, and especially not when he knows Brewer is coming.

We do the usual round of hugging and somewhat-manly back slaps, and I formally introduce Troy to the others. I can tell he's a little star struck, but he holds his own as we grab some hot dogs from the best hot dog vendor in LA. He even manages to hold a more-or-less intelligent conversation with Campy, who turns out to be a big-time gamer like Troy himself. Who knew?

"What's your favorite game?" Campy tries to drag me into their conversation.

I scratch the stubble on my chin. "Erm, *Angry Birds*?" I joke. "I haven't played video games since high school, for real. And even back then, it wasn't really my thing. But I love these arcade games."

Campy mumbles something about me being a heathen, whatever that means, but Troy merely laughs at me. "You just haven't found the right game yet," he says with confidence.

We make our way inside the arcade, and my eyes are drawn to a huge, old-fashioned pinball machine. "Now there's a game I love," I say with deep satisfaction. "You game?"

Troy nods. "Bring it on."

I do pretty well on my first try, but when it's Troy's turn, he absolutely slays it. I watch him while he's playing, completely focused on what the balls are doing. He even whispers encouragements that turn into louder cheers as the game progresses. Hot damn, he's good at this.

"Is he your boyfriend?" Pixie asks me softly.

I hadn't even noticed him standing next to me, totally engrossed in watching Troy. "No," I say quickly. "We're friends with benefits, sort of."

"He's hot," Pixie observes. "I'd totally let him fuck me."

My head shoots sideways, and my eyes meet Pixie's, who's grinning. "Just friends with benefits, huh? Keep telling yourself that."

"It's complicated," I say defensively.

"It always is," is Pixie's answer. There's too much wisdom and sadness in his voice, considering how young he is.

"You're new to this, baby-boy, but having a relationship is hard when you're doing porn. Most men have a big issue with their boyfriend having sex with others, even if it's for a job."

His gorgeous misty eyes turn sad. "Yeah, I can imagine. Then again, having a relationship is hard even when you're not doing porn, you know?"

I want to hug him, but instead I rub his neck a little. He

lets out a little sigh. He's a tactile one, our little imp. Does he even realize himself how much he loves being touched? Even with this little gesture of my scratching his neck, he steps closer to me, as if to make sure I have full access.

Troy raises his hands and lets out a loud cheer. "I broke my record!"

I let go of Pixie and step closer to look at his score. My eyes grow big. "That's your score? You didn't just break your own record, you broke the record on this damn machine!"

He spins around and suddenly lifts me in a bear hug, smacking a fat kiss on my lips. "I sure did, babycakes!"

Babycakes? What alien has taken over Troy's body and mind? He lets out a happy laugh and lets go of me to take in high fives from the others.

"I'm not even gonna bother after that," Campy says, laughing.

"Come on, I'll let you beat my ass on this retro Pac-Man they got," Troy says.

"And such a fine ass it is," Brewer says, licking his lips. I smack the back of his head in true Leroy Jethro Gibbs style —I love me some *NCIS*. If I'm the stern Gibbs, that would make Brewer the goofball and playboy DiNozzo, and damn, that fits him to a T.

"You guys fighting over my ass now?" Troy asks, turning around and shaking his butt. "Keep going, this does wonders for my ego."

"There is nothing wrong with your ego," I grumble.

"Nothing wrong with your ass either," Brewer fires back.

"Mine or his?" Troy wants to know.

Brewer pretends to think about it. "Well, Rebel here has got a nice ass, but I've tapped it already. I'm always interested in fresh meat."

For some reason, his incessant flirting suddenly irritates

me. It's irrational, because I don't have exclusive rights to Troy. Hell, we haven't even mentioned the word exclusive. I can pretty much guess how fast he's gonna run when I utter that red-flag word.

Still, I want Brewer to stop, because he's really hot, and he's got all these cool tattoos, and he's the perfect happy fuckboy for Troy, and what if Troy decides he likes him better? I run out of breath in my head to think, and all that time Brewer is studying me with a look that says he knows. He knows this is messing with my head, and he's thoroughly enjoying this.

"I'm so gonna propose a scene with you and Tank to Bear," I say and watch with satisfaction as Brewer pales.

Troy sends me a cocky grin and saunters off with Campy. "Just friends with benefits, huh?" Pixie repeats his earlier remark, and I don't know whether to slap him or hug him.

14

TROY

Lazing in bed on a Sunday morning is never complete without my Ballsy Boys. But I hesitate for a second before clicking over to the site because I'm worried it'll be weird if Rebel has a new video. I know he doesn't do scenes often anymore so if a new one is up, it probably means he filmed it since we've started hooking up. And in theory that doesn't bother me—it's his job after all—but I don't know if it will freak me out to actually see it.

Hanging out with all the guys last weekend at the arcade was a blast and totally surreal. I always figured you probably didn't want to get to know porn stars in real life, the whole *watching the sausage get made* principle. But those guys are chill as hell, especially Campy. He knew his shit about gaming, and he even asked if I wanted to hang out and play sometime.

I snort a laugh to myself remembering Rebel's expression when he overheard just the last part when Campy asked if we could play sometime. I swear his head looked like it was about to explode.

Wait...was he jealous?

The thought stops me in my tracks for a few seconds. That can't possibly be right. What would Rebel have to be jealous of? We're not *together*. We're fuck buddies, friends with benefits, whatever. But none of those rambling thoughts brings me to any sort of conclusion about whether it's weird to watch porn when I'm hooking up with the guy in it.

Dammit, just because I'm getting some prime porn star cock doesn't mean I'm going to give up checking out my favorite porn site on a relaxing weekend morning. I click the link on my favorites bar and, sure enough, there's a brand new scene up with Rebel and Heart.

The thumbnail has the two of them lounging on a bed together in just their boxers. I stare at it for a few seconds, waiting to feel a flare of jealousy, but all I feel is horny as hell...and honestly a little curious to compare Rebel's performance with what he's like one on one.

I click on the video and settle back against my pillow to watch. It starts like most Ballsy Boys videos do, with a few minutes of flirting and banter between the two men and the off-screen director.

"Heart, you told me you were looking forward to working with Rebel. Are you nervous at all?"

Heart blushes a little and glances at Rebel. *"Nah, I think I can handle him,"* he answers and then gives Rebel a playful wink.

"Good, then I won't promise to be gentle," Rebel teases.

I smile, watching my man in his element, clearly having fun. Wait...*my man*? No, Rebel isn't *my man*. He's *a* man that I happen to be fooling around with, nothing more.

The chatting ends and the men get down to business, kissing and touching each other. Still, I don't feel any jealousy. I certainly wish I was there to join in, though.

As they start getting into it, I notice Rebel's moan is different, more over the top than how he moans in private. And, for some reason, that makes me feel a little smug. I know something about Rebel that most people don't know. Sure, millions of people have watched him fuck and get fucked, but very few know how he really sounds when he's overcome with lust.

I stroke myself as I watch Heart deep throat Rebel, and my mouth waters. The pleasure on his face is fucking gorgeous.

My phone rings on my nightstand, and I almost decide to ignore it, but so few people call me that it's almost certainly Rebel. I pause the video and grab my phone.

"Hello?" Even to my own ears my voice is breathless and a little rough.

"Hey, baby. Am I interrupting something? You sound out of breath."

"Um..." Is it weird that I was jerking off watching a video of his? Hell, my barometer of what's fucked up sexually isn't exactly fine-tuned, I'll be the first to admit that.

"Oh, shit, you have someone over? Well, this got awkward... I'll just let you go and call you later."

"Rebel, wait. I don't have anyone over, I was watching...something."

"Something?" I can hear the teasing in his tone. "Were you watching one of my videos and jerking off?"

"Yes, I was. Are you happy now?"

"Very. Which video was it?"

"The new one with you and Heart."

There's a long pause on the other end of the phone, and I start to wonder if I should've lied.

"Is that weird?" Rebel asks cautiously. "I mean...you know I filmed that like two weeks ago, right?"

"Yeah, I figured. Why would it be weird? It's your job."

"True, but I didn't know if you'd feel...I don't know, jealous or something?"

"Honestly, I thought I might, but once I started watching it, all I felt was turned on. You look hot as fuck."

"You know, I could be over there in five minutes."

"Then why are we still talking on the phone?"

Rebel chuckles, and then the line goes dead.

I glance at the freeze frame one last time and admire the flush of arousal in Rebel's cheeks and the way his lips are parted on a moan. Then I force myself to close my laptop, because if Rebel is on his way over, I don't want to waste a good orgasm jerking off alone.

As promised, there's a knock on my door six minutes later. I open the door in nothing but my boxer briefs, my half hard cock filling them out nicely.

"Mmmm, hey sexy," Rebel greets me, not hiding his slow perusal of my nearly naked body, his eyes lingering on the bulge of my hardening cock.

"Hey yourself. I'm starting to wonder if this is some sort of coma dream, because there's no way this is real life that I can be watching my favorite porn star get blown one second and have him on my doorstep the next."

"You must've done something *very* good in a past life," Rebel says with such a serious expression that I can't help but laugh.

"I must've been Mother Teresa," I agree as I step aside to let him in.

Rebel makes a bee-line for my bed, shedding his clothes haphazardly along the way.

"Way to make a guy feel easy," I tease.

"I assumed we were having a lazy Sunday in bed, am I wrong?"

I smile at the innocence in Rebel's expression as he dives between my sheets and settles in like he owns the place.

"That's exactly what we're doing," I agree, following suit.

"So how do you normally spend a Sunday in bed? Or do I even need to ask?" Rebel waggles his eyebrows at me.

"I usually alternate Netflix and porn."

"I'm game."

"Netflix or porn?"

"Surprise me," Rebel suggests.

I open my laptop, and the Rebel/Heart video I was watching is still up.

"Do you ever watch your own videos?"

"Nah, I end up nitpicking them too much. I watch the other guys' videos though."

Just for fun I go back to the main site and pick another recent upload, this one with Pixie and Brewer. I set the laptop between us and settle back to watch as the two men flirt and chat, and then Pixie climbs onto Brewer's lap and they start to make out and grind against each other. They started the scene in just their underwear, but they lose those quickly enough, and Brewer takes both their cocks in his fist and jerks them together. Rebel shifts beside me, and I glance over to find him with his hand down the front of his boxers, lazily stroking his growing erection.

"Mmmm," I hum and then shimmy my own underwear down and kick them away.

Back on screen, Brewer is on his knees sucking Pixie's cock with noisy slurps and dirty groans. I wrap my hand around the base of my cock and slowly tug from root to tip, spreading my legs wide and flexing my muscles to put on a good show for Rebel.

I can feel his eyes boring into me, and it makes me hot as hell. The smell of sweat and pre-cum fills the air as we lay side by side jerking off in my bed. His arm brushes against mine, and he presses his hairy thigh against mine.

I don't know about Rebel, but the clip playing on my laptop is nothing more than background noise since I can't tear my eyes away from his cock as it grows darker and firmer in his grasp. Rebel flexes his hip and fucks into his fist, and I'm done for. With a deep moan, I spill into my hand, a few spurts making their way into my happy trail and my belly button. Rebel gets up onto his knees and kneels over me. With a few quick jerks, his cum covers my stomach, mixing with mine.

When he's got nothing left, Rebel leans over and laps our combined release off my stomach. He crawls up the bed until we're face to face, and then he opens his mouth to show me our cum on his tongue. I grab him by the hair and tug him to me, shoving my tongue into his mouth to get a taste. Rebel moans into my mouth as we share a filthy kiss that leaves us with cum sticky lips and dirty, satisfied smiles.

"Can I ask you a question?" Rebel asks when we're laying side by side again.

"Sure."

"Do you ever like to top? I kinda pegged you as vers when we met, but since we've been fucking, you haven't said anything about wanting to switch it up."

"Oh, yeah I'm vers, but it usually depends a bit who I'm with. I don't let randoms top me usually, so I guess I've been indulging with you since you're so damn good," I admit.

"Oh," Rebel breathes out, and I can tell by his expression that my answer surprised him.

"I want to fuck you, but I didn't think there was any big rush."

"No rush at all," Rebel agrees, rolling onto his side, facing me, and tucking his arm under his head.

"Good." I nod, scooting a little closer to Rebel. "What's your favorite thing to do in bed?"

"On camera or off?" Rebel clarifies.

"Off. When you can do whatever you want, what do you like to do?"

"Rimming," he answers without hesitation.

"Really? Not getting a blowjob or...I don't know, something really kinky?"

"Don't get me wrong, that's all great, too. But there's just something about having a man on his hands and knees, quivering, waiting. Taking the firm globes of his ass in my hands and parting them to expose a tight little pink hole. Then, running my tongue up and down his crack until he starts to soften and welcome me in. Licking and fucking his ass with my tongue until he's begging for my cock."

My spent cock makes an effort to take interest in this conversation, but it's not happening so soon, unfortunately.

"Damn, that's fucking hot."

"Mmhmm. You going to let me eat your ass?"

"Anytime you want. Just not until I get a few minutes of recovery time. How about some Netflix in the meantime?"

"Works for me."

15

REBEL

"And Hendrix, I do not want to see you show up by yourself, you hear me, honey? Find yourself a hot date. We're gonna dance all night, and your dad and I want you to have fun!"

I sigh, biting back a cringe as my mom waves at me on FaceTime once more and ends our session. I close the screen with a tired move. She means well, my mom, but fuck my life for having parents who not only fully accept me being gay, but also wholeheartedly support my chosen career. They're weirdos, both of them.

Wait, that didn't come out right. I love my parents, don't get me wrong. They're kind of a rare commodity in the gay community: accepting, loving parents who couldn't give a shit about who I date, fuck, or love, as long as it's consensual and safe. Yup, that's the exact speech my mom gave me when I came out.

Not that they didn't know before, even though I thought it was this huge secret. Turns out, my mom had started suspecting when I was, like, eight or so. I knew they wouldn't freak—my parents are the classic hippies from the seventies—but I still needed to gather my courage for months before I told them.

My dad patted me on the back and told me he loved me no matter what. Bless his heart. My mom gave me a massive hug and then lectured me on safe gay sex. Judging by the level of detail, she'd done some research. I was thirteen, mind you. No wonder I ended up in porn.

Free spirits as they were, they did get married pretty young—they were both nineteen. At twenty-one, my mom had my older sister Marley, and two years later I was born. Wanna take a wild guess who we were named after? Bob Marley and Jimmy Hendrix. As I said, fuck my life. They're pretty great, though, seriously, even if they embarrass the shit out of me at times.

And now they're getting ready to celebrate their twenty-ninth wedding anniversary. They were supposed to throw a bash at their twenty-fifth, but my mom had breast cancer, so they wanted to wait with celebrating until she was given a clean bill of health. She's been declared cancer-free, so they're planning the mother of all parties. That means tons of food and booze, all-night dancing, and I wouldn't be surprised if some strippers show up. Plus, of course, weed. They live in Colorado, just saying.

And I'm supposed to bring a date. Fuck my life.

There's only one person I can ask, really. Well, technically, I could ask one of my Ballsy Boys co-stars, but I'm not that stupid. My mother has no filter and zero sense of what's appropriate. I swear, she'd ask Brewer for tips on how to suck cock, and don't even get me started on her weird obsession with Tank. It's...super awkward.

It's one thing to know your mom watches gay porn, but quite another that she's watching the guys you fuck. Or get fucked by, same difference. Thank fuck she at least has the common sense to not watch my videos.

But yeah, that date? I'll have to swallow some serious pride and ask Troy. My Banana Boy is the only guy I know who's crazy and self-confident enough to survive meeting my family.

Wait...what?

My Banana Boy?

What the ever-loving fuck?

Oh, god.

I refuse to think about what this means, but instead pull up his number and call.

"Hey, you miss my tight ass?" Troy jokes as he picks up.

I give a half-assed attempt at a laugh. "Always."

Really? *Always?*

Troy laughs. "Says the guy who fucks the most desirable asses ever."

"It's just sex, you know," I say quietly. "It's my job. It's fun, sure, but it's not the same as..."

As with you, I want to add, because thinking of him as *my* Banana Boy and admitting that I always think of him weren't sappy enough. Holy hell, I need to stop talking. For real.

"I know," Troy says, then hesitates. "Are you okay?"

I sigh. "Yeah. No. I don't know."

Troy waits a beat, then asks, "Do you want to talk about it?"

My first instinct is, of course, to say no. But before I realize it, I find myself opening up. "It's my parents. They're celebrating their 29th anniversary next weekend, and they want me to come."

"Of course, they want you to come. What's wrong with

that? Aren't they nice? Do they have an issue with you being gay or with what you do?"

"No, that's not it. They're great about all that, really, and so is my sister, Marley. She's married to a dentist, for fuck's sake, the most boring guy you'll ever meet, but he loves her to pieces, and for some weird reason she has stars in her eyes when she's with him. No, it's more that they're all so...happy. They're stable and happy and committed, and I don't know why the hell I'm telling you this when all I wanted to do was ask you on a date."

It's very quiet at the other end of the line. "You want to ask me on a date?" Troy repeats slowly.

It's then I realize that the connection in my head between the party and the date never made it into actual words. "For the wedding anniversary," I add quickly. "My parents. In Colorado."

"Dude, I feel like I'm on some game show, trying to guess a word but coming up short on vowels. Use whole sentences, Rebel, 'cause you're not making much sense."

"I wanted to ask you if you wanted to be my date to my parents' anniversary party, which is next weekend in Colorado," I say, grateful my brain is finally shifting to the right gear.

Troy is quiet for a long time. "Rebel, I don't know about this... Meeting the parents, that's some serious commitment, man."

"It's not. I'm not proposing marriage, for fuck's sake. I just need a date to this party so I don't look like a total loser. Plus, you know, we could have fun together. There's food and booze and weed, and we'll have a hotel room where we can hang out if it gets too much for you."

On a scale of one to ten, I'm at major pathetic now. If he doesn't agree soon, I'll start begging, and it will get ugly.

God, what the fuck is wrong with me? I used to be cool and I dunno, detached. For some reason, Troy is fucking with all that. It's like my brain is short-circuiting where he's concerned and out comes the stupidest shit.

"Hang out. Is that code for sex?"

I smile, because I can hear laughter in his voice now. Thank fuck. He's starting to come around. "Yes. I will fuck you six ways into Sunday, whatever you want. I swear, I'll do a fucking lap dance, if that's what you want."

"Your ass, that's what I want. My cock in your ass."

"Deal," I say, not even hesitating a second. Are you kidding me? Getting fucked is rarely a chore for me and especially not with Troy. I can't wait.

"You'd damn well better pay me in sex, and then you'll still fucking owe me," Troy says.

"Whatever you want, baby."

Baby.

Holy hell.

Kill. Me. Now.

16

TROY

I shouldn't have agreed to a fifteen-hour road trip to a family function with my fuck buddy. This is too intimate, it's too boyfriend-y. So why did I agree to it? And why do I feel just a little bit excited?

I grab my bag—packed with a week's worth of clothes—and fling it over my shoulder. I check the time, Rebel should be outside waiting, so I lock my door and head down.

As expected, Rebel is waiting in his idling car just outside my building. I toss my bag into the back seat and climb in.

"Hey," Rebel greets me by leaning over the center console. Without thought, I press a quick kiss to his lips, and then I freeze, my stomach jolting.

That wasn't a *let's get down to business* kiss, that was a *nice to see you, boyfriend* kiss. And the scary thing is it felt so natural. I pull back and paste on a smile. Rebel looks just as surprised and unsure as I feel.

"Hey, listen, I know I told you to call me Rebel, but I think that might be weird in front of my family."

"Oh, yeah I guess that makes sense. So...I should call you Hendrix?"

His real name on my lips feels strange but somehow also a little thrilling. I can imagine rasping it as he pounds me from behind.

His eyes widen a fraction, and the slightest hint of a blush rises in his cheeks. "Yup, is that okay?" he asks, his brisk tone out of balance with his shy expression.

"Yeah, it's cool."

An awkward silence settles between us for a few beats before a genuine smile returns to Rebel's face. "Guess what we'll pass right by on our drive."

"What?"

"Vegas." Rebel waggles his eyebrows at me, and I do a fist pump.

"We're going to stop, right?"

"Fuck yeah, we're going to stop," Rebel agrees. "It's only five hours to Vegas. So we'll head there and spend the night, then we can split the rest of the eleven-hour drive from there."

"Works for me, let's do this."

"Thanks again for coming," Rebel says, the hint of vulnerability leaching into his expression again.

"No thanks required, just the sex you promised."

"Oh yeah, we're definitely doing that. And feel free to entertain yourself during the first portion of our journey by giving me road head, if the spirit moves you."

"I'll keep that in mind."

As we pull out of the parking lot, Rebel selects a playlist, and I relax into the passenger seat.

Even once we're outside the city proper, traffic is at a standstill. Rebel and I entertain ourselves singing along with the radio, pointing out random road signs or anything that gives either of us a chuckle, and talking about nothing and everything.

"Tell me about losing your virginity," I prompt with a wicked smile at Rebel, who throws his head back and laughs at my question.

"Oh man, this is a really awkward story. I dated this guy, Justin, my junior year of high school. He wasn't the love of my life or anything, but he was hot and one of the few other openly gay guys. Anyway, we'd been dating for a few months and done everything else so we figured it was time to go where neither of us had gone before. We argued for over a week about which one of us would bottom. Both of us were nervous about being the one to take it. We ended up agreeing to flip a coin for it, I flipped and it came up tails..."

I laugh at the grim way Rebel recounts the story. "Aw, poor baby," I tease.

"Oh, yeah, just wait. With the important details decided, we made a plan for him to come over to my place after school when I knew we'd have the house to ourselves. We clumsily undressed each other, like we weren't already well practiced at getting each other naked. Once we were naked, things took a turn for the worst. We'd watched porn to figure out technique, and as I'm sure you might realize there's one thing that's missing from a porn education."

"Oh, my god, you poor thing," I gasp, guessing where this story is going, and doing a terrible job of stifling my chuckle behind my genuine sympathy.

"Yeah, no prep, no lube, I just bent over, and he went right for it. It felt like my ass was being torn in two. Luckily, he wasn't the most well hung guy ever, but it was still not awesome. After about thirty seconds, I told him to stop, and he said 'give me a second.' When he didn't stop, I got pissed and shoved him off me and then punched him in the jaw."

"Oh my god, how is this a real story?"

"I know, it's crazy, right? That's not the embarrassing part, though. Apparently, my mom had come home at some point and overheard us. After Justin left, she sat me down and talked to me about lube and prepping for, and I quote, anal play."

"Yeah, that's awkward," I agree, trying to catch my breath from how hard that story made me laugh.

"She's a great mom. Both my parents are awesome. I wasn't sure how they'd take it when I started doing porn, but they were cool about it."

My good humor sobers as talk turns to his parents.

"What about your family? You haven't mentioned them before."

"I grew up in foster care," I answer with cool detachment.

Understanding dawns on his face. "What happened to your parents?"

"Who knows, who cares," I snap. "They weren't around a lot when I was young. When they were home, they slept a lot and fought all the time. In hindsight, they were probably drug addicts. When I was six, my mom dropped me off at a police station. She said she'd be right back. That was the last time I saw her. I bounced around to different foster homes until I aged out of the system."

"I'm sorry."

The pity in Rebel's expression is enough to make me want to hit something. "Don't be. I was fine on my own. I don't need to rely on anyone but myself, and I'm good with that. I don't need to be coddled."

"I get it," Rebel assures me. "What about your first time?"

The tension in my shoulders relaxes. Bless Rebel for the subject change.

17

REBEL

Foster care.

I can't even imagine. I mean, I curse my parents at times, especially my mom. There is such a thing as parents who are too supportive, so I've discovered. But I wouldn't trade them for anything, and I can't possibly imagine what my life would have been like without them, who I would have been without that foundation of love and support.

I'm no shrink, but even the little bit of info Troy gave me on his background explains a lot. No wonder he has a hard time building friendships and relationships. No one has apparently ever stuck around long enough for him to even know what those words mean.

I guess I'll have to show him.

The thought warms my heart. I like him, this emotionally closed-off guy, who is so sexy and wild and free. And now the strange urge I've had to be his friend is even stronger, at least until that constant weariness in his eyes is gone.

"At this rate, we're never gonna make Vegas tonight,"

Troy says. He perked right back up after entertaining me with the story of his first time—convincing a guy he'd had a crush on that yes, he'd done this dozens of times, while praying he wouldn't fuck up his first time topping. I swear, this guy was born to fuck.

I eye the endless traffic jam ahead of us. Traffic is an eternal curse here in LA, but it seems even worse than usual. We've been in the car for two hours, and we haven't even reached Azusa yet. "There must be some kind of accident," I say.

"There's always some kind of accident."

"True. A bigger accident, then. Bigger than normal."

Troy smiles. "You know what else is bigger than normal?"

I groan. "Seriously? You're making a dirty joke out of a potential pile up?"

Wrong choice of words. Troy's grin widens. "I bet we could create a really big pile up."

"I give up. You're determined to turn everything into sex, aren't you?"

Troy shoots me an innocent look. "Sex? Who's talking about sex? I never even mentioned sex."

The traffic has been at a complete standstill for minutes now, which means I can send him a long glare. I don't think it's very effective, because he keeps grinning at me.

After a few more minutes of no moving, I sigh. "Wanna get off the freeway and see if we can grab a bite somewhere? This seems pretty useless."

He nods, then points at a sign, a hundred yards or so ahead. "There's a mall here. I'm not sure how big it is, but usually if there's a mall, there's something to eat, right?"

I swear, it takes us ten minutes to make it to the next exit, and we both sigh with relief as we get off. The mall turns out to be a small one, but there's a couple of restaurant options, so it works.

When we step out after wolfing down a delicious burger, there's a guy on the phone in our way. "I'm begging you, Austin, you have to come. You fucking promised me!" he pleads. "I'm gonna be a laughingstock if I show up by myself."

Apparently, Austin decides to hang up, because the guy locks his phone with an angry gesture. "Motherfucking asshole," he mutters.

He's cute, an adorable little twink with a pale face, black hair that's styled into a careful mess, and a tight little body. He's also obviously gay. I mean, my gaydar is plinging like a freaking weather alert.

"You okay?" I ask.

He looks up from his phone. His eyes slightly widen when he spots us, but he's not embarrassed, which I like. "Yeah. No. It's nothing serious, let me put it that way. Nobody's dying, not literally at least."

My curiosity is piqued, I can't help it. "You got stood up?" I ask. "Sorry, we overheard that last bit."

He shakes his head, obviously still frustrated. "Yeah. For a Paint and Sip party, can you imagine?"

"A what?" Troy asks the same question that's on my lips.

"A paint and sip. It's where they show you how to paint some stupid dumbass painting on two hours, meanwhile serving you alcohol so you don't realize how shitty your painting really is."

"Sounds...fascinating," Troy says.

Actually, it sounds stupid as shit, but I like his version better.

"It's not," the twink says. "It's, like, the most dumbass, asinine thing ever, and I've done some weird shit in my life."

"So why do it?" I ask.

He sighs. "It's my bitchy cousin's bachelorette party. She puts the desperate in desperate housewives, and she wanted this for her bachelorette. So, of course, her equally dumb-as-dogshit Barbie friends obliged. And since I'm the token gay, and I can't make it to the actual wedding because of work, I was lucky enough to get invited. This guy I've been seeing lately, Austin, was supposed to come, but he canceled on me. So now I have to face this horrendous bitchfest by myself, and there's not enough liquor in the world to make this fun, trust me. Especially when I show up alone, 'cause they're gonna get on my ass about that after assuring them I'd show up with a date."

During his explanation he gets more and more riled up, and he's a little firecracker. I decide I really like him, and I shoot a quick look over at Troy. Our eyes meet, and he nods. We're totally on the same page.

"Hi," I say, extending my hand. "I'm Hendrix and this is Troy. We'd be honored to accompany you to this illustrious party."

The little twink's eyes spread open wide. "You're shitting me, right?"

He takes my hand on reflex, and I shake it. "Nope, we're dead serious. We're fun, we've got nowhere else to be right now, and if I do say so myself, you could do worse than showing up with the two of us in tow."

His face splits open in a big grin, as he shakes Troy's hand with far more excitement. "Holy motherfucking yes, please. I'm Byron." He sees my face and adds, "My mom loved poetry. Don't ask."

"I'm named after Jimmy Hendrix, so I feel you."

"So, you want us to pose as a threesome or what?" Troy asks.

"Hell, yes," Byron replies. "I can't imagine anything better than that to stick it to my stuck-up cousin. Her name is Barbra, by the way, and her unlucky man is Dennis."

I mentally rub my hands. This is gonna be so much fun. "Give me the Cliff Notes version of you."

"I'm 23, I'm a teacher's assistant in third grade, and I'm almost done with my degree in education so I can become a full-fledged teacher. I'm an only child with two great parents, divorced and both remarried with new families, so lots of half-siblings. Let me see... My hobbies are ballet, which I've done since I was seven, and designing and decorating shoes. I'm gay as a unicorn, so sue me."

He's a happy, bubbly little twink, and he makes me smile. I'm so glad we'll be able to help him save face...and have some fun in the process.

Troy gives him the rundown on both of us, though he omits the "adult" part in my "acting career". Two minutes later, we walk into a large space, filled with dozens of tables, all with mini-easels set up, holding a blank canvas.

"Byron!" a blonde woman greets our new BFF. She looks like something pink vomited all over her, and the slightly-too-tight hug she gives Byron informs me this must be bitchy Barbra.

Then she spots us and her face transform into an almost comical look of confusion. "Who are they?"

Byron steps back and takes both our hands. "Barb, honey, these are my men. This gorgeous specimen is Troy, and this other hunk is Hendrix."

I swear, it's a good thing Barbra's eyes are firmly attached somehow, because the way they pop, I almost fear we'll see one rolling over the floor any second now. It's obvious she did not see this coming.

"You're with..." She swallows. "...two guys?"

Byron sends me an adorable look, then does the same with Troy. "I am."

"This little firecracker is too much for one guy," I say with a sexy smile aimed at Byron. "It's so nice to meet you, Barbra. Congrats on your upcoming nuptials."

She opens and closes her mouth a few times before finally finding her voice again. "Yeah. Thank you. Thanks for coming?"

The last part comes out a question, and I suppress a smile at how flustered she is. Mission accomplished, two minutes in.

Byron referred to his cousin's friends as Barbies, and we soon discover that's an apt description. Women don't do much for me anyway, but holy hell, this blatant explosion of all things fake is something else entirely. It's like the LA version of *Jersey Shore*, and it ain't pretty or even entertaining.

I don't even bother trying to remember any of their names, because the Candys, Tiffanys, and Heathers all blend in together after five of them. Troy is as amused as I am, and we both keep a close eye on our little twink to make sure no one gives him any shit.

The instructor gives us a short and sweet inspirational speech about how anyone can paint. She doesn't mention to what degree of quality, though, so I'm not convinced I'm not gonna suck badly at this.

The painting she demonstrates to us is some sappy beach scene with rolling waves and a dog playing on the beach. I was hoping for something a little more cultural, but I'll take it. I'll be happy if anyone can recognize it's a beach when mine is done. Bonus points for the dog.

I gotta say, adding booze to an event like this is a great idea. Absolutely terrific, in fact. There's a reason they call it liquid courage, and after three glasses of wine, I think my painting is fabulous. Isn't it, like, the prettiest beach ever?

Troy grins as he studies my painting with suspiciously clear eyes. "It sure is. Best damn beach I've ever seen."

I nod with satisfaction. I knew there was a reason I liked him enough to take him home to meet my parents. I frown. Well, not like that. Not exactly. Plus, I can't say that to Troy because he'll get all scared and standoffish. I gotta keep it light.

I reach out and grab his collar, pull him in for a wet kiss. God, he tastes so good. He always does.

"You're such a lightweight," he grins after I break off the kiss. "Three glasses of wine and you're three sheets into the wind."

I nod. "One glass for each sheet," I say solemnly.

His smile widens, and he kisses me again.

"I'm starting to feel left out," Byron says. We break off the kiss, and he's watching us with an adorable pout.

"We can't have that," I say. I grab him by his hand and yank him toward me. He's such a little thing that he falls onto my lap easily, and then my mouth is on him, and I kiss him until we both run out of breath.

"Mmm," he says with a dreamy look in his eyes. "You're such a good kisser."

"Better than me?" Troy asks, before lifting Byron off my lap and to his feet, proceeding with devouring his mouth.

It's not till I watch them that I start wondering. Was it weird that I kissed Byron? Should I have checked with Troy? We never said we were exclusive, and I'm pretty sure even mentioning that word would send him into a state of panic, but should I have asked anyway? He's kissing Byron as if he's starving right now, but is that because he's jealous or angry with me?

Oh, dammit, I've had too much wine to think. I can't deny watching him kiss that cutie is hot as fuck, though.

"You guys need a room?" one of the Barbies calls out. Troy and Byron break off their kiss and laugh. Troy sends him back to his easel with a playful swat on his butt.

I finish my painting, while making short work of my fourth glass of wine. I think. I may actually be up to five.

"That doesn't look half bad." A female voice startles me. It takes a few seconds for me to push through the alcohol-daze. Barbra.

"Thank you," I say, deciding to take it as a compliment.

"I'm so happy to see Byron so happy with you two," she says.

That's a lot of happy for one sentence, I think, but I decide to go with the flow. "Thank you. He makes me happy. Us. Both."

"So the three of you are really together?" she asks, lowering her voice. I blink a few times because she creeps closer to me, and it's weirding me out. I lean as far back in my chair as I can, but there's a table behind me, so I can't go much farther.

"Erm, yeah?"

Her manicured, pink-polished hand comes at me, dragging down from my cheek to my... I don't know where her move ends, somewhere on my chest. I'm pretty sure, even in my somewhat inebriated state, it's supposed to be sexy, but to me it's creepy as fuck. Didn't this woman get the memo that gay means not being interested in women, at least not sexually?

"How does that even work, with three guys, I mean? How do you keep it...equally satisfactory for all parties involved?"

She's kidding, right? She did not just seriously ask me

about my sexual activities with her cousin, did she? Oh, she's gonna get it now.

"Oh, honey, there's all kinds of ways. We've done a three-way sixty-nine, which is fabulous, but there's also the classic option of using his hole for one cock, and his mouth for another. Or Troy's, or mine, 'cause we're equal opportunity guys—with other guys, at least."

She takes a step back, but I lean forward 'cause I'm just getting started. "Good heavens, girl, there are all kinds of delicious things we do to each other. Rimming is one of my favorites."

Troy steps in, puts a hand on my shoulder. "He's an expert at it," he fake-whispers to the bitch. "His tongue in my ass, it's pure heaven."

"Not as good as his cock in my ass, though," Byron says, parking himself on my lap. He grinds his ass a little, and I let out a happy groan. He's a little tease, but I don't mind. Especially not when I see Barbra pale even more.

I nibble a little on Byron's ear, for Barbra's benefit, obviously. "One of these days, we'll convince our little firecracker here to take both our cocks at the same time."

Byron lets out a little moan, and grinds his ass again on my cock. "I can't wait."

Well, neither can I. My cock hasn't gotten the memo that this is all play, and is ready for action.

"That's all...fascinating," Barbra says, then gives up all pretense and hightails it out of there.

"Good riddance," Troy says. "Time to get you to a hotel, Re—Hendrix. You need to sleep it off."

I sigh. He's probably right that it's best to leave before my inhibitions are completely gone, and I start fucking someone right here, right now. "Can we at least take the firecracker?" I suggest.

Byron climbs off my lap and kisses me gently. "Any other time, I would've happily obliged, but you're drunk. Ask me again when you're sober, okay? I can appreciate a good man-sandwich."

I pout, sending Troy a pleading look. "I'm really horny, and I want to fuck something."

Troy pulls me up, then slings his arm around me to keep me steady because I'm wavering a little. Maybe it was six glasses of wine?

"The only thing you'll be fucking tonight is your own hand, though I doubt you'll be able to pull that off. Come on, Mr. Lightweight. There's a Marriott right next to the mall. We'll get a room there."

Byron accompanies us to the hotel, as Troy needs both his hands to keep me steady and can't carry our art. Troy gets us a room, and ten minutes later, we're inside the most boring room ever. Troy gently lowers me on the king size bed and proceeds to take off my shoes.

"Thanks so much, guys. You gave me the best night I've had in a long time," Byron says.

Troy bends down for a quick kiss, and then Byron walks over to me and kisses me. "You're a class act, Hendrix. A fucking amateur when it comes to drinking, but a class act. Have fun on your Vegas trip."

I'm snoring before he even leaves the room.

18

TROY

Living in LA my entire adult life, you'd think I'd have been to Vegas by now. But it seemed like the type of place to go with a friend, get drunk and crazy, and make memories. Going by myself would've been pathetic. I'm a little embarrassed by how wide-eyed I am when we hit the strip.

"This is insane." I look around at all the huge buildings and all the people on the streets. "I've never been here."

"I'm glad we stopped then." Rebel puts an arm over my shoulder, and we head into the hotel Rebel had the foresight to book ahead of time.

"Holy shit, this room is amazing. This must've cost a fortune."

Rebel shrugs and tosses his suitcase down beside the couch. "I make plenty, and I don't spend much, so I figured I'd splurge a little."

I swallow around the lump forming in my throat. There's no way I can repay Rebel for all this. I'm barely making enough to get by, and the last thing I want to do is be in anyone's debt. Rebel is watching me carefully like he can tell how much I'm struggling to accept the gesture, waiting to see if I flip out.

"Guess I'll have to find some way to pay you back," I tease, shaking my ass in his direction to lighten the mood.

Rebel's shoulders relax, and an easy smile spreads across his lips. "You don't have to pay me back, but you know I won't turn down that ass."

Rebel gives me a quick smack to my left ass cheek, and I yelp in surprise, straightening up and rubbing the abused flesh.

He heads over to the window, and I join him to check out the view. Our room overlooks the crowded pool and all the lights of the city. I can even see the Eiffel Tower.

"So, one night in Vegas, what's the plan?" I ask, excited to get out and get into some trouble. I can't think of anyone I'd rather be in Sin City with than Rebel. The dude is wild, and I love it.

"I'm thinking we hit a casino for a bit, because we're in Vegas, so it's basically a law we need to lose some money gambling. Then we'll do dinner and drinks, strip club, and check out the pool later tonight."

"I didn't bring a swimsuit."

"I didn't either," Rebel says with a wink. "Now I'm going to hop in a cold shower real quick, because I'm already melting in this heat and then we can get this night started. You coming?"

"Hell yeah."

I strip down where I'm standing and follow Rebel into the bathroom. After the *hottest* cold shower of my life, we both get dressed in fresh clothes and head out onto the strip again.

The casino downstairs is exactly what I would've pictured if you'd asked me to imagine what a Las Vegas casino looks like. It's bright with all kinds of flashing lights and chiming machines. There are waitresses in short skirts and little black vests over white shirts, offering complimentary drinks to keep people playing and always putting money into the machines.

"What's your game?" Rebel asks.

"Uh, not a clue. Blackjack maybe?"

"All right, let's give it a shot."

It turns out Blackjack is *not* my game. I lose a hundred dollars before I decide to try slot machines instead, where I lose even more money. I cringe inwardly knowing how much time and effort it took to make that money.

"Okay, I'm calling it. Apparently, I'm unlucky, and now I'm a few hundred dollars poorer. I say we move on to the dinner and drinks portion of the evening."

"I'm good with that. I could use a big slab of meat and a stiff drink," Rebel agrees.

"If you wanted something stiff, all you had to do was ask," I tease, leaning over and flicking my tongue along the shell of his ear. To my satisfaction, Rebel shivers and lets out a quiet groan.

"I never thought I'd meet a man who could match my sexual appetite, but damn dude, you are one horny fucker."

"I'll take that as a compliment," I chuckle.

"Good, that's how it was intended." Rebel slings an arm over my shoulder and guides me outside.

I blink a few times, surprised to find that the sun has already set. People are right when they say time passes differently inside a casino. I feel like I've stepped into another dimension. And if the strip was something to see in the daylight, it's unbelievable at night, all lit up.

As we walk down the street, Rebel tells me about the

porn convention he and the guys were at last year in Vegas and all the trouble Brewer managed to get into.

"Wait, he didn't know the guy was a prostitute?" I laugh at the end of the story.

"No, he gets propositioned everywhere he goes. He had no reason to think this guy was working him. Oh my god, Tank has never let him live that one down."

"What kinds of shenanigans did you get into?" I ask, bumping my shoulder against Rebel's.

"None, actually. With the guys and at the studio, I sort of feel like I'm supposed to set an example, be a role model, I guess. I think it's because I've been with Bear and Ballsy Boys since the beginning, so it sort of feels like it's my baby as much as it's Bear's. So, I've been to Vegas, but I've never really let loose, because I had to make sure I was being a good boy."

"Sounds like we have to make up for that tonight. Drinks and then debauchery," I declare. "Who knows, maybe we'll even get a prostitute."

"No, thanks," Rebel laughs. "I'm perfectly happy with this ass at the moment."

He grabs my ass, and I tense for a second. Not because I have a problem with PDA or anything, but because that sounded kind of *exclusive* and *couple-y*.

"Why wouldn't you be, it's a fantastic ass," I joke to hide my discomfort.

Luckily, we reach the restaurant before I can reach epic levels of awkward avoidance.

"Tell me more about the degree you're working on. It's video game design, right?"

"Yeah," I clear my throat and reach for my glass of water as we wait for the steaks we just ordered. "Some people think it's kind of a pipe dream, because it's not an easy industry to get into. I mean, every other frat boy thinks he wants to play video games for a living, right?"

"But, you're not every other frat boy," Rebel points out. "What appeals to you about it?"

"I guess it's the challenge of combining the technical aspects of coding with the creativity of telling a story through images, character development, level design, and so on. It's very complex, but it also seems so rewarding to have this story in your head that you want to tell, and be able to turn that into something millions of people can experience. I know that probably seems weird…"

"Not at all, I think that's amazing. I know it's not exactly the same thing, but it's similar with porn, the behind the camera aspect anyway. Bear has let me do some work with him from that end of things, and having this idea and being able to see it come to life, it's really surreal."

"Yeah, exactly," I agree.

Rebel smiles at me, and I feel a warm flutter in my chest. It's like he really *gets* me. I've never had that before. If I'd known it would feel this good to have a friend, maybe I would've tried it a long time ago.

I have the strange urge to lean across the table and kiss him just for the hell of it, but luckily, that insane notion is interrupted when the waitress drops off our drinks—a Jack and Coke for Rebel, and a Seven and Seven for me—and a basket of bread.

A handful of drinks and a giant slab of meat each later, and we're both feeling a bit giggly and a lot ready to hit the strip club. Yet another thing I've never done before, because it felt too pathetic to do alone. If you go to a strip club with friends, you're having fun. If you go by yourself, you're a creep with your hand in your sweatpants.

"Hunk Mansion?" I laugh at the name of the strip club when we reach it.

"Yes, and there will be hunks galore, I assure you."

"Good, I need to see some naked men."

Rebel smacks my ass again, and I nearly fall over laughing. How crazy is it that the porn star I was crushing on from afar just a few months ago is now the best friend I've ever had? I feel like it shouldn't be this easy to let go and have fun with him, but he's just as crazy as I am, so there's no judgment. It's so...freeing.

Inside Hunk Mansion we grab seats near one of the stages with a good view of a cute little twink working the pole. And it only takes a minute for a buff waiter—wearing nothing but a pair of shiny underwear and a healthy dose of oil glistening on his muscles—to come over and take our drink order.

"Are you two going to get your fine asses up there in half an hour when amateur night starts?" the waiter asks Rebel and me with a flirtatious smile for each of us.

"What?" I ask with surprise.

"Amateur night," he says again. "You just sign up at the bar, and then you get a chance to get up there and shake your money maker for some cash."

"Oh my god, we have to do this," Rebel says in a giddy tone, grabbing my arm excitedly. "Let's go sign up right now."

"Sure, why not," I agree. "But you'd better make my drink a double, so I'm drunk enough to do this in a half hour," I add to the waiter.

I save our spot while Rebel goes and signs us both up to take our clothes off in front of a bunch of strangers. I guess for him this is no big thing. I'm not exactly body shy myself. I'm more worried I'm going to dance like a spaz or freeze when I see a bunch of eyes on me, or worse yet, suffer the humiliation of not getting any tips.

Rebel returns a few minutes later, as does the waiter with our drinks. The twink who was dancing on the stage in front of us hops down and makes his way in our direction.

"Sorry if this is super rude, but are you Rebel?" he asks with hearts and stars in his eyes.

Rebel gives him a charming smile. "I am, nice to meet you."

"This is so cool! My friends are never going to believe I met you. Do you, um, want a lap dance?" he offers with fluttering eyelashes and a cute little blush.

"Um..."

Rebel looks over at me like he's asking for permission, and I bristle a little. "Dude, I'm not your boyfriend, do what you want."

There's a little too much venom in my tone, but the implication that I should have a say in who touches Rebel has my chest tightening and my palms sweating.

"Sure, I'd love a lap dance."

"Oh my god, this is so cool. You can call me Glam, by the way."

Glam wastes no time straddling Rebel and working his hips in mesmerizing circles. His hands are all over Rebel's chest and combing through his hair.

A flash of something hot and possessive flares in my gut as Rebel smiles at the kid and runs his hands up the back of Glam's thighs to cup his ass. Apparently, Glam's not going to enforce the *no groping the dancers* rule that was posted at the entrance.

Glam leans close and whispers something in Rebel's ear that makes Rebel smile and shake his head. *What did he ask?*

Maybe he was asking if Rebel and I are together or if Rebel has a boyfriend.

I swallow the bile in my throat. What do I care, anyway? Rebel can fuck anyone he wants. He's a porn star. He fucks people for a living and that doesn't bother me. And he's *not* my boyfriend.

When an announcement cuts over the music that amateur night is about to start and that all those signed up should claim a stage, I jump up and tap Glam on the shoulder. "Sorry, man, Rebel and I are signed up to dance."

"Oh." Glam's face falls as he climbs off Rebel's lap. "If you change your mind, here's my number." He slips a piece of paper into Rebel's pocket, and I have to bite back a growl.

"You okay?" Rebel asks, clearly noticing the tension vibrating off me.

"I'm great; let's get up there and make some money."

Rebel and I climb up onto the nearest stage, and immediately, we have a few bachelorette parties and a horde of men gathered around to watch us.

"Uh, this is a little daunting," I whisper to Rebel.

"Just relax and have fun," he suggests as he tugs his shirt over his head and tosses it into the crowd.

I shrug and follow suit, and then we start shaking it to the music. With the strange, hot, territorial feeling still lingering, I reach for Rebel and start to grind up on him like I'm staking a claim in front of the whole club. I run my tongue along his neck, and I hear a cheer go through the small crowd we've amassed.

Rebel's hips work in perfect time to the beat, and he doesn't falter as he makes quick work of getting my pants open. He drops into a crouch, tugging my jeans down with him, and then twerks it for the ladies directly behind him.

Another cheer goes up and money starts landing on the

stage. I step out of my pants and kick them over so I have room to move but don't lose them. Then I help Rebel get his pants off, much less elegantly than he managed for me, but we get the job done.

I catch sight of Glam beside the stage watching us, and out of sheer pettiness, I grab Rebel and shove my tongue into his mouth, grabbing his ass and pressing our bodies close together as we move to the music.

We're met with whistles and cat calls.

"Not sure we're supposed to put on a live porn show," Rebel jokes, giving me one more quick kiss before pulling away.

In just our briefs, we dance our way toward the edge of the stage and are met with tons of groping hands, trying to shove money into our underwear and stealing a quick grab of our asses and junk when they can manage it. By the time the song ends and we have to give up the stage to the next guys wanting a chance, we've made back at least three times what I lost at the casino.

"Okay, that was fun," I admit, pulling my pants back on.

"Hell yeah, it was," Rebel agrees.

Our shirts are long gone, so when we leave the club after a few more drinks, we do it with our glistening abs on full display.

"So, uh, what did Glam ask you?" I blurt as we walk back to the hotel, both more than a little tipsy.

"What?" Rebel asks, his eyebrows scrunching.

"When he was giving you the lap dance, he asked you something?"

"Oh," Rebel nods. "Yeah, sorry, I forgot. He asked if I wanted to meet up after his shift. I said no thanks."

"Oh." That hot flare hits my gut again. "Did you *want* to? If you just said no because of me, you can totally call him."

"I'm having fun with you, why would I go out of my way to hook up with someone else when I'm enjoying what we've got going on?"

"I guess," I agree.

"Now, let's go see about swimming. I'm all hot and sweaty. I'd love to jump in the pool."

We head through the lobby and out back to the pool, which, to my surprise, is completely empty.

Rebel looks one way and then the other before kicking off his shoes then dropping his pants and underwear. He smirks at me and shoots me a wink over his shoulder before doing a cannonball into the pool. I hurry to follow suit, adding a flip to my jump just to show him up a little.

"Show off," Rebel accuses when I break the surface of the water.

"Don't be jealous," I tease and then splash water at his face.

"Oh, you're going down."

Rebel launches himself at me and we tussle, trying to dunk each other. Until we both become acutely aware of our naked bodies rubbing together and the fact that our dicks are getting very interested in the action.

"Too bad we don't have any lube down here with us," I lament, cupping his balls and then wrapping my hand around Rebel's fat shaft and giving his a few slow strokes beneath the water. His head falls back, and his lips part on a silent moan.

"Mmm, guess we'll have to find another way to entertain ourselves. Or just tease until we get back to the room. A little edging action is always fun," Rebel says, pinching my nipples and then nibbling along my jaw.

"I've always been too impatient for edging, maybe you'll have to show me."

"I'm not going to say no to that."

His lips find mine, and I back Rebel up against the side of the pool. His legs wrap around my waist, my hands moving to his ass, his still playing with my nipples as our tongues meet in a teasing dance.

I groan into Rebel's mouth when he flexes his hips, rubbing his hard cock against mine.

"You're so fucking hot," he murmurs against my lips.

A throat clears behind us, and we jump apart.

"What do we have here?" A stern looking security guard stands over us at the edge of the pool. "You two do realize that public indecency is a crime, even in Las Vegas, don't you?"

"Oh shit," I mutter, sure this big dude with a stick up his ass isn't going to go easy on us.

"We're sorry, sir. We got a little carried away," Rebel apologizes with that charming smile back in place.

The guard glares down at him, and then suddenly his expression changes. "Wait, you're not...?"

Rebel's smile brightens. Damn, does everyone in this town know who Rebel is?

"I take it you're a fan?" Rebel asks, straightening up a bit.

"Uh, yeah, you could say that." The guard blushes. Then he looks around like he's making sure no one else is out here. "Listen, I'll let you off with a warning, but you can't do this again. There are still rules here, and it's my job to make sure they're enforced."

"We understand," Rebel assures him.

Then he hoists his hard, wet body out of the pool and stands before the security guard stark naked with a semi like he doesn't have a care in the world. The guard's eyes widen as he takes in Rebel's body. Poor guy didn't even get any warning before Rebel unleashed the beast on him.

"Do you think...um...could I get an autograph?" he stammers.

"Sure thing, man." Rebel claps him on the shoulder. "Do you have a pen? As you can see I don't exactly have a place to carry one at the moment."

"Oh, yeah."

He whips out a pen and a pad of paper. Rebel writes something and signs it with a flourish.

"Here you go, and thanks for being cool. Now, if you don't mind, we'll just head up to our room before we get into any more trouble out here."

Rebel winks at him, and the guard quivers a little. I stifle a laugh. The guard leaves, and I climb out of the pool as well, and Rebel and I hurry to dress.

"Well, this was a night for the history books," Rebel jokes as we ride the elevator up to our room, our jeans sticking to our wet skin. "And it's not even over yet. I promised to school you in the ways of edging, which means we have a long night ahead of us still."

19

REBEL

Considering how early we need to be on the road to make it to Colorado tonight, we really should've gone to bed earlier. Correct that: gone to sleep earlier. We did go to bed. We just didn't do a whole lot of sleeping till much later.

Turned out Troy sucked at edging, so I had to show him again. And again. And then he had to prove to me he'd learned, so he drove me to the brink of insanity before he finally let me come.

I sigh as I take in my red-shot, small eyes. My hair is such a hot mess, I'm not going anywhere near it until I can take a shower and wash it properly. It will have to wait till we reach Colorado. For now, I just tie it into a sloppy man-bun. It will have to do.

Troy stumbles into the bathroom, and he doesn't look much better. "Fuck," he mumbles. "It's too early to be up."

He looks adorable with his hair sticking up in every direction, and I grab his hand and yank him toward me for a morning kiss. He protests a little, probably because we haven't brushed yet, but I don't care. Like a little morning breath is gonna bother me.

"Morning, sunshine," I tease him when I'm done thoroughly kissing him.

I pull him close for a hug, his morning wood poking me. I don't know if it's because he's still half-asleep or what, but he returns my hug with more enthusiasm than usual, and even snuggles close for a bit. I nuzzle his neck. "Want me to take care of that for you?" I ask, sneaking my hand between us to rub his hard cock.

"Mmm. Would you?" he asks. "You don't have to, but..."

I've already sunk to my knees, and I free his cock from his boxers. "My pleasure."

It takes me less than two minutes before he comes with a deep sigh. He's messed up my bun, of course, but it was totally worth it.

"You look like shit," he says when he gets a good look at me.

"Wow, that's some kind of thank you." I rise off my knees, lick the last remnants of his cum off my lips.

"Sorry," he says, then shoots me one of his sexy grins. "Thank you for the blowjob. You look like shit."

"Have you looked in the mirror?" I say indignantly. "You don't look much better, dude."

He turns to study himself in the mirror. "I still look twice as good as you."

I slap his ass. "Have your eyes checked, man. Nobody looks twice as good as me, not even on my worst day. Now, put on some clothes so we can go downstairs for breakfast, 'cause I need to mainline some caffeine."

Troy halts in his moves. "I figured we'd do a drive thru somewhere for coffee and unhealthy breakfast sandwiches."

I walk into the room, grab a T-shirt and a fresh pair of

jeans from my weekend bag. "No, I booked a full breakfast for both of us with the room. Figured we'd need the fuel for a whole day of driving."

I get dressed quickly, and it doesn't hit me till I'm putting my socks on that Troy hasn't responded. I look up to find him watching me with a strange look on his face. It's not anger. More like...panic?

"I can't afford breakfast here," he says. "I need that money for tuition. It was stupid of me to even gamble with it, and I got lucky I made it back with the stripping thing." He starts to make a move like he wants to jam his hands into his pockets, but then apparently realizes he's not wearing pants, so he ends up with clenched fists.

"That's okay," I say carefully, sensing I need to tread lightly here. "I told you this hotel was my treat. That includes breakfast."

He doesn't look reassured. "How much is the breakfast?"

I shrug. "I dunno. It's usually between fifteen and twenty bucks in hotels like this."

He relaxes a little. "That's not too bad," he says. "A coffee and a breakfast sandwich will run you close to eight bucks already."

"Twenty bucks each. Not including tip," I add. I could lie to him, but that will only end up biting me in the ass.

"For that much money, they'd better serve, like, caviar or something," he mutters.

"It's probably a breakfast buffet," I say. "Maybe with some fresh options, like waffles or pancakes, or they may have an omelet bar."

He finally starts putting on some clothes. "I don't even know what that is."

It's starting to sink in that this is a whole new experience for him. I travel regularly for Ballsy Boys events, and while we don't always stay in the most expensive hotels, we've outgrown the cheap-ass motel phase. When clients bring us out, for instance for a photoshoot, they need to put us up in respectable hotels. As a result, I've stayed in hotels like this all over the country and even in Europe. Troy hasn't, and that's probably embarrassing him.

"It's like an area where you can gather fresh ingredients for an omelet, or point them out, and they'll cook a made-to-order omelet for you."

"Oh."

That one word is filled with so much emotion, it's almost tangible in the room. What do I do? Do I ignore it to avoid making him feel even more uncomfortable? Or do I address it, try to take away his shame? I opt for the second one, but still choose an indirect approach.

"Before I started working for Ballsy Boys, I had never stayed at anything more expensive than a Motel 6. My parents were big on camping, so all family vacations were done in tents. We used the cheapest motels my mom would find for things like trips to Disney, or when visiting family in big cities. The first time Bear booked a Marriott for me, I was blown away. I'd never seen a bathroom that big, and I sure as hell never had a bed that size for me alone. And that breakfast... Man, I completely stuffed my face. I get it, Troy. This was new to me as well a few years ago."

He sighs. "I'm struggling to keep my head above water, financially. I can't afford shit like this, but I feel like crap for letting you pay for it."

I walk up to him, approaching him like a skittish rabbit. "I get that, but there's no need to feel guilty. I can afford it. I come from a long and proud tradition of frugal people, so I've invested my porn earnings wisely. Trust me, one night here won't make a dent in my savings. And we had fun, didn't we?"

When he doesn't bolt, I slowly pull him close to me, hug him tightly. He allows it, but his body is tense. Maybe I need to distract him a bit. Sex usually seems to work with him, so I lower my hands to his ass.

"Don't tell me you didn't have fun with our edging lessons."

He harrumphs. "That wasn't fun. It was hot as hell, but I seriously hated you for a few minutes."

"Our striptease, then. That was fun, wasn't it? Or skinny-dipping in the pool?"

"We got lucky that guard was a fan of yours," Troy grumbles, but his voice sounds less upset.

"Everyone who's seen me is a fan," I joke. "Once they've seen my cock, they're hooked."

I feel Troy's face break open in a smile against my cheek. "Don't forget your long and sexy hands. Pixie could write a sonnet about them, probably."

I squeeze those hands around his ass cheeks to demonstrate the accuracy of his statement. "Damn right. Then there's my mouth..."

Troy hmms. "That did feel pretty nice wrapped around my cock a few minutes ago."

"So, I think we can safely establish you don't like me for my money, right?" I go in for the kill.

He freezes for a second, then relaxes again. "No, I don't," he says softly.

He allows me to hug him for a minute or so, before he steps away. "Thank you," he says.

I watch him with a warm feeling in my belly. "You're welcome."

20

TROY

We pull into the quiet truck stop in the middle of nowhere in either Utah or Colorado…I'm not sure at this point. As the car rolls to a stop, I bolt from the passenger seat, my bladder full to bursting. Rebel is a few seconds behind me into the bathroom, which is exceptionally clean for a truck stop.

We finish up and turn back to the door to leave, when something catches my eye as I pass a stall with the door swinging open.

"*Hellllo.*" I grab Rebel's arm to stop him.

He follows my gaze, and at the same moment, we both turn to look at each other. I imagine my expression mirrors his, a little goofy and a lot dirty.

"Oh, we're so doing this. Go in there, I want to suck your dick." He shoves me toward one stall, and I go without protest.

I unzip my pants and free my already hard and aching cock. My pulse races at how fucking dirty this is. And maybe because I never thought I'd meet a guy as spontaneous and fun as Rebel.

I grab the base of my cock and angle it toward the crudely made hole, a duct tape padding all around the edges. There's a strange sort of thrill in not being able to see what's happening on the other side of the wall, as I wait for Rebel's mouth.

He doesn't play coy or tease. A scorching pair of lips wrap around the head of my cock and slide toward the base, engulfing me in wet suction. I ball my fist and pound lightly against the flimsy plastic wall, trying to keep myself from blowing it too quickly.

Rebel's tongue strokes firmly around my head, not missing a beat on the descent and retreat. My breath comes out in a fast huff, and my fingers flex, wanting to be buried in the thick tangle of Rebel's hair.

"Holy fuck," I gasp as he presses his tongue flat to the spongy V of nerves and pulses it.

My body trembles as my nerve endings all come alive. My hips press hard against the wall, wanting to be deeper inside the heat of Rebel's throat. His tongue continues to flutter against almost the entire underside of my shaft.

"Yes, fuck, Rebel," I shout as my balls draw tight, and my ass clenches.

The assault from Rebel's lips and tongue continue as I empty myself in his throat. When he finally releases me, a shudder races through my body, and I sag against the stall for balance.

"That was fucking hot," Rebel says from the other side of the wall.

"Eh, it was okay," I feign a bored voice.

"Hey!" he protests, and we both chuckle.

I tuck my spent dick away and zip my pants. When I step out of the stall, Rebel is there waiting to kiss me. I moan as he shoves his tongue into my mouth, my flavor lingering inside his mouth.

"You're fun," I say when our lips part.

Rebel smiles, and his fingers tease along the millimeter of exposed skin between my shirt and jeans.

"We'd better get going. I promised my mom we'd be on time for dinner, and we've still got two hours ahead of us."

I nod, shaking off the haze of orgasm and follow Rebel back out to the car.

The last stretch of the trip flies by as I take in the breathtaking mountains in the distance, and we cruise down the open roads. I crack my window and breathe in the crisp, clean air that's sorely lacking in LA.

But as each mile falls behind us and we near his parents' house, I find my stomach twisting itself in tighter knots.

It's not that I think his parents will have an issue with me. I'm a grown ass man. I don't need the approval of other adults that I don't even know.

Except...maybe it would be kind of nice if his parents approved of me? And therein lies the cause of the cold sweat trickling down my back. I don't know what I want them to *approve* me for, but I *do* want it.

The closest I ever came to parental approval was this older lady who took me in for a year when I was twelve.

Her name was Elise, and when I was first placed with her I thought it was some kind of joke. What did a sixty-five-year old widow with too much perfume want with a twelve-year-old boy who'd already been rejected by two prospective adoptive parents and kicked out of two other foster homes for fighting?

I still remember the first day I arrived at Elise's house. I stepped into her living room and decided that there was no way I'd last a week with her. She had too many glass figurines and knick-knacks, there was a basket of knitting beside a worn in recliner, and the whole house smelled like cooked cabbage. This wasn't a person equipped to deal with a kid with my level of issues, or so I thought.

It took exactly two days for Elise to put me in my place.

On the second night, she caught me trying to sneak out after she went to bed. She sat me down, looked me in the eyes, and told me something I'll never forget. *I know life dealt you a shit hand, but that doesn't mean you get to treat other people like they're beneath you. As long as you're under my roof, you're going to respect me and respect my rules. If you can manage that, you'll have a much brighter future ahead of you.*

No one had ever been so blunt with me, but the words weren't what startled me. It was the way she looked at me, like she actually cared what happened to me.

It wasn't smooth sailing from there by any means, but I did try, and Elise and I fell into a comfortable routine together. She was more of a mother to me than my own had ever been, and to this day I know she's the reason I didn't end up in jail or worse. I had been headed down a bad road, and she set me straight.

When I was thirteen, Elise passed away from a heart attack while I was at school, and I was shuttled off to a new foster family. This one had too many foster kids and not enough shits to give. I was there until the wife caught her husband trying to sneak into my bed one night, and then I was sent away again. Such is the life of a foster kid.

"You're awfully quiet over there," Rebel says, startling me out of my reminiscences.

I clear my throat and try to be stealthy as I wipe a stray bit of moisture from my cheek. It was totally from the wind in my eye.

"I'm fine." My voice cracks a little at the end, and I hold

my breath to see if Rebel's going to call me on it and press the issue. The crazy thing is, if he pushed it, I think I'd tell him everything. I'd tell him about Elise and all the shitty foster homes where there were wandering hands and harsh words at worst, and indifference at best. I'd tell him about the fights I got in because of all the rage I had inside me and because asshole little kids like to pick on the outsider. I might even tell him how tired I am of holding the world at a distance.

But, he doesn't push it. He just gives me a reassuring pat on the knee and lets me lapse back into silence.

When we pull into the driveway of a large, white two-story house with a well-kept lawn, I've got myself half-convinced again that it doesn't matter what his parents think of me.

We climb out of the car, and I take a second to appreciate the captivating lines of Rebel's body as he stretches his arms over his head, exposing a little bit of fuzz on his belly that makes my mouth water.

Head in the game, I remind myself.

Rebel shoots me a wink when he catches me staring, and I shake my head at him with a smile.

"Ready?" he checks.

"As I'll ever be."

"Dude, it's dinner with some aged hippies, not a firing squad. You'll survive, I promise."

The front door of the house flies open before we even reach it, and a middle aged woman with long, dirty blonde hair comes running out and tackles Rebel in a hug.

"Oof!" He catches her with a smile and hugs her back. "You know, Mom, you could greet me like a normal person with a polite hug once I've entered the house."

"Normal people are so boring," she retorts. "And I miss

my son too much to wait a whole thirty seconds for him to enter the house."

"I missed you too, Mom." He gives her a kiss on the top of her head, and a weird hollow feeling blossoms in my chest, making it almost difficult to breathe.

A man—I'm assuming Rebel's dad—appears at the door as well.

"You couldn't keep your wife under control?" Rebel calls to him.

"She's been pacing in front of the door all day. There was no reining her in."

"Oh my gosh, how rude of me, you brought a young man with you, and here I am acting like a basket case." She turns to face me with a smile. "I'm Susan, and you must be Troy."

"Actually, it's Mike. Who's Troy?" I ask, looking over her shoulder at Rebel, my expression as serious and confused as I can manage.

Susan's face pales, and I immediately feel bad for the joke.

"He's being a dick, Mom." Rebel assures her, and I offer a sheepish smile in apology.

"I thought a joke might break the ice."

"You're going to fit in here just fine," she declares.

Susan ushers us toward the house, and Rebel's father, Joe, greets me with a firm handshake. I can see what Rebel meant when he said they were aged hippies. They look more or less like your average middle age couple, but there's something about them that hints at a wild and carefree youth. His mom especially still looks like she has a flower child trying to break through.

Inside the house I'm introduced to Rebel's sister, Marley, and her husband, Doug. Susan tells us all to sit down because dinner is ready and waiting.

"So how did you and Hendrix meet?" Marley asks as she settles into the seat beside me at the table.

"Uh…" I look at Rebel for a little help, but he just chuckles and shoves a roll into his mouth.

"Don't be embarrassed; it can't be that bad. I know you don't work with Hendrix, so where did you meet?"

I cock my head and catch Rebel's eye with my silent question.

"She knows you don't work at Ballsy Boys, because she's an avid viewer," Rebel explains. "Not my videos though, of course."

"Of course," I agree sarcastically. "Well, we met when this guy Reb—Hendrix was dating hired me to do his dirty work of dumping him. I recognized him as soon as he opened the door, and I was a bit star struck, to be honest, and the rest is history."

"That's like a romantic comedy; I love it," Marley declares.

"No, it's not romantic though," I argue quickly. "Hendrix and I are just friends."

21

REBEL

I catch the quick look that passes between my parents. They've got this whole wordless communication down to an art.

Just friends.

I know what they're thinking: there's no way these two are just friends. And they're right, because we're not. And a few weeks ago, I would've been bothered by Troy saying something like this, probably, but ever since he told me he'd been in foster care, something clicked. He's not afraid of commitments because he wants to play the field or because he's not ready to settle down or some shit.

He's scared.

He's deathly afraid of being rejected, again. And it makes sense for him to keep people at bay, because if you don't let anyone in, they won't be able to hurt you. I get it. Doesn't mean I have to like it.

"Friends with a lot of special benefits," I say, winking at Troy to make sure he knows I'm joking.

"Oh, god," Doug says. "Here we go again with the sex

references. Is it too much to ask to have one meal without talking about sex?"

Marley sends him a blinding smile. "When we're back home, we can talk about root canals and wisdom teeth extractions, but I kinda like the sex talk, babe."

I grin. Doug is a good guy, but he's a little on the dry and dusty side. I'm still not sure what my formerly wild sister sees in him, but they're obviously happy together. Still, I can't help jerking his chain a little.

"What do you mean, sex? I wasn't talking about sex. I was talking about him hooking me up with some seriously good weed."

"And don't forget the bananas," Troy plays along. "I've introduced him to the best bananas ever."

"We found a new supplier here," Mom says, and I'm pretty damn sure she's not talking about bananas. "All organic homegrown from a family operation and it's the best."

Troy's eyebrows shoot up. Yes, Troy, my mom's talking about weed. Welcome to the crazy reality that is my parents' house.

"It's true," my dad adds. "They don't add any additives, and it makes it so pure. Best damn weed I've ever had."

Doug looks like he's about to slam his head on the table, but Marley pats his shoulder. "It's legal here, honey."

"Like that's ever stopped them," he mumbles.

"It did wonders for my pain throughout my cancer treatment," my mom says, her tone a little sharper now. She likes Doug well enough, but she does not tolerate criticism on the choices she and dad make. Rightly so.

"So, Troy, what do you do?" Marley asks, as always excelling in dissolving tension.

"I'm working on my degree in video game design."

He says it as if he's expecting criticism on that choice, but that's not gonna happen. Not in this house.

"You mean to develop games like *Call of Duty*?" my dad wants to know.

Troy's eyes widen slightly at the interest, but I'm not surprised. My dad is the biggest reader I've ever met, and he reads books on every subject known to man. I'm sure that while he's never played a video game in his life, he can tell you the names of at least ten popular games. Hell, he probably knows more about it than I do.

"For example," Troy says. "Personally, I'm not the biggest fan of first person shooter games, but both the complexity and the design of that game are undeniable."

"What kind of games would you like to develop?" Dad asks.

Troy drags a hand through his hair. "Erm, I'm working on a mobile game right now with a friend. It's a good way to start for us, because we don't have much experience yet. Mobile games are way easier to develop than complex games for consoles or MMORPG games. That takes years of experience and way more skills than I possess right now."

"You have to start somewhere," Dad says. "I bet you the folks who developed *World of Warcraft* or *Elder Scrolls* started small as well. They didn't create games like that overnight."

Troy's eyes light up. "Do you play, Joe?"

I love how he skipped the whole formal Mr. part and went right for informal. My dad loves it, as he's the most relaxed, casual guy you'll ever meet.

"God, no, son. I don't even own a computer. Susan has a laptop to do everything that needs to be done online, like paying bills and what not."

"And watching porn," Mom deadpans, causing Troy to almost choke on his food. "My god, that new boy you found is cute."

"Which one, Pixie or Heart?" I ask with my mouth full, meanwhile keeping an eye on Troy as he bravely tries to recover from coughing up a bit of food, his eyes watering.

"Pixie. Heart's not cute. He's fucking sexy, but not cute."

I quickly swallow. "True. They're both great additions, and I love working with them, too."

"Susan, we were talking about games. Don't get distracted by sexy boys all the time," Dad admonishes her.

Her face lights up, and her eyes sparkle. "But they're so much fun to talk about!"

Dad lets out a passive-aggressive sigh, before refocusing his attention on Troy. "But is that your goal, to work toward designing a big game?"

There's something in Troy's eyes, as if he can't believe my dad is interested in him. I could've told him he would be, because my dad is interested in everyone. He's a people person, always enthusiastic to get to know people better. I guess I get that from him, because I'm pretty much the same.

"I don't know, really. For now, I'm excited about working on this game with Mason, because we work well together, and we complement each other."

"How's your work been?" Mom asks me, as if I have a regular nine-to-five job.

"That video with Campy, Heart, and Tank was a-ma-zing," Marley gushes. "Holy fuck, it was so fucking hot!"

Really?" Doug says, more resigned than mad. "More talk about porn?"

"I seem to remember you reaped the benefits of that particular scene," Marley states. "We had a hot—"

Doug yanks her toward him and kisses her, probably the most effective way to shut her up.

"I have to agree with Marley. That video was smoking hot," Mom says.

I'd love to say that this is abnormal, the way they gush about porn, gay porn specifically, but it's not. This is how my family rolls. I'm pretty sure Troy can take it, though, once he stops being weirded out.

"Reb—Hendrix came up with the idea for that shoot," Troy says, and the pride in his voice is unmistakable. It does strange things to me inside, to hear him express admiration for what I do. Not only does he not have a problem with me shooting porn and working in this industry, he's actually proud of what I do. It's such a foreign concept to me after having so many boyfriends and potential boyfriends who broke up with me over my job, that I get all warm and fuzzy inside.

"Bear had the basic idea of the exchange between Campy and Heart," I say, not wanting to claim false glory.

Troy fires me a look that shoots straight to my balls. It makes me want to drag him into a room, drop my pants, and bend over. I love it when he gets all bossy on me.

"Shut up," he says. "That idea was yours, and you know it."

"Hendrix working in porn is not an issue for you?" Mom asks.

I hold my breath as I wait for him to answer this.

"Not at all," he says. "He's really, really good at it, and I love watching him. Hey, I'm as big a fan of gay porn as anyone, so nope, all fine with me."

I exhale. As Marley and Troy get into a heated discussion over the best gay porn video ever made, my mom's eyes meet mine. She smiles at me. He didn't see through her trick question. If he and I had been just friends, as he claimed, the fact that I'm in porn wouldn't even have been an issue. He didn't answer that question as just a friend. He answered it as a boyfriend, and my mom and I both know it.

22

TROY

After dinner, we head back to our hotel room on the other side of town. My thoughts are spinning over the entire evening. I don't know what I expected after Rebel told me how cool his parents were, but I didn't expect them to be like *that*. What must it have been like to grow up in a household so obviously full of love and support?

I glance over at Rebel. The street lights play across his features as he drives, giving him an oddly ethereal look. I'm not sure I deserve to know someone as amazing as Rebel, but I'm going to appreciate it as long as I have the privilege. I just hope that eventually, when he's gone from my life, he'll still think of me from time to time. The thought of Rebel forgetting me entirely makes my stomach clench.

"So, what'd you think of my family? Did they scare you off?" Rebel asks as we pull into the parking lot of the hotel.

"Nah, they seem really great. Thanks for inviting me; this has been a lot of fun."

"It's not over yet. You still have to be subjected to my entire extended family tomorrow."

"I think I'll survive," I assure him with a chuckle.

Once we're checked in, we haul our bags up to our room and both flop down on the bed.

"Oh man, I'm wiped," Rebel says, punctuating it with a loud yawn to illustrate his point.

"We didn't sleep much last night," I agree with a yawn of my own.

Rebel tilts his head back and forth and rolls his shoulders a few times before tugging his shirt off and tossing it aside.

"Are your shoulders stiff?" I ask.

"A bit. I think it's from all that time in the car."

"Lay on your stomach," I instruct.

"Ooo, is this going to be kinky?" Rebel asks with hope.

"You were about to fall asleep two seconds ago, and now you're awake enough to mess around?"

"I'm always up for messing around."

"Sorry to disappoint, but I'm going to give you a shoulder massage."

"That is the opposite of disappointing."

I straddle Rebel's ass and start working his shoulder muscles with my hands. He lets out deep groan of pleasure as I work out a tricky knot behind his shoulder blade.

"Keep those noises up and this might turn kinky after all."

"Do whatever you want with me, just don't stop rubbing," Rebel moans into the pillow.

"Hey, you know what would feel even better on your muscles? A hot bath."

"Only if there's enough room for both of us in there."

I climb off the bed and check the bathroom.

"Definitely room for both of us," I call out.

Less than a second later, Rebel's arms wrap around my midsection from behind. "I'll start the water, you get naked."

I strip, leaving my clothes in a pile just outside the bathroom. And as soon as the tub is full of hot water and a splash of something that made floral scented bubbles, I climb in and spread my legs for Rebel to sit in front of me. A shiver of pleasure zips over me as our slick skin slips and slides against each other.

I resume the shoulder massage, not bothering to hide the way his sounds of pleasure affect me.

After a few minutes, Rebel melts against me, making it difficult to rub his shoulders. So I let my arms go around his waist, and trail my fingers up and down his chest and stomach. I lick a few water droplets off the side of his neck, and a deep rumble of contentment comes from deep in his chest.

I slip my hand lower and find his thick erection just waiting for my attention. I tease him a little, dragging my index finger from the head of his cock down to his balls and then cupping them in my hand.

Rebel sucks in a breath as I gently roll his balls in my palm, not in any rush to finish him. I'm more content to play and enjoy his warm, wet body in my arms. It only takes a few minutes for his balls to tighten and his body to start trembling against me. I back off, and he lets out a frustrated grunt.

"Don't be mad, I'm just proving how much you taught me in Vegas," I say, referencing his lesson in edging last night.

I've never been one for delayed gratification, but I have to admit that he was right about how much harder you can come if you hold it off a bit first. When I feel him relax a little, his orgasm no longer right on the edge, I wrap my hand around the base of his cock and give it a slow stroke from root to tip. My return journey is equally as measured. And I repeat the unhurried motion until Rebel is squirming against me, my name falling over and over from his lips in equal parts pleading and curse.

"Do you want to come?" I ask in a bored voice, and Rebel growls in response and flexes his hips.

I tighten my fist and jerk him faster while reaching around with my other hand to play with his balls.

"Fuck, Troy, so good."

Rebel's head lolls back against my shoulder, giving me perfect access to the pulse point in his neck. I bite down, not quite hard enough to leave a mark, but hard enough to make Rebel cry out. His cock pulses in my grasp, and I slow my strokes to milk the cum from him. Rebel shudders and lets out a sigh full of deep satisfaction.

I kiss the red flesh on his neck where my teeth have bruised him just the slightest bit. "I don't know about you, but I'm ready to pass the fuck out."

"Mmmm, let's go to bed," Rebel agrees.

We climb out of the tub and towel ourselves off before crawling between the sheets together. Last night, I was too exhausted to think much about sharing a bed with Rebel. But as soon as we're lying down, Rebel rolls toward me and puts his arms around me; my whole body tenses.

"Sorry," Rebel says, immediately pulling back and scooting over to give me a little breathing room.

"Sorry, I'm not much of a cuddler," I apologize.

"S'okay, babe." Rebel presses a quick kiss to my cheek and then backs off again. "Get some rest. You have a whole clan of crazy to face tomorrow, and you're going to need your strength."

I STAND in front of the mirror buttoning my shirt and then trying in vain to smooth out every minute wrinkle.

"Relax, babe." Rebel appears behind me and presses a quick kiss to the back of my neck.

I shiver at the intimacy of the gesture, and my heart thuds erratically. "I'm relaxed," I argue.

"No, you're not. That's okay, though, because it's cute that you're so nervous."

Rebel puts a hand on my shoulder and turns me to face him. He fiddles with my collar, arranges a few rogue strands of my hair, and then he smiles. My already thundering heart can barely take it. This is too much. It's too risky.

"Thanks," I say, clearing my throat and taking a step back.

Rebel's face falls for a second before he recovers with a forced smile. "Don't mention it; that's what friends are for. Now, let's get going, so we don't miss all the fun."

We ride in silence to his parents' place, and when we get there, I'm floored to see how many cars are lining the street. "You weren't kidding about this being a big thing."

"My parents don't do anything half-assed."

I take a deep breath, and we both climb out of the car and head for the front door.

Inside, it's a blur of handshakes and hugs from overzealous family members who don't realize they don't even know who I am. It's warm and happy in a way I've never experienced before. And it's impossible not to get just a little lost in the moment.

23

REBEL

He's so damn gorgeous. I know I've had a little too much to drink, also because of the altitude, so undoubtedly, it's clouding my judgment. And I'm tired and horny as fuck, so that probably doesn't help either.

But dammit, look at him. Look at that perfect man, making my stomach swirl and my hands all clammy. He's dancing with my cousin Sarah in the sun room, which has been transformed into an impromptu dance floor for the occasion, and he's being the perfect gentleman to the flustered fourteen-year-old who knows he's gay, but thinks he's super-hot anyway.

I can't blame her. The blue dress shirt he's wearing makes his eyes pop. Every time he laughs, he gets these wrinkles around his eyes that are so cute I have to sigh a little. His body is perfectly outlined in the tight shirt, and I can't take my eyes off his chest and arms as he twirls Sarah. He can't dance worth shit, but he's trying for her, and damn if that doesn't make him even more adorable.

What the hell is he doing to me? This is more than just

the drink and the altitude and being tired from the road trip.

"You got it bad, brother-mine," Marley says, plopping down in a chair beside me.

With effort, I rip my eyes off the man-candy on the dance floor. "What do you mean?"

"Your Troy. You're a goner for him."

I huff. "He's not mine at all, and we're not serious. I told you, we're just friends."

"Friends don't stare at one another the way you looked at him just now. Or the way he looks at you when you're not watching him."

All my bravado seeps out of me, and I sigh as I lean back in my chair. "I don't know how I feel about him. I've never felt this way. It's unnerving."

Marley smiles and slings her arm around my shoulder. "I know, Jimmy."

I smile at the use of her nickname for me. "Was it like that for you when you met Doug?"

"God, no. He bored the crap out of me for the first few months I knew him. But after a while, I realized I liked that feeling."

I frown. "You like being bored?"

"I love mom and dad, but they're not exactly normal—no offense to them. The way they raised us was perfect in many ways, but after all the moving we did and the constant change, I desperately craved stability. Doug is that to me. He's predictable, safe, dependable, and what seemed boring to me at first is now exactly what I need."

"I'm not like that," I say, still frowning as I'm trying to process what this means to me. Do I want boring? Hell, no.

"I know, Jimmy. You're more like mom than you realize.

Like her, you're a free spirit, and you don't give a fuck what anyone else thinks."

"I never did. Until…" I swallow, my throat suddenly constricted. "It's not easy, you know, with my job. Troy is super cool about it. He was a fan, actually, before we met in real life. He's never once asked me to quit or consider doing something else."

Marley scrunches her nose as she tries to follow my reasoning. "That's a good thing, yet you make it sound like… Oh, god. You want him to ask you."

"It's stupid, right? But if he really liked me, wouldn't he ask me to stop doing porn?"

She shakes her head at me, her eyes soft and kind. "Honey, he's damned if he does and damned if he doesn't. If he asks you to quit, he'll always be the one that held you back in some way. And yet if he doesn't, you question if he cares enough. You can't ask him to take on that responsibility. Whether or not you quit porn should be your decision, not his."

"I don't even know if he wants me to. He's quite the commitment-phobe. Every time I even hint at us being more, he balks."

Marley smiles. "Even worse than you? I didn't think that was possible."

"Well, believe me. I have to walk on eggshells here, because if I move too fast, he'll be out of here faster than you can say Usain Bolt."

"What do you want, honey? Do you want to quit?"

Suddenly, there are tears in my eyes that I can't explain. "I think I do, though I love working there. Not for the sex, though I still love that part, but the boys, they're kinda like a family, you know? I'd hate to miss that."

Marley pulls me close, and I put my head on her shoulder. "Isn't there something else you could do for Ballsy Boys beside being an actor? Doesn't your boss need a right-hand man or something?"

He does, actually, and I'm it already. In all honesty, I have been doing fewer shoots than I used to, and Bear has been using me more and more for other shit. I still break in newbies, but he also has me consulting on ideas for shoots, assisting him while filming, and coaching new guys through their shoots. It doesn't pay as much as the shoots in terms of per hour pay, but I make more hours, so it adds up to pretty much the same amount.

Plus, I really enjoy it, maybe as much as being in shoots. It's creative, and I love that Bear listens to my suggestions and takes me seriously. Like that idea I had for the shoot with Heart and Brewer, pulling Tank in, Bear loved what I came up with and gave me a percentage of the profits for that video.

An idea bubbles in my head. The studio is doing really well, and Bear keeps getting more and more busy. What if I propose to him that I want to be his right-hand man for real? Like, full time? There's certainly enough work, and the studio would definitely benefit if Bear could concentrate on what he's best at. Would he be open to that?

A wave of excitement rolls through me, and I smile. I'm onto something here. If Bear says yes, this could mean Troy and I... I'm hesitant to finish that thought. Even if I do get out of shooting porn myself, it doesn't mean he'll want me. He's been pretty damn clear about not wanting a relationship. Hell, I had to practically bribe him with sex to even get him to come here.

My smile widens. Maybe that's my best strategy. Persuading Troy with great sex until he realizes he likes me as much as I like him.

24

TROY

The song ends and Sarah is all blushes and stuttered thanks.

"It was my pleasure," I assure her. She seems like a sweet kid.

All of Rebel's family is really cool, actually. It's weird as hell in a kind of nice way. The warmth and love filling the house is causing a strange aching pain in my chest. And every time I look over at Rebel—apparently in the middle of a serious conversation with his sister—the ache gets deeper, fuller.

I swallow against the thick lump in my throat. I have the inexplicable urge to walk over to Rebel and slip my hand into his. But, why the hell would I do that? Holding hands isn't something I've ever wanted to do. I mentally mock people who hold hands. Don't they know they're on the road to heartbreak? No one stays forever. If there's one thing life has taught me, it's that.

No, I don't need to hold Rebel's hand. I need to enjoy all the hot sex and have fun while it lasts.

"Troy, would you mind giving me a quick hand in the

kitchen?" Rebel's mom, Susan, asks me, placing a gentle hand on my shoulder.

"Of course."

"So, you and Hendrix seem close," she comments once we're in the kitchen.

I flounder for a second, trying to think of how to respond as she turns to the refrigerator and starts to pull out a few trays of desserts. What does *close* mean? Is this going to be a *don't hurt my child* speech? Is this a *when's the wedding* speech? Or is she just making conversation?

"I guess?" I finally answer with obvious uncertainty in my tone.

"Relax, I'm not trying to grill you," she assures me with a laugh. "Hendrix is a good boy. He was always a good boy. Don't get me wrong, he was a handful when he was young. But he was always loving and generous. I know he's grown into a good man, too. I like seeing the smile on his face when he looks at you. And I like that you seem to accept him for who he is and what he does."

Her words strike at the ache in my chest, intensifying it. *What* is that?

"I don't mind what Hendrix does for a living. And he is a very good man," I agree.

Without warning, her arms wrap around me, and I freeze. It's stupid, but when I was little and bouncing around foster homes, I always wondered what it felt like to be hugged by a mom. It seemed like it would be so warm and comforting. Sometimes, I would close my eyes tight and try to imagine it, try to conjure what the sensation could possibly be. It never came close to what it feels like right now to have Susan hugging me tight. I can feel the love she has for Rebel pouring out of her. She loves him so much that I can almost believe she cares about me by extension.

When she releases me, there's a tight, burning behind my eyes and an even bigger lump in my throat than before. I knew coming here with Rebel would be dangerous. It's making me yearn for things I learned as a child aren't meant for me.

She hands me two of the trays of food and nods me toward the living room. I force my emotions under control and follow her out.

"Are you okay?" Rebel asks after I've set out the desserts where Susan directed me.

"Of course," I lie.

Rebel narrows his eyes at me and then takes my arm and leads me toward the stairs. He takes me to a bedroom right at the top of the steps that I have no doubt was his as a kid. There are a few dusty sports trophies on a shelf and posters still on the wall. His parents kept his room how he left it. Another wave of emotion washes over me.

"I can tell you're freaking out; what's going on?" Rebel asks again now that we're alone.

"This is a lot, that's all."

Rebel's eyebrows furrow. "Do you want to leave? We can go back to the hotel if you want."

"No, we came for your parents' anniversary. We're not going to miss it. I told you on the way here that I don't need to be coddled," I grumble. "I'm good at being alone. One day, you'll be gone, and it'll just be me again, and I'll be fucking fine."

I wince as the words leave my lips. They're too harsh, but they're also like a shield, protecting my heart from Rebel.

Undeterred by my outburst, Rebel wraps his arms around me and pulls me against him. I can feel my body vibrating at his touch, too many emotions overwhelming me at once until they start to spill over as frustrated tears.

"You're not alone anymore. We're friends, and I'm not going anywhere."

"Yes, you will," I argue, disgusted by the flair of hope his words cause in the pit of my stomach. "You'll leave like everyone else."

I try to push him away, but he hangs on tighter. "I know I'm not about to convince you that I'm not going anywhere, so I guess I'll just have to show you. And, in the meantime, we can keep doing what we do best."

Rebel tilts my chin up so my face isn't buried against his neck anymore, and his lips devour mine with a hungry desperation. Relieved to be back on familiar footing, I part my lips and thread my fingers into his hair, kissing him back with urgency. Rebel groans against my lips and presses his hard length against mine.

"Should we be doing this in your childhood bedroom?"

"You think I never fooled around in here? I got plenty of action in high school, babe."

I chuckle, trying to imagine a younger version of Rebel back when he really was only Hendrix. "Oh yeah? So you weren't all pimply and dorky?" I tease, walking him backward toward the bed.

"Pssh, no way, I was a total stud. What about you?" Rebel pulls me down so I'm straddling him on his narrow bed.

"I was a shy loner, but I was secretly hooking up with a few jocks," I brag.

"That sounds kinda hot." Rebel tugs up my shirt and runs his fingers along the ridges of my abs. "Wanna play?"

"Hendrix, your parents are right downstairs. What if they hear us?" I feign a protest as I unbutton his pants.

"I guess we'll have to be quiet." Rebel works on my pants as well, at the same time kissing and nipping at my throat. "I've seen you checking me out in the locker room after gym. But no one at school can know, can you keep a secret?"

"I'm very good at keeping secrets. In fact, I'd say it's my second-best skill, right after my oral skills."

"Is it true what they say? Are guys really better at giving head?"

"I'll show you, and you can decide for yourself."

"Boys, sorry to interrupt, but we're going to cut the cake, and your sister wanted to give a speech," Rebel's mom calls through the door.

He winces, and I stifle a laugh. "We'll be right there," he calls back. "I guess this will have to wait until later," he adds to me in a much quieter voice.

"Mmm, looking forward to it."

I zip Rebel's pants back up—which is a much more depressing direction—and climb off him.

I hold my hand out to Rebel to help him up, which he takes, but he doesn't drop the touch immediately. A small tingle of awareness at the pleasure of the innocent contact runs up my spine. I yank my hand back quickly, and Rebel gives me an apologetic smile.

"Glad you boys could join us," Rebel's mom says with a knowing smile when we make it back to the living room, where everyone is congregated waiting for speeches and cake.

"Sorry," I mumble.

Marley stands with a champagne glass in her hands and faces the full room of people.

"Thank you all for coming today to celebrate my parents' anniversary. I want to say a few words about my parents before we cut the cake. Growing up, I thought my parents were extremely weird. Instead of McDonalds and Mac and Cheese, we were getting kale burgers. Instead of family vacations to Disney World, we were going on meditation retreats. But in spite of all the weirdness, I always knew we had something special. I could and still can see the love pour from both of you whenever you look at each other. In most things, I've wanted a different life than you two built together, but in love, you are my absolute role models.

"Maybe you didn't know that Hendrix and I could always see the little things you did to show your love, but every single thing imprinted on me, and I think it did on Hendrix as well. Because love isn't about grand gestures and being perfect, it's about leaving the last of the organic orange juice because you know your wife will want some when she wakes up, or leaving each other notes with dirty pictures drawn on them, or holding your wife's hand when she hears that she has breast cancer and then standing by her every day of her recovery. You two are the embodiment of love, and I'm so blessed to have learned how to love from you."

Hendrix's hand flexes against mine, and I realize we're holding hands again, and I'm not sure how or when that happened. His gaze is fixed on his sister, and there's a slightly glassy look to his eyes.

He looks over at me like he can feel my gaze on him and gives me a lopsided smile. My gut clenches in a mixture of fear and... I'm not actually sure what the other emotion is exactly. All I know is it feels warm, makes me want to be as close to Hendrix as humanly possible, and intensifies the fear tenfold.

Marley's speech comes to an end, and I blink myself back into reality. I tug my hand out of Hendrix's and clap along with the rest of the group, just so it looks like I had an excuse to pull away.

My heart pounds in my ears. I need to get a grip. I'm

getting too close to the edge, and I need to correct course. And there's only one way I know how to do that.

"When can we head back to the hotel?" I whisper, letting the suggestion drip into my tone.

"Cake and then we'll leave."

∼

"Strip and bend over the bed," I growl against Rebel's lips as we kiss and lick at each other's mouths.

I swallow Rebel's groan of approval. He pulls back to comply, but I stop him with a firm palm on his left ass cheek.

"I can't wait to have this tight ass."

"Me too, baby. You have no idea."

I take a step back and strip my shirt over my head, keeping my eyes on Rebel as he scrambles out of his own clothes.

I can't get used to how perfect he looks. I mean, duh, he's a porn star, so of course he's completely hung. But, perfect cock aside, his body is everything I'd picture if you asked me to describe my ideal man. He's in shape but is devoid of bulging muscles. The dusting of blond hair on his chest and down his stomach feels incredible against my own naked body, and I need to feel him again right the fuck now.

I don't pay any attention to where my clothes fall as I strip out of them. And Rebel seems to feel the same way as he tosses his pants on the floor and sends his underwear flying over his shoulder.

He wastes no time bending over the bed, bracing his hands against the mattress and arching his back.

I wrap my hand around my cock and give it a few lazy strokes, gathering the leaking pre-cum on my thumb. I lick my lips as I step up behind Rebel, unable to tear my eyes away from his round, powerful ass. I know exactly what he looks like when it's flexing with each powerful thrust. And I know what he looks like spread and taking it. But, I don't know what he feels like hot and tight around my cock, and I can't wait to find out.

I spread his cheeks with one hand and lift my slicked thumb to his tight pucker. He spreads his legs a little wider and leans farther forward.

Rebel's asshole easily softens under the small circles I make with my thumb. The small amount of pre-cum I used dries quickly, so I spit into his ass crack and spread it with my fingers. Rebel groans at my touch.

"God, you're fucking filthy; I love it," he grunts as I use the new moisture to work two fingers inside.

"I know you do."

I lean over and run my tongue along Rebel's spine as I fuck him open with my fingers. His hands clutch fistfuls of the bedsheets, and his breath is coming out in heavy pants.

"You're sexy as fuck." I nibble at the back of his neck, and he whimpers. "Are you ready for my cock?"

"Fuck, yes."

I pull my fingers out and reach for my bag to grab my condoms and lube. Spit may be enough for finger fucking, but I'm not going to try to shove my cock into him without any lube. I suit up and then squeeze a generous amount into my hand and cover my cock with it. I spread what's left around his hole and wipe my hand on the edge of the bedsheet.

Rebel groans as I line up and slowly press inside. There's little resistance as he relaxes expertly to take me. His smooth inner muscles grip my cock and suck me into his hot channel.

My fingers dig into his hips, hard enough to leave bruises. The thought sends a shiver down my spine and straight to my balls as I imagine thousands of viewers watching a video featuring Rebel and noticing finger shaped purple smudges on his waist and thighs, wondering where Rebel got them. I can picture watching the video myself and trying to hold back from coming too quickly, remembering this moment, pounding into him from behind as he wails and begs for me to give it to him harder.

I lean over him and suck his neck, desperate to leave marks all over him as my hips snap forward and drag back over and over again.

"Troy, ungh, fuck," Rebel rambles random combinations of words and pleas while meeting every one of my thrusts. "Harder, rougher, please."

I wrap my hand around his throat from behind, not obstructing his airway, but just hard enough to feel the rumble of each word and gasp escaping his lips. And then I fuck him harder, until he collapses forward onto the bed. I follow, falling on top of him but doing my best not to miss a beat.

"So good, Hendrix, you feel so fucking good." I don't realize my slip up until the words are out, but it doesn't seem to give Rebel any pause as he cries out, humping against the bed as I hit that spongy pleasure spot inside him.

His ass clenches so hard around me that my vision blurs around the edges for a second as I lose my breath. I grab onto his firm, chiseled ass cheeks for leverage and thrust deep, emptying myself with a deep moan. When my legs are shaking too badly to hold me up any longer, I collapse on top of Rebel, who seems just as drained as I am.

"Holy fuck, you are a goddamn god," Rebel mumbles in a tired, sated tone.

Pride swells in my chest, along with another emotion I can't name. I roll off of Rebel so I can lay beside him without crushing him.

"Well, look at the tools I had to work with," I point out, giving his ass a resounding smack.

25

REBEL

I wait till Bear is done thanking Brewer and Pixie for their stellar performance in the shoot. The colorful tats on Brewer's arms shimmer with the sweat he worked up while fucking Pixie into the mattress. The little imp took it like a champ, though. That lithe body of his was made to be fucked, rude as it may sound. And he's still so fucking eager. This is gonna be a popular one, I can tell.

We already had hundreds of requests to see more of Pixie—quite a few demanding Tank have a go at him. I can see why, the difference in their personalities and body types makes for an interesting contrast. Besides, Tank is such an obvious top and Pixie such a total bottom that it fulfills that stereotype as well. So far, Bear has been reluctant to book those two together, though.

Brewer had a great time, I can tell. He hugs Pixie, then slaps him playfully on his ass before walking over to the locker room to take a shower and get dressed. It's funny, but as soon as he's gone, Pixie transforms back into the shy guy he was when I first met him. He looks at Bear from between his lashes, wringing his hands. It's almost as if he has to fight the urge to cover himself up, which makes no sense because we all just watched him get ravished.

He gives Bear an awkward wave as he all but runs to the locker rooms, and Bear keeps staring at him until he's out of sight, a frown on his face.

"Something wrong?" I ask, stepping closer.

Bear jerks as if I shock him, then turns his head my way. "I don't know." He looks back at the locker rooms, then at me. "Do you think Pixie likes it?"

"Working for us? For Ballsy Boys, I mean," I quickly say to cover my mistake. "I think so. He loves to be fucked, that much is clear."

"Yeah," Bear says, his eyes once again trailing toward the locker rooms. "Every time I try to make small talk, he clams up."

"He's shy," I offer. "And I don't think he's fully used to being naked around us yet."

Bear seems to give himself a mental shake. "Anyway, you said you wanted to talk to me. What's up, kiddo?"

I gesture toward his office. "Can we talk in private?"

Bear frowns. "I'm not gonna like this conversation, am I?"

My stomach rolls as I follow him into his office. What if he doesn't think I'm good enough for this?

Bear signals me to sit down, and I plop down on one of the chairs before I realize it. Most of the time, the guy is pretty laid back, but he's got this dominant edge that pops up every now and then that makes you want to obey.

"Talk to me, Rebel," he says, his tone serious, but kind.

"I wanna quit," I blurt out, starting in the exact wrong way. "Wait, no, that's not what I meant." I sigh, frustrated with myself for fucking this up, even though I'd rehearsed exactly what I wanted to say. Bear is still patiently waiting for me to get my brain into the right gear. "I love working for you, for Ballsy Boys. I'm proud of what we do here. At the same time, I think it's time for me to move on. I was hoping you would be interested in taking me on as an assistant. Full time. Or at least, enough hours so I could stop doing shoots."

Bear's face breaks open in a smile. "That's it? Fucking hell, Rebel, I thought you were gonna tell me you were moving on to another studio. That would've broken my fucking heart."

"I would never do that. This is my... I love working here, Bear. You know that. These guys, they're my friends. Family, more like. I don't wanna leave, but I..." I sigh. "I met someone. He's... He's special to me, and I need to put that first."

"Did he ask you to?" Bear asks.

I shake my head. "No. We didn't even discuss it. He knows what I do, obviously, but he never asked me to quit. But I want to."

Bear's smile is much softer now, almost fatherly. "You're in love."

My heart skips a beat. Am I? It's all so fucking confusing and complicated, not the least of which is I know Troy won't wanna hear it. If I even mention the word "love" he'll either freak out completely or run for the hills. Or maybe both. I sigh. "It's complicated."

"It always is, kiddo. That's why there are millions of songs about it and countless books and movies. Love is complicated."

Before I know it, I ask him. "Have you ever been in love?"

Bear's eyes sadden. "Once. He..." I watch him swallow, his eyes saddening even more. "He got sick and passed away. But that was years ago."

"Would you do it again, knowing what you know now?"

It's an awfully personal question, but Bear doesn't seem to mind.

"Honestly, I don't know. For myself, probably. I loved him with all my heart, and I wouldn't have wanted to miss out on our time together, brief as it was. But I wouldn't wish it on my worst enemy, to have to watch someone you love slowly die. It's the most horrific, helpless feeling, because all you can do is watch."

We sit there for a few beats, but the silence is strangely comforting. "Do you think there's a spot for me as your assistant?" I finally switch back to the topic I wanted to talk to him about in the first place. "Or do you think I'm not ready? Or lack the talent?"

I hate that I sound so hesitant and insecure, but I need him to be honest. If I have no business even attempting this, I need him to tell me straight to my face. I mean, it'll break my fucking heart, but at least I'll know.

He gently shakes his head. "Rebel, you already are my right hand. You've barely done any shoots these last months, except with new guys, and the one with Heart. Truth is, I should have talked to you about transitioning into a more formal role as assistant creative director, but I've just been too busy. We're growing like crazy, and I more than need you full time."

Something warm opens in my heart, and I have to swallow. "You think I have the talent to do this?"

"You've got more talent for it than I do. Seriously. I may be better at the business end and the technical details, for now at least, but you have great vision and creativity. Did you see how many hits we got on that video with Campy, Heart, and Tank? It blew up, man, and that was all you. I love that you wanna come on board for this full time. Consider yourself hired."

My face lights up, and I'm probably beaming like a Christmas tree. "Really?"

Bear leans in and puts a hand on my shoulder. "Kiddo, it's not charity. I'm not hiring you out of the goodness of my heart or something. My biggest fear these last months has been that you'd get snatched up by a rival company."

My mouth drops slightly agape. "But... Why didn't you ever say anything?"

He squeezes my shoulder before he lets go and leans back in his chair. "Part of it was because I was too busy and didn't make the time. But part of it was also because I didn't want you to feel beholden to me. If I had asked you, you might have said yes out of obligation, and I wanted you to choose this out of passion, because it was what you truly wanted."

Why are my eyes getting watery all of a sudden? "This is what I want. I love Ballsy Boys, and I want nothing more than to be a part of it in the future. Thank you for giving me this chance." My voice breaks in an embarrassing way, but Bear merely smiles at me.

When I've composed myself a little, he asks, "So now that you're officially hired, tell me what ideas you have for shoots."

Without hesitation, I open up and share this crazy idea I had for a video with Tank and Brewer.

26

TROY

Mason and I are lounging on my couch working on our game when my phone rings on my nightstand. Since no one calls me aside from Rebel, the sound immediately brings a smile to my face.

Mason glances over at me and gives me a knowing look. "Boyfriend?" he asks as I reach for my phone.

My nose scrunches, and I shake my head rapidly. *Boyfriend?* No, fuck no.

"What's up, stud?" I answer.

"Hey, babe. Can I come over?" he asks.

"Sorry, I've already got a man in my bed at the moment," I tease, shooting Mason a wink and trying not to laugh at his horrified face.

"Oh, seriously?" Rebel asks, sounding a bit disappointed.

"Yeah, but not in the way you're thinking. My...uh...friend, Mason is here."

It feels weird calling anyone a friend, I've spent so much of my life keeping everyone at a minimum fifty-feet distance. But, I can't deny that the more time Mason and I have spent working together, the more I've grown somewhat attached to him as a person. It's kind of gross. Maybe I need therapy.

"Aw, you have a friend. I love that."

"Shut up," I grumble. "Now, what's up? Is this a booty call or what?"

"No, I have some news." Rebel sounds nervous, which immediately piques my interest.

"Stop over, Mason and I are almost finished. Maybe the three of us can go grab something for dinner?" Then an idea strikes me, so I slide off the bed and walk toward my living room area so I can lower my voice and Mason won't hear me. "Actually, this poor dude desperately needs some fun, know anyone you might want to bring along to introduce him to?"

Rebel snorts a laugh, catching my drift instantly. "I'm sure I can rustle someone up. Want to meet somewhere? I can tell you my news later when we're alone."

"Oh, yeah, that's fine."

We make a plan of where to meet and I hang up.

"That kind of sounded like a boyfriend," Mason points out as soon as I return to my bed.

"No, just a friend I fuck around with," I correct. "You up for grabbing something to eat with him? He's cool, I think you'll like him."

"Oh? Um, sure." Mason pushes his glasses higher on the bridge of his nose.

Mason and I wrap up our work for the day and head over to the bar and grill Rebel suggested, only a few blocks away. Inside, my stomach gives a weird flutter when I spot Rebel next to the bar smiling and talking to Mason's surprise blind date. He brought Heart, not exactly who I would've chosen for shy, nerdy Mason, but he'll do. There's no way Mason won't spring a boner for the tattooed porn star.

Rebel's eye catches mine, and he straightens up and waves us over.

"Oh my god," Mason hisses as he grabs my arm. "Are you fucking kidding me right now? I thought you were joking about the porn star thing."

"Why would I be joking?" I ask. "Wait, I thought porn was *so* skeevy? How do you even recognize them?" I challenge.

Mason's cheeks burn bright red, and he glances around like he's trying to find an escape route.

"Oh my god, I'm a living male; of course, I watch porn."

"If you can watch porn, you can hang out with porn stars. Don't be a snob." I put an arm over his shoulders and steer him in Rebel and Heart's direction.

"Hey," Rebel reaches for me, before catching himself and shoving his hands into his pockets. The gesture somehow makes me both happy and twitchy.

I introduce Mason, and I notice the blush in his cheeks deepening when Heart gives him a friendly smile and holds out his hand to shake. I bite down on the inside of my cheek to keep from laughing at his discomfort, and Rebel shoots me a wink like we're sharing some sort of inside joke.

The hostess comes over to take us to a table, and Rebel's hand finds the small of my back, and a shiver runs up my spine. I want to drag Rebel to the bathroom and suck his dick. Or force him out to the car to fuck me in the backseat. Hell, I'll take a handjob under the table.

"By the way, after we're finished here, I'm having your ass for dessert," he whispers in my ear, and my cock pulses in the confines of my jeans.

Mason is quiet during dinner, only talking when Rebel

or Heart ask him a question. I start to feel kind of bad for springing a sort of blind date on him without telling him. Maybe he isn't ready to date again after his break-up. Or maybe he was serious when he said he wasn't into casual sex. Whatever the case, I owe him an apology when I get him alone. Heart seems like a cool guy, though. He spends the meal telling jokes and stories, flirting with our waiter, and basically entertaining anyone within a ten-foot radius of our table.

And Rebel is practically glowing over whatever his news is. He tends to smile a lot in general, but tonight, it's like happiness and light is pouring from him. He keeps touching me under the table. They're innocent touches, a brush to the knee or forearm, but they're making me so hard I'm about to go insane.

By the time we're finished eating, my sole focus is making our exit so I can be alone with Rebel.

"You don't live far from here, right Mason?" I check as we pay and start heading toward the door.

"Only a few blocks east, I won't have a problem getting home," Mason assures me.

"Oh hey, I live over that way too. Mind if I walk with you?" Heart asks, and Mason looks startled.

"Um...yeah...I mean, if you live that way anyway, I can't really stop you." Mason laughs with obvious discomfort.

"Cool. Catch you later, Rebel," Heart says, clasping hands with Rebel and then giving him a pat on the back.

Outside, I climb into Rebel's car.

"Think we made a love match?" he asks, glancing one last time at Mason and Heart's retreating forms.

"I'll be happy with a lust connection. Poor Mason needs it."

"Yeah, Heart obviously isn't lacking in the sex department, but I get the feeling he could use a friend, so hopefully they'll both find what they need."

"All right, let's stop worrying about our friends' sex lives and get back to focusing on our own," I suggest.

"Good thinking." Rebel pulls out of the parking space, and we drive the short distance to my place.

As soon as we're back at my apartment, Rebel is all over me with his hands and mouth. His fingers thread through my hair, and he tilts my head, forcing his tongue into my mouth with a filthy moan. With greedy hands, I reach for the button on his jeans, but he slaps me away and then shoves me down onto my bed.

"I told you, I want my tongue in that ass."

My hole flutters, and my cock throbs as a groan escapes my lips. I tug my shirt off while Rebel rids me of my jeans. My breath catches as his hungry gaze roams over my naked body, his eyes half-lidded and his tongue running along his plump bottom lip.

"Flip over, baby," Rebel commands, and I waste no time obeying.

I settle onto the mattress, folding my arms around a pillow and spreading my legs enough for Rebel to crawl between them. A shiver of anticipation runs up my spine as I feel the bed dip.

Obviously, I've been rimmed before. But ever since Rebel told me that rimming is his favorite thing to do and the filthy way he described it, let's just say I've been looking forward to experiencing it first-hand.

Rebel's big hands rest on my ass, kneading and spreading my cheeks. I shiver as cool air hits my hole. My pucker twitches at the sensation, and Rebel lets out an appreciative moan.

One of his hands disappears, and I hear the sound of

sloppy sucking. Seconds later, Rebel is running a damp finger down my crack, brushing briefly over my hole and making me squirm. I press up slightly on my knees, seeking more friction, and Rebel's palm comes down hard against my ass.

"You know you have a fantastic bubble butt?" Rebel comments. "It has such a nice jiggle. And when I'm fucking you...ungh, so perfect."

The rough pad of his finger traces my rim slowly, maddeningly. I flex my hips, dragging my leaking cock against my cool sheets. Rebel abandons my rim, and his finger wanders over my taint and then teases just behind my balls, already high and aching.

"Please," I gasp.

Rebel grabs my hips and tugs them up until I'm up on my knees, my face still on my pillow. And then his hot breath ghosts along my hole, and my cock pulses, already missing the friction from the bed.

The tip of Rebel's tongue taps against my tight pucker, and I groan into the pillow. My skin tingles, and heat radiates from my balls to the pit of my stomach. I want to feel Rebel's monster cock stretching me. But I also *really* want his tongue licking and fucking me.

"Oh my god, you know what would be hot?" I blurt.

"Huh?"

"A dildo mold of your cock, then you could fuck me with it while you rim me."

Rebel pauses for a second and then lets out a little huff of a laugh, tickling all of my sensitive nerve endings. "You are one kinky fucker. That must be why we're so good together."

Then he dives back in, this time dragging the whole flat of his tongue from my balls to my hole. He licks and nibbles around my rim, and my ass clenches, desperate to be filled. My cock drips steadily, pre-cum pooling on the sheets beneath me. Rebel taps at my entrance with his tongue again, but this time when I soften for him, he shoves inside.

"Holy fuck," I moan, clenching my fists around the pillow.

His tongue plunges in and out, eating my ass like it's his favorite dessert. When his large hand wraps around my cock, I can't breathe. The pleasure is so close to the surface, a single movement would shatter me. Rebel moans and licks deeper inside me as he jerks me hard and fast.

"Oh Jesus, so good," I gasp. "I'm going to...oh, fuck."

My ass clenches down hard around Rebel's tongue, and my balls draw up. I scream Rebel's name over and over into my pillow, and not just his porn name, a few *Hendrix's* slip out as well. My legs give out as the last of my pleasure leaks onto the sheets, and I collapse into my wet spot.

Rebel climbs onto the bed beside me and pulls me into his arms. The dude really loves to snuggle, and I guess if I'm being honest, I don't *hate* it.

"God, that was good," I hum against Rebel's neck.

My whole body feels warm and tingly as I wiggle closer. I sigh in contentment and absentmindedly run my fingers along the exposed skin on Rebel's stomach, where his shirt is just riding up. His scent surrounds me and beckons me to nap curled up against him. That jolts me out of my post orgasm haze like a cold slap.

"Oh, hey, what was your big news you were all excited about?" I ask, grappling for something to ground my emotions that are too big right now.

I watch as a smile slowly spreads over Rebel's lips. His arm tightens around me, and his fingers trace small circles on my hip.

"I quit porn."

"What?" I shout, bolting up and examining Rebel's face, expecting him to start laughing any second before yelling *gotcha*. "You did *not* quit porn. Tell me you're joking."

He looks back at me with a surprised expression, like he doesn't understand my reaction, and then a resigned sadness settles into his eyes. "I didn't *quit* quit, but I won't be doing scenes anymore. I'm moving to behind the camera."

My stomach clenches, and I struggle to untangle myself from the sheets as I scramble out of bed.

"What the actual fuck, Rebel? Or...fuck...are you even Rebel anymore? Do I have to call you Hendrix now?" I ask as I pace by the foot of the bed in all my naked glory. I'm sure I look insane right now, but I feel a little crazy, so I guess it fits.

"You've called me Hendrix before," he pipes in quietly.

I stop in my tracks and spin to face Rebel. "Is *that* what this is about?" My heart beats wildly in my chest like a bird in a too small cage. "Is this some sort of *gesture*? We agreed this wasn't serious. The first time we fucked around, we both said we weren't looking for anything serious. I *thought* we were on the same page."

Rebel runs a hand through his wild hair and shakes his head at me. "I don't think I ever said I wasn't looking for serious. I said I didn't think I'd ever find someone who'd be cool with my job, and that I was capable of casual. I didn't expect—"

"Nope, no, uh-uh." I hold my hands up and shake my head, rapidly backing away. "I can't do this. It's too much, I just...*can't*."

I grab the first pair of pants and shirt I find and tug them on, avoiding looking over at Rebel. I can't bear to see his emotions written all over his face. None of this is how it's supposed to be. Anyway, whatever he thinks he's feeling for me won't last. I'll disappoint him, I'll drive him away, I'll do whatever it is I do that makes me unlovable.

As soon as I'm dressed, I'm out the door without a backward glance or a second thought to the fact that I'm leaving Rebel alone at my apartment.

27
REBEL

I've waited a whole week, but not a peep from Troy. I'm starting to wonder if he's gonna be the seventh guy in a row to dump me. And in this case, it would even be more ironic because of his insistence we weren't even dating in the first place.

Just friends. Friends with benefits. Fuck-buddies. I don't know how many terms Troy has used to describe what we are, but not one of them was boyfriends or anything resembling a serious relationship.

After the little he explained to me about his background, I understand where he's coming from. Sort of. I get that he has a trauma because of nobody wanting him, nobody sticking around long enough. I don't know shit about psychology other than the occasional self-help book I read, but you don't need to be a genius to figure that one out.

My question is if he'll ever get past it. I'm a pretty patient guy by nature, but I need to know if we even have a shot together. If he can't get past this fear of being rejected again, I don't know how long I can keep doing this.

I miss him. I really, really miss him. Not just the sex,

though I will readily admit my own hand is a sorry replacement for Troy, but the friendship. The relationship. Because I know despite all his protests, we were in a relationship. We still are, as far as I'm concerned. I just need to keep that little detail hidden from Troy, because he'll freak out for sure.

I'm not ready to give up on him just yet. How can I, when my heart is fully invested? I need to figure out a way to ease him back into our thing, whatever it is. He needs to feel safe and unthreatened, which means I need to keep my mushy feelings in check.

Sex. Sex has always worked for us, right? I'm gonna do an old-fashioned booty-call, see how he responds.

Should I call him or text him? Calling is more confrontational and gives him less time to think it over. That might mean he'll say no faster. Maybe texting is better. I could try to...entice him?

Within minutes, I have my phone's camera set up on a mini tripod in my bedroom. I check the lighting to make sure it's light enough to see, but not so bright it kills the sexy vibe I'm going for. Yup, this should work.

I hit record and let myself fall backward on my bed. My cock is already hard, and I squirt a little lube in my hand and stroke it slowly, reveling in the slick sensation. My balls are full and heavy after not jerking off for a whole day, and roll them in my other hand, first the left, then the right. I let my legs fall open, then pull them up so the camera will show everything.

Despite being completely used to having sex on-camera, this is a little awkward. Aside from my Fleshjack video, I haven't done any solo videos. We have them up on the Ballsy Boys site, guys who have made jerking off into an art. Hell, we even have a guy who is so flexible he can suck his own dick. I gotta say, after watching that, I seriously considered taking up yoga.

Solo shoots are not my thing, I guess. I much prefer playing with a partner. I gotta make this one work, though, so I slowly stroke my cock and play with my balls.

"Mmmm," I moan softly. "That feels nice. Can you tell how full my balls are? I haven't jacked off in a day, and I'm so fucking horny…"

I rub my thumb over the head of my cock, where a drop of pre-cum has welled up.

"You know what I'm picturing right now? You, Troy. I'm picturing your golden eyes, which get so much darker when I'm fucking you. Your hair that's all messy and disheveled after I've pulled you down on my cock. Your arms that are so strong when they hold me down as you fuck me with your thick cock. I'm seeing you in my mind when you get all desperate, right before you come. You get this fire in your eyes, this determination. So fucking hot."

Every single observation is the truth, except that I'm leaving out so much at the same time. The way my stomach drops when he smiles at me. The way his hands feel when they explore my body. How sweet his lips taste, his mouth, his tongue. How happy I am when we're in bed together, even when we're sleeping. There's so much I say, and yet so much I hold back.

I open my legs wider, let my left hand travel down lower, to find my hole. I push in with ease, courtesy of a lot of practice. Another soft moan escapes me as my body remembers how good it felt to have Troy breach me, fill me. God, I miss him.

With slow, deliberate actions, I drive myself to the brink, prepping my ass until it's stretched and ready. Then I turn around on all fours, my ass toward the camera, looking over my shoulder with my trademark sultry look. "Wanna come over? I'll be here waiting...ready for your cock."

I edit the video slightly so it starts and ends at the exact right moment and send it to Troy without allowing myself time to reconsider. It's a risk, sure, but above all an emotional one. One of the advantages of being a porn star is that I'm not concerned about sending videos like this. First of all, I trust Troy to not make this public, but even if he did, who cares. There are hundreds of videos of me out there, naked, fucking, doing whatever. This is mild and tame compared to what I've done.

Now all I can do is wait to see if my bait gets his attention.

When he hasn't replied after fifteen minutes, my stomach sinks. Dammit, I was so sure he wouldn't be able to resist a booty call. Now what? I'm about to put my clothes back on when the doorbell rings.

My heart jumps up, and I quickly throw on a pair of shorts. Is it Troy?

I yank the door open, and there he is, his cheeks slightly red and his hair a glorious mess. We stare at each other for a few seconds before he pushes me inside and kicks the door shut behind him.

He looks at me again as if he's trying to find something on my face, in my eyes. I don't know what he's looking for, and all I can do is smile because he's here. He took the bait, and he's here, and hot damn, I want him.

His right hand shoots out and finds my hair. He pulls me toward him, not too gently, but I willingly let myself be dragged. One more stare, his eyes drilling into mine, and then he crushes our mouths together.

His mouth tastes salty, as if he recently ate chips, and I dig in deep, licking and sucking until I've explored every little bit of his mouth. I've missed that taste, his soft lips, that addictive tongue, his stubble chafing my skin.

His hands slip under the waistband of my shorts, then yank them down. He cups my ass, his big hands possessively splaying my cheeks, molding, rubbing, pinching. I moan into his mouth. My little session for him has left me incredibly horny, so I really hope he came here to fuck.

His right hand dips between my cheeks into my crack and finds my hole with ease. I'm still wide open and slick with lube, so he slides right in. He hums his approval into my mouth, while still ravishing my mouth.

His left hand wriggles between us to unzip his jeans. With quick moves he drops his pants and his boxers. His wet cock rubs against mine and pleasure zings through my balls.

He breaks off the kiss, and we're both panting. He turns me around with strong hands and pushes me down until I get the hint. I put my hands on the wall, spread my legs, and arch my back to create the perfect angle. His hand grabs my throat with just enough pressure to feel it, and then he enters me with one swift thrust.

I cry out, as much in pleasure as in shock. Somehow, I expected him to be slower, more careful, though I love it that he isn't. He pulls out, surges back in, and another low moan falls off my lips.

He fucks me hard, raw, with big, deep thrusts that make me brace myself against the wall to provide enough counterforce. His one hand stays on my throat, the other digs into my hip, probably leaving bruises. Holy hell, he feels so good. So deep, so close.

His balls slap wet against me, and he grunts every time he pushes in. I breathe in deeply, his scent enveloping me. And then he shifts his position slightly, causing him to target my prostate head-on, and I stop thinking at all.

He fucks me relentlessly, not even stopping when I explode all over the wall, until he comes with a loud groan. It's then I fully realize he isn't wearing a condom, because his hot release scorching up my insides is a completely new experience.

I let my head drop to my hands with my eyes closed, crashing against the wall, no longer able to hold my weight. My breath comes out in short pants as his cum drips out of my ass.

When I open my eyes and weakly turn around, half-hanging against the wall, it's just in time to see him zip up. He bends over for one last wet kiss, both our faces slick with perspiration, and then he's out the door.

This was the single hottest fuck I've ever had. And throughout our whole encounter, we never spoke a word.

28

TROY

I *just fucked him without a condom.*

What the actual fuck was I thinking? I wasn't thinking, that's the problem. I haven't been thinking at all when it comes to Rebel. Time and time again, I've let my dick make the calls, and while that's usually not an issue for me, it seems to get me into a lot of trouble where Rebel is concerned.

"Troy, wait," Rebel calls from his doorway, halting my progress down his hallway. "Get your ass back in here."

Part of me wants to give him the finger and keep walking. He's the one who lured me over here for a quick fuck, now he's going to try to talk about our feelings or some shit again. I don't know what makes me turn around and go back into his place, aside from the fact that I've obviously lost my ever-loving mind where Rebel is concerned.

I step back into his foyer and shut the door behind me. Tension radiates between us, vibrating and pulsing in the air all around.

"You want to smoke some weed?" I ask, grasping for

anything to ease this unprecedented awkwardness between us.

"Sure." Rebel points me to the living room and heads to the kitchen, I assume to get drinks or snacks.

I roll a joint and take a hit while I wait for him. And while I wait, I start to think about how fucked up things suddenly are between us. In the blink of an eye, this thing went from the best sex and most fun hanging out I've ever had, to an awkward fucking mess...pun intended.

"You fucked everything up," I accuse Rebel when he returns with two sodas.

Rebel raises an eyebrow at me in question and holds out a hand for me to pass him the joint. "How do you figure that *I* fucked everything up?" he asks after he takes a hit and passes it back.

"Because everything was perfect until you decided to quit porn and declare your feelings for me or whatever."

"I didn't declare anything," Rebel counters. "I told you I was stepping back from porn, that was it. You're the one who freaked out and blew everything out of proportion."

"Are you saying you don't have feelings for me, more than just as friends with benefits?"

Rebel opens his mouth and then closes it again, his eyes filled with silent pleading. "No, I'm not saying that," he mumbles after several strained seconds.

"This is total bullshit. You can't change the rules in the middle of the game," I complain, my chest almost too tight to breathe. "Now you've gone and ruined the best..." I trail off and shake my head at my shaking hands and strained voice.

"Nothing has to be ruined. Can't you give this a chance between us? I know you're scared—"

"You don't know shit. What, just because I told you I was in foster care, now you think you know my whole life story?"

"Tell me then. I *want* to know your life story." Rebel's voice is pleading, almost desperate, and it only makes me want to scream at him. I want to fucking hit something, even if I learned the lesson too many times that violence isn't the way to make anything better. I clench my fists, willing the shaking to stop.

"I don't *want* to tell you. Don't you get it?" I lash out.

Push him away now to save us both heartbreak later, that's the best thing to do. It's kinder to both of us. Even if it does feel like my heart is bleeding in my chest.

"I don't believe you," Rebel challenges, fixing me with a steady look. "You can throw a tantrum all you want, but when you're done, I'm still going to be waiting here for you to realize that what we have is so much more than just a good fuck."

"I can't deal with this," I stand abruptly. The walls feel like they're closing in. I need to get out of here.

"Listen, I'm going to New York in two days with all the guys. We're nominated for an award, and it's a big deal. Why don't you take a day to calm down and then come with me? We can explore New York and have fun like we did in Vegas."

"I don't think that's a good idea."

Rebel looks like I kicked his puppy, and it makes me feel like complete dog shit.

"If you change your mind, the offer stands."

"Yeah, I'll think about it. I'd better get home."

"Yeah," he nods and follows me to the front door to see me out. "By the way, I, and all the guys at the studio, take PrEP, so don't worry about the condom fuck up."

"Thank fuck for that at least." I breathe out a sigh of

relief. I almost lean forward to kiss him goodbye, but I stop myself at the last second and settle for an awkward head nod before booking it out the door.

Back at home, I crawl into bed fully clothed and pull the blankets over my head. I promised myself I wouldn't let myself get attached to anyone ever again after Elise passed. And here I am, halfway in love with some gorgeous, adventurous, perfect man who's bound to break my heart eventually.

Who am I kidding? My dumb ass is a lot more than halfway in love with Hendrix.

Maybe if I just hide out here under my covers, I won't ever have to face this, and I won't have to admit to Hendrix or myself that there's nothing left of my heart to protect, since it's already in his hands.

The only solution is to cut him off. I won't go to New York. I won't get tricked into another booty call. I'll go completely cold turkey. And eventually, I'll get over him, and he'll get over me, and we'll both be better off.

29

REBEL

I still don't like flying, I affirm on the flight to New York City. I just don't like being cooped up with too much crazy and on an airplane, there's always too much crazy. Thank fuck me, Brewer, and Campy at least got seats in the same row, meaning we're plastered against each other, instead of some smelly dude.

We know each other well enough to chat for a bit, and then leave each other the fuck alone. I listen to my music, Campy is on his phone, as usual, playing some game, and Brewer is reading a book I can't even pronounce the title of. Something about biochemistry? No fucking clue why he wants to read something like that, but if that's what he likes, it's fine with me.

Tank, Bear, and Pixie are a few rows behind us, also sitting together. I had to smile a little when I looked back a few minutes ago, because the sight of the cute, innocent-looking Pixie between grumpy, hairy Tank and silver fox Bear was...interesting. Not that Tank has been giving him a hard time or anything. No, he's been nothing but kind to the shy little imp. He reserves all his grumpiness for Brewer, it seems. This, of course, makes the idea I had for a shoot with the two of them even more epic—and Bear absolutely fucking loved it. Now, all I have to do is convince those two of cooperating. To say that's a challenge is the fucking understatement of the year.

I saw Bear make an effort at engaging Pixie in a conversation, so that took some of my worries away about him feeling left out. I was surprised Bear even wanted to bring him, but he insisted Pixie was part of the core group now. So is Heart, but apparently, he had other obligations and couldn't make this trip. I wonder what he had that was more important than a free trip to New York.

Just like I wonder what was more important to Troy than joining me. Rationally, I know that it was too much, too soon for him. He's a wounded soul, my banana boy, too hurt by the people who left him in the past to dare to give himself to someone else. I get it, but fuck, it hurts.

This is a proud moment for me, whether we win or not, and I wanted him with me. I wanted to share this with him as one of the hopefully many beautiful moments we'll get to share together. I guess I'll need even more patience to wait until he's ready. If he'll ever be. At what point do I decide I can't wait anymore for him to start trusting himself, trusting me and us? I don't know, but even the thought makes it hard to breathe. I never thought I'd be in this position, but the idea of spending life without Troy is so painful, it physically hurts. I guess that's why they call it a broken heart.

After a meal has been served, I doze off with my music relaxing me, until Campy gently shakes me awake. "Look," he says, pointing out the window. The plane tilts to turn, and Manhattan displays itself in all its glory. It's a bright sunny, though supposedly chilly day in the city, and the sun reflects off the iconic buildings I can easily identify. It's not my first time here, but every time, this city takes my breath away just a little. Campy told us it was his first time in New York, so we had to promise him we'd do at least some sightseeing.

"It's stunning, even from the sky," Brewer says, leaning over me and Campy to catch a glimpse.

We join Bear, Pixie, and Tank as we make our way to the luggage carousels. We catch a few curious looks, but the various subtle disguises we're wearing so far seem to do their trick. Brewer and Campy are wearing baseball caps, and I'm clean shaven—a true rarity, and one Troy would undoubtedly get on my ass about—and wearing my hair up in a man bun. It's not my best look, but it does make me look completely different. Pixie's hair is unstyled, which interestingly enough completely changes his appearance. Bear is pretty much himself, but since he's rarely on camera, people won't recognize him unless they're die-hard fans.

The only one who can't help but stand out is Tank. His body is just too damn tall and broad to miss, especially with that dark look he's always sporting and the tattoos peeking out from under his shirt. The guy's too intimidating to pull off a disguise, but on the plus side, usually too intimidating to approach, even for fans.

Luckily, our suitcases arrive quickly and a driver is waiting for us with a discreet sign. Bear learned through trial and error that putting "Ballsy Boys" on a sign wasn't the smartest idea in a big city like New York, and neither was using our porn names. We have quite the fan base, both amongst gay men and women, and after two incidents where we were pretty much run over, Bear told us to use fake names for the trip as much as we can. Along with the aforementioned disguises.

Our luggage is quickly loaded into a small shuttle bus,

and we crawl inside and find a spot. I let Campy sit near the window, so he can look out the window on our shuttle from JFK to our midtown hotel.

As soon as we start driving, I check my phone for messages. Nothing. I sigh. Had I really expected anything else?

Brewer gently bumps my shoulder with his own. "Nothing from your man?"

I shake my head. "No. I'm not even sure if he's still my man at this point, to be honest."

Everyone grows quiet, and what should be intimidating, opening up like this, feels safe instead. These are the men who know me better than anyone else. Like brothers, if not for the fact that I've fucked every single one of them, with the exception of Bear.

"Is it the porn thing?" Campy asks, turning away from the stunning view outside toward me.

"No. Surprisingly, that has never been an issue for him. It's the relationship in general thing. He's been hurt in the past, and it's hard for him to commit. Me asking him to join me for this was too much, I guess."

Brewer's hand finds my shoulder, and he squeezes. "Maybe all he needs is time."

"Yeah, maybe." I hear the disbelief in my own voice.

"Don't give up on him," Brewer urges me. "Sometimes people have been told a certain message so many times that they've internalized it to the point where it has become their truth. It takes a repetition of a different message to break through that old conviction. Keep telling him and showing him you love him until he starts believing it."

The advice is so out of character for happy-go-lucky Brewer that I blink a few times. It's spot on, though, because it's exactly what happened with Troy. He's been left so many times that his conviction is I will leave him, too, at some point. I need to keep showing him I won't. No matter how long it takes, I can't give up. He loves me—he just can't admit it yet.

I try to shake off the mood I'm in as we slowly make our way to our hotel, which is smack dab in the middle of Manhattan, a block or two away from Times Square. The actual ceremony tomorrow is at another hotel, but was already sold out when Bear decided all of us would go, so we're staying a few blocks away. Brewer's nose is pretty much plastered to the window as Campy and I try to point out landmarks to him. He's like a kid in a candy store, and his enthusiasm definitely improves my mood.

Check in is smooth, and then Bear tells us we're off till the next morning, when we're expected at breakfast at eight sharp. "And guys, no excessive drinking tonight. It's a work day tomorrow, and I need you looking bright and sharp."

We all nod in agreement, as he told us this beforehand. A trip like this sounds like way more fun than it actually is. As I said before, being a porn star is damn hard work for the most part.

"Who's rooming with who?" Campy asks.

Huh. I never even thought of this. There's six of us and three rooms.

"I'm not rooming with him," Tank and Brewer say almost simultaneously, pointing at each other.

Bear lets out an exasperated sigh. "The two of you need to grow the fuck up. This is getting really old."

"I'll room with Tank," I offer to keep the peace. I don't mind, and honestly, I kinda prefer him over Campy and Brewer. Brewer is a total flirt, and we've fooled around on more than one occasion. Campy and I have done dozens of shoots together, and we're all too familiar with each other.

No matter what the current situation with Troy is, I'm not fucking it up by getting too close with any of the boys. Tank is safe, at least for me.

"I'll take Brewer," Campy quickly says.

That leaves Pixie and Bear, and oh, fuck, I should have realized it would be awkward as fuck for the little imp to room with the boss. Why didn't I offer to room with Bear instead? That would have been fine with me.

Bear shuffles his feet, obviously acutely uncomfortable with the whole situation. No wonder; he just got maneuvered into sharing a room with someone he'd probably rather keep a distance from, considering how he's a new employee and all that.

"I can..." I start, but Pixie quickly cuts me off.

"It's fine. I don't mind."

Okay, then. I don't know how to interpret the blush that's staining his cheeks, but I'm gonna go with major awkward. Bear gives Pixie a look as if the kid has sprouted angel wings all of a sudden, then clears his throat.

"That's settled then. I'll see you all tomorrow at eight."

30

TROY

I glance at the day-old text for the millionth time.

Rebel: I know I freaked you out, and for that I'm sorry. But I'm not sorry that I broke our agreement and developed feelings for you. If you change your mind about New York, the offer stands.

My stomach pitches and rolls every time I read the words. He's sorry he freaked me out? But he's not sorry that he has feelings for me. I don't even know how to process that. What kind of feelings does he have? And surely the offer to try to work things out must have an expiration date. If I blow him off for six months and then try to talk things out, he'll have found someone who's less of a head case than I am.

A knock at my door startles me until I remember that Mason is supposed to be coming over so we can put the finishing touches on our mobile game. I shove my phone roughly into my pocket and open my door.

"Hey, man."

"Hey," Mason responds, stepping into my apartment with just a bit more confidence than the last few times he was over. It might take some time, but eventually, he's going to be comfortable around me. I don't know why that matters to me, but it does. He strikes me as the type of person who hasn't had many friends in life, and I can more than relate with that.

"I'm surprised you didn't go to New York with your man," Mason says as we get settled on my sofa with our laptops and our notes spread out around us.

"Rebel isn't my man," I snap, the words like a sharp knife in the pit of my stomach. "And how did you know about New York?"

A blush creeps up Mason's neck and into his cheeks. "I've been texting with Heart a little bit. He couldn't go to New York, and he was bummed about it."

A smile twists on my lips. As miserable as I feel right now, I'm happy Rebel made the right call introducing him to Heart. Who knows, maybe they'll fall in love and live happily ever after. I don't know why I'm suddenly able to even think those words without rolling my eyes, but there you have it.

"I think I fucked things up with Rebel," I admit.

"What happened?"

"He told me he was stepping back from filming scenes and is only going to do behind the camera work from now on, and I kind of freaked out on him."

"Why?" The confusion on Mason's face almost makes me chuckle.

"Because it felt like some sort of *gesture*, and maybe it

was. I don't know, he says he has *feelings* for me, and I don't even really know what that means." I struggle to explain.

"Hold on, let me see if I'm getting this. You got scared because you thought Rebel was taking the relationship more seriously than you were?"

"Yeah, that's a way easier way to put it."

"You don't have any feelings for him?" Mason asks, cocking his head to one side.

"What does that even mean?" I grumble. "What are these elusive *feelings* everyone keeps referring to?"

"It means you like him for more than just sex; you like just being around him, and you like him as a person. Like, if you have a mental checklist of things you look for in a long term partner, *feelings* usually means the person checks a lot of those boxes. It means you can see a future with them."

Oh.

"Yeah, maybe some of that."

My heart pounds as I think back over the past few months and all of the non-sex time Rebel and I have spent together. If I'm being honest with myself, there are some definite warm fuzzies when I think about the time we've spent watching Netflix, talking on the thirty-hour road trip, the fun we had in Vegas...and then when I think of how I felt seeing him with his family...

"I think I have feelings for him," I admit in a whisper like I'm confessing an illness. "Fuck. What do I do now?"

"Tell him how you feel."

"But I was such a dick. Not just when I freaked out at him, but I've been pushing him away all this time while he's been letting himself fall for me. I don't deserve him, but if I'm going to try to make things right, I can't just call him and tell him I want to be his boyfriend or anything lame like that."

"Go to New York," Mason suggests. "I can find out from Heart where they're staying, and you can go tell him how you feel. Maybe even consider the word *love*?"

My heart jumps into my throat. "We'll see about that last part."

"But you'll go to New York?" Mason asks.

"Yeah, I don't think I have a choice. I need to win Reb— Hendrix back."

Mason whips out his phone and presses a few buttons. "Hey, Heart, I need a favor."

~

AFTER MASON GOT me the information on where the guys are staying in New York and where the awards ceremony is being held, I booked the earliest flight I could get and spent a restless night mentally rehearsing what I could say to Hendrix to make things right between us.

When I get off the plane, my hands are shaking, and I feel like I'm on the verge of a massive panic attack. What do I do if I lay it all out on the line and he tells me he changed his mind? Or what if I misinterpreted everything and Hendrix doesn't want me the way I want him? Propositioning him for sex when he was just a stranger was so much easier than asking him to be my boyfriend now.

I hail a cab and tell him which hotel I need to go to, and then I sit back and try to enjoy the sights of a city I've never been to. But the entire time, all I can do is count down the miles dissolving as I get closer to my man.

The one thing Heart didn't know was the room number, so when I get to the hotel I stop at the front desk.

"Hi, I'm supposed to be meeting my friends, but I forgot to get his room number. Would you happen to know which rooms the Ballsy Boys are staying in?" I ask with a charming smile.

"I'll have to call up and make sure it's okay to tell you. There've been a few *fans* trying to gain access after they heard they were staying here."

I nod in understanding and wait as she calls up to their rooms. I wanted this to be a surprise, but I guess it still will be in a way.

"No one is answering," she says apologetically after a minute or so of trying to call.

"Oh, shit. What time is it?"

I whip out my phone and realize they're probably already at the award ceremony. I take off again, hailing a cab and hoping to hell I'll be able to find Hendrix there.

When I hop out of the cab at the hotel where they're holding the awards thing, I realize I'm going to stick out like a sore thumb as soon as I enter, in my casual clothes, carrying a duffle bag with my stuff in it. But I don't care. All I care about is getting to Hendrix.

Inside isn't exactly what I was expecting, as people mingle while food and drinks are being served. It looks more like a bit of a party than a stuffy awards ceremony like I was imagining. And, it turns out I'm not really underdressed after all, considering some of the stars in attendance are practically naked.

It only takes a second for my gaze to zero in on Hendrix across the large hotel ballroom. I push my way through the crowd, calling half-hearted apologies to those who seem particularly offended. I come to a stop in front of Hendrix, and the moment his ice-blue eyes meet mine, every word I practiced over the last twenty-four hours is blown from my mind, and I stand there gaping at him like a complete moron.

"Troy, what are you doing here?" he asks, his expression seeming to war between worried and happy to see me.

"I needed to talk to you."

"Okay, let's talk," he agrees.

"Could we go somewhere private for a minute?"

Hendrix glances over his shoulder at all his friends, seeming to realize for the first time that all eyes are on us. His hand finds my lower back, and he leads me out of the convention hall, into a quiet hallway.

"Okay, let's talk," Hendrix prompts as soon as we're alone.

I take a deep breath, desperately grappling for my scattered thoughts. I knew exactly what I wanted to say, but now I'm at a loss. "I was a dick," I blurt and Hendrix smiles.

"Go on."

"I've held people at arm's length my whole life, because I was afraid to get hurt. It's worked well for me for the most part. But, you had to go and fuck that all up by making me fall for you. I don't do relationships, but with you, I think...I think I want to try."

"You want to be my boyfriend?" Hendrix asks with a slight teasing lilt in his tone.

"Yeah, I do. I want to be exclusive and committed and all that shit."

"You have such a way with words."

"Hey, you can't make fun of me; I'm your boyfriend," I complain, stepping close to Hendrix and reaching for him. I need to touch him. I need to feel that this is real.

"That's not a rule at all; I can totally make fun of my boyfriend." Hendrix opens his arms and pulls me in, and all I can do is melt against his chest, basking in his heat and distinct scent.

"I lo—" I try to tell him what Mason suggested, but the

word catches in my throat. I don't think I've ever said it out loud. My parents never even told me they loved me that I can remember. "Sorry, that's hard."

"That's okay," Hendrix's hand runs up and down my back soothingly. "We'll get there. And when you're ready to say it, I can tell you that I do, too."

My heart leaps into my throat, and I nod. "Wow, this is getting heavy. I feel like we need a quickie or something to make this easier."

"We're not going to use sex to hide from our feelings now. Don't get me wrong, we'll still have tons of sex, because sex is awesome, but it's okay for things to get heavy. Okay?"

"Okay," I agree before grabbing Hendrix by the back of the neck and pulling him into a deep kiss.

"Sorry to bust up this love fest, but you're going to miss the award announcements," Brewer says from behind Hendrix.

He presses a few more kisses to my lips before releasing me and then twining our fingers together and leading me back into the crowded room.

31

REBEL

He loves me.

Troy loves me.

It's all I can think of when we make our way inside, together, our hands linked. My heart is doing some weird dance inside my chest, like a disco inferno, only better.

He loves me.

He can't say it yet, but the fact that he flew in from LA to tell me he wants to be with me says enough. I mean, that must have cost him a good portion of his savings, and from what I can gather, he didn't have much of a reserve to begin with. It's the best declaration of love I could have ever dreamed of receiving from him.

The words will come, that I am certain of. It'll take time, but one day, he'll have the courage to say them. And when he does, I'll be ready with mine.

We join the other boys, and they all smile at me with happiness, knowing how much it means to me to have Troy with me.

"They're coming up on our category," Bear whispers,

and I focus on what's happening on the small stage they've set up in the front of this huge hotel ballroom.

The yearly Porn Awards are a biggie, even if most categories are more or less exclusively aimed at straight porn. Gay porn is rapidly growing in popularity, as women are discovering it. They tend to find it way more attractive than straight porn. Duh. If I were a straight woman, I'd prefer watching two men to a man and a woman. I mean, tits are really not that interesting if you're not attracted to women.

"To announce the winner in our next category, please welcome Big Boss!"

I smile as I applaud the tall man entering the stage. Big Boss is like the granddaddy of gay porn, one of the first stars in the genre. He's long since retired, enjoying life with his three partners. Yes, you heard me correctly: the man is in an actual foursome. Good for him. I've seen a documentary about him and his men, and I swear, they're all crazy in love with each other.

"I am beyond pleased to announce the winner in the next category: Best Gay Porn Production," Big Boss says in his deep, low voice. "I am truly proud to see this genre develop, and I've thoroughly enjoyed the high-quality productions that have been released this year. We've come a long way since grainy, hand-shot videos in basements, and I couldn't be prouder. The winner of this year's Best Gay Porn Production is…"

I squeeze Troy's hand as Big Boss opens the envelope in his hand and slowly pulls out the card. His face breaks open in a huge smile, and I hold my breath. "Ballsy Boys with *Extortion*! Congratulations!"

We won. Holy mother of all, we won. And not only that, we won with the video I helped produce. Adrenaline floods my veins, and I turn around to kiss Troy with so much force he staggers back before holding on to me. Before I can break off the kiss myself, I'm pulled away from him by Brewer, and we all hug and kiss and let out more than a few undignified whoops.

Bear makes his way to the front, and we all link arms as we watch him accept the award, his face beaming in a way I've never seen before. Then Big Boss steps back, and Bear takes the mic.

"A big thanks to the organizers and members of the Porn Awards for recognizing our hard work to create something beautiful that we're truly proud of. As Big Boss said, we've come a long way in gay porn, and I am grateful that our desire to produce high quality porn has been valued by this organization. I'm exceptionally proud that *Extortion* won, but I would be dishonest if I accepted this award as if it were my accomplishment alone. First and foremost, this story was the creative concept of my assistant creative director, Rebel, who built on my idea and made it ten times better."

Troy sends me a proud look that reaches deep inside me. He's so proud of me, and it makes me feel like I could fly. He sees me, the real me, both Rebel and Hendrix—and he loves me.

"But the video would not have been this good without the terrific acting and hard work of Campy, Heart, and Tank. So, I dedicate this award to my Ballsy Boys."

He holds it up, and we cheer, whistling our approval. When he arrives at our group with the award, another round of hugs and cheers and kisses follows. Hell, even Tank and Brewer hug, before they realize what they are doing and shoot each other a scowling glare to make up for it.

The after-party is exactly what you would expect from an event like this, with male and female strippers holding a lap dance competition, a drag queen fashion show, and a leather and fetish expo in one of the other ballrooms, including all kinds of demonstrations.

"That looks cool," Troy says, and before I realize it, he's dragged me into the expo.

"Excuse me, you *were* joking about that dildo of my cock, right?" I check.

He laughs. "Somehow, I think a dildo will be about the tamest thing we'll find here."

He's right. Seriously, I'm a fucking porn star, but some of what they show here has me paling and my stomach rolling uncomfortably.

"What the hell is that?" Troy whispers, pointing toward a big contraption that looks like a torture device, with big leather straps and spikes everywhere.

Before I can say anything, the salesman has spotted me, and his eyes light up in recognition. Oh, fuck.

"Rebel!" he says excitedly and hurries over to shake my hand. "I'm so happy to meet you in person! I'm your biggest fan!"

"It's nice to meet you, too" —I squint to read his nametag— "Donald."

"Can I interest you in a demonstration of one of our products? I've got great cock rings and spreaders as well as brand new ball gags, the best on the market. And of course, we have a wide range of leather products for your pleasure, ranging from whips and floggers to all kinds of restraints."

Troy is fighting hard to suppress his laughter, and I can feel his body shake with the effort. He knows how I feel about shit like this. I mean, to each his own, but this kind of stuff is a big no for me. I like my sex in all positions, and I don't mind a little rough, but other than that, I'm as vanilla as it gets.

"I'm not really an adventurous type, sexually speaking." I try to discourage Donald politely, but he won't budge.

"Psh, nonsense. A hot gay porn star like you, of course, you like a little kink."

Troy gives him a manly slap on the back. "You're absolutely right, Donald. Rebel should live a little, experiment, right?"

Donald nods enthusiastically and starts a lengthy discourse on whatever the fuck he's trying to sell me. Troy turns away from us, and I know he's laughing his ass off, the fucker. I will so get him for this.

"You know what," I say sweetly, "I'll take a ball gag and a pair of handcuffs, please."

"Excellent!" Donald beams and quickly grabs them for me. "Promise me to give us a shout out in a video if you like them!"

Troy turns to face me, looking distinctly less amused now.

"I will after I've tested them thoroughly."

Troy narrows his eyes. "You wouldn't dare," he hisses.

I waggle my eyebrows. "Keep provoking me and you'll find out."

We walk around the rest of the expo, but Troy is a lot less cocksure, and I can't suppress a grin. For all his bravura, he's as much averse to that kinky shit as I am. Still, watching all the sexual toys has me hard as a rock, and as soon as we've reached the end of the expo, I drag Troy into a more or less empty hallway.

"What—"

My mouth is on his before he can even utter another word, and within seconds, I have him moaning into my mouth and thrusting against me. I back him against the wall and dig in deep, pressing myself against him everywhere. The bag drops out of my hand onto the floor.

"Mmm," I groan, dragging my mouth finally away from his. "I missed you. I missed this."

His eyes find mine, quick breaths coming past his swollen lips. "Me too," he says, and I know that's as good as another declaration of love.

"Wanna head back to my hotel? If we go now, we can get a quickie in before Tank shows up."

He nods immediately. Hand in hand, we walk back to the lobby. In one of the ballrooms, we pass Tank, and I tap him on the shoulder.

"Please give us at least an hour?" I ask, and I'm rewarded with one of his rare smiles as he nods. "Thank you. Here, you can use this on Brewer the next time he pisses you off."

He looks in the plastic bag and laughs even harder. He's truly a beautiful man when he smiles like this, and I quickly kiss his cheek. "Thanks, Tank."

Tank gives us a couple of hours before coming into the room, and by that time, we're both sated, already dozing in each other's arms. Best day of my life.

He loves me.
Troy loves me.

32

TROY

I tense when I wake up with a body plastered to mine. It's a habit that's going to be difficult to break. But I'll have to get used to sharing a bed because I'm pretty sure that's what boyfriends do. *Boyfriend.* I still can't believe I'm someone's boyfriend, and he's mine. Not just *someone*, a sexy, smart, amazing man like Hendrix.

I roll over and find him looking at me through sleepy, half-lidded eyes. A smile tips the corner of Hendrix's lips, and my heart skips a few beats. I reach up and run the tips of my fingers along his lips and across his jaw.

"Did you sleep okay?" he asks.

"I would've slept better if Tank didn't snore so loud."

"I heard that," Tank gripes from the adjacent bed. "You're lucky I even agreed to let you stay in our room."

"He's grumpy when he first wakes up," I whisper to Hendrix, and we both laugh.

"He's always grumpy. You should see him after he films a scene, you'd think fucking that hard would mellow him out, but it doesn't seem to help."

"I can still hear you," Tank grumbles again, and Hendrix and I laugh like teenage girls at a sleepover.

By the time we get ourselves together, I can hear my stomach starting to growl, but there's one thing that was weighing on my mind last night as I was falling asleep that I need to get an answer to.

"You want to go check out that continental breakfast before we have to catch our flight in a few hours?"

Hendrix and I had an argument before bed when he insisted on covering the cost of switching my flight, so I could fly back with them. He said I'll have to get used to him sharing his money with me if we're a couple. *Fat chance*. I guess that's an argument for another day.

"In a minute, I have to ask you something first."

"Yeah, what's up?"

"Why did you want to quit filming scenes? Was it just because you thought you would have to in order for us to get serious?"

"In a way it was because of you, but not because I thought you'd give me an ultimatum or anything."

"Why then?"

"Because I didn't want to do it anymore when I had someone like you to come home to. Plus, it's not like I was going to do it forever. I'd already reduced the number of scenes and was doing more of the creative work; I can see a future behind the camera. This is what I want, and falling for you gave me a little push to finally go after it."

I let out a breath I didn't realize I'd been holding, and then I press my lips against Hendrix's stubbly chin. "That's all I needed to know. I would never make you choose. I want you to do what makes you happy, always."

"And that's why I chose you."

His words send a shiver down my spine. I don't understand how he can feel this way about me, but I'm going to do my damndest to earn it.

"Breakfast?"

Hendrix nods and stretches, yawning loudly.

I get out of bed wearing the boxers I went to sleep in, and Hendrix gives my ass a hard smack.

"Can the two of you either stop flirting or at least start fucking so I have something interesting to watch?" Tank complains.

"I've never fucked with an audience, could be fun," I tease Hendrix.

"Sorry, babe, I'm retired. I'll only be fucking behind closed doors from now on...although I'll still make exceptions for swimming pools in Vegas and glory holes." Hendrix winks, and my belly quivers. This is love, right? It sure as hell feels like love.

∼

"Do you want the window seat or do you prefer aisle?" Hendrix asks as he takes my bag from me and puts it into the overhead compartment.

"Aisle please. I never got over that damn *Twilight Zone* episode with the creature on the wing of the plane."

"Oh yeah, that was a freaky one. Thanks for the reminder, now I'm going to have to avoid looking out the window, too."

We settle into our seats and all the other Ballsy Boys claim their seats around us as well. Brewer and Tank end up in an argument over an armrest that I swear nearly comes to blows before Bear breaks them up and sits between them.

"You ever think those two should just fuck out whatever

their issue is with each other?" I whisper to Hendrix, and he snorts a laugh.

The flight is uneventful and when we land and start to deplane, I find myself reaching to twine my fingers with Hendrix's. Maybe holding hands isn't as pointless as I always thought. It is nice to have a small physical connection for no reason other than the pleasure of contact.

"Do you have anything you need to do tonight, or can I take you on a proper date now that you're my boyfriend?" Hendrix asks as he pulls me close and nibbles along a pulse point, causing heat to flare in the pit of my stomach and a pleasant warmth to settle in my chest.

"A date sounds nice." My voice comes out a little shaky, and I'm sure Hendrix can hear it, but he doesn't call me out on it.

"Great. I'll drop you at home to get showered, changed, whatever. Then I'll pick you up in a few hours, because baby I'm going to wine and dine you."

"Then sixty-nine me?"

"We'll see how the night goes," he winks and presses a kiss to my lips. "I wouldn't want you to think I'm easy, putting out on a first date and all."

"Don't you dare tease. Before yesterday evening, I've had nothing but my hand for *days*," I complain.

"Poor thing," Hendrix teases.

It takes about forty minutes to get to my place from the airport, which isn't bad considering LA traffic. I lean over the center console to give Hendrix one last parting kiss, my pulse spiking with each small contact. I hope love isn't always this gross. I'm smiling way too much for my own taste...but maybe I don't hate it so much.

~

I'm embarrassed by how much time it took me to settle on what to wear on our date tonight. To be fair, this *is* my first date, and I didn't want to be a dweeb who overdresses, but I also didn't want to be a dick who underdresses either. I ended up settling on an emerald green polo and a nice pair of jeans that hug my ass just right. And I spent a little extra time styling my hair.

When Hendrix buzzes my apartment, my stomach flutters with nervous excitement. With a deep breath, I pull open the door and try not to jump all over my *boyfriend* standing in the doorway looking all sexy in a tight red t-shirt that clings to his muscles in all the right ways, and a pair of worn jeans that I swear I can see the bulge of his dick through if I catch it at just the right angle. And then there's the way he's smiling at me... It's a little too much and exactly the way I always hoped someone would look at me.

"Ready to go?" Hendrix asks as he looks me up and down and then licks his lips.

"Keep looking at me like that, and we won't be going anywhere except my bed."

"Can't have that." Hendrix grabs my arm and yanks me out of my apartment, pulling the door closed behind me. "There, now we're safe from sex interrupting our first date."

"Spoilsport," I complain.

Hendrix takes me to a seafood restaurant downtown that I've never been to, due to it being massively out of my price range. But he waves me off when I comment about this place being way too expensive.

"Let me do something nice; I have enough money. You can treat next time and take me anywhere you want."

"Hello and welcome," a cute little twink host greets us when we enter. His eyes fall to our joined hands, and he smiles at both of us, not bothering to hide the serious *I'd love to be the meat in your masc sandwich* vibe.

And, like with the dancer in Vegas, an odd, hot jealousy snakes through my veins. My grip on Hendrix's hand tightens. We're lead to our table, and before he leaves, twink cutie fixes Hendrix with a sultry look.

"Please, let me know if you need *anything*."

"Thank you, we will," Hendrix replies politely while I bite back a growl.

"What was that guy's problem? It's obvious we're together," I grumble as soon as he's gone.

"Huh?" Hendrix cocks his head in confusion, and then understanding dawns in his eyes. "Were you jealous he was flirting?"

"Psh, no," I scoff, reaching for the menu to hide my face before it can give me away.

"You totally are. That's so cute; I love it."

"It's not cute," I argue. "And, it doesn't even make sense. Why am I jealous of strippers and hosts, but I can jerk off to videos of you fucking and getting fucked?"

"You were jealous when I got that lap dance in Vegas?"

"That's not the point."

"You're right. I'm sorry, but I like hearing that you're a little jealous. I like that you didn't mind me doing porn, but I think part of me needed to hear that you wouldn't be cool with me messing around with whoever."

Just the thought of Hendrix with some random dude at a club, in his apartment, anywhere other than in the studio has my blood boiling. "Yeah, really not cool with that at all. But, I still don't understand why the porn doesn't bother me. The porn is still fucking hot."

"Because porn isn't the same thing as sex I'm choosing to have. Don't get me wrong, I enjoyed doing porn, but there was no emotion or anything there. Does that make sense?"

"It does. Just to be clear, being boyfriends means we're exclusive now, right?" I check, keeping my tone carefully regulated so I don't sound too needy.

"It better, because I'm pretty sure I'll break the fingers of any guy I catch touching you. Don't get me wrong, if you ever wanted to pick up a third for a night or something, I'd be up for discussing that, but I definitely don't want either of us with anyone else."

"Good," I breathe a sigh of relief.

Our waiter appears, and we both order and then fall into comfortable conversation while we wait.

"Can I ask you something I've been wondering about?" Hendrix asks, looking slightly nervous.

"Sure."

"Have you ever thought about looking for your parents?"

I freeze with my glass of water halfway to my lips.

"Why would I do that?"

"To get some answers and maybe some closure?"

My hand shakes a bit as I set my glass back down.

"I don't know if that's a good idea."

"Why not?" Hendrix presses.

"Because I don't want to," I snap.

"That's not a reason."

"I can't believe we're having this conversation." I shake my head and move my silverware around fruitlessly. "I don't see what looking for them would accomplish. I'm supposed to take time out of my full life to look for people who probably have a bunch of new kids they never wanted to give up?"

Hendrix's expression softens, and he immediately gets up to come around to my side of the table. He sits beside me and puts an arm around me. I didn't realize I was trembling until he starts to soothe me with his touch.

"Listen to me, *nothing* you did caused them to give you up. Even if they did have kids after you that they decided to keep, that is not a reflection on you. Do you understand?"

I nod. "I'm afraid."

"I know. I won't push you to do anything you don't want to do. But if you do want to find them to try to get some closure, I'd be happy to help you, and I'll be with you the entire way. It's your call. Okay?"

"'Kay. Thank you." I kiss his shoulder, and then he gets up to go back around to his side of the table. "I'm not a date expert or anything, but are we doing this wrong? I doubt discussions about insecurities and arguments about emotional demons are normal first date fare."

"You're right. Let's back it up a bit," Hendrix agrees. "So, tell me Tony, what do you do for a living?"

"Are you pretending like you're a date who forgot my name? Because that's worse than the other stuff," I laugh.

"You're right; this is a failure of a first date. The company is good though." Hendrix bumps his knee against mine under the table and I smile.

"Yeah, the company is good," I agree.

33

TROY

"I have to get going; I'm supposed to meet Mason this morning, and I'm already late," I insist as Hendrix tries to pull me back into bed for the second time. The first time I didn't bother to resist since I was just as interested in a little bit of morning fun as he was. But now that we've both come and I've had a few hits of weed, I'm seriously behind schedule.

"Just one more blowjob," Hendrix tries to tempt me, trailing his hot lips over the back of my neck as I sit up and swing my feet onto the cool floor.

I stand and grab a pair of jeans off the floor. And when I bend over to pull them on, I feel a quick slap against my left ass cheek.

"Hey!" I protest, standing up quickly and whirling to face Hendrix with only one pant leg on.

My man smirks at me with a playful glint in his eyes, and my stomach somersaults, and my heart trips. *I love you.* The words are on the tip of my tongue, but they can't make it past my lips.

Everyone leaves, one way or another, everyone leaves, the malicious voice in the back of my mind whispers.

"Come back to bed," Hendrix says in a husky, sleep rough voice.

A shiver runs down my spine, and I'm sorely tempted to drop the damn pants and crawl back between the sheets with him. My phone vibrates on the dresser, reminding me that Mason is waiting for me.

"Babe, I'm unbelievably late."

I resume getting dressed so I can get out the door, and a slow smile creeps over his lips.

"You called me *babe*."

"Oh, sorry, is that weird?" I ask, pausing my effort to pull my pants on to examine his expression more closely. "I've never used a pet name, did that not work?"

"No, I liked it."

I reach for the closest shirt, and it's not until I'm pulling it on that I realize it's Hendrix's shirt, not mine.

"Oh, sorry." I start to remove it, but Hendrix calls out to stop me.

"Wear it."

I swallow around a lump in my throat and nod. I lean over the bed and press my lips quickly to Hendrix's and pull back before he can grab me and convince me to stay home.

"Lock up when you leave and text me later," I call over my shoulder as I jog out the door.

I run the mile across campus to the student union.

"Sorry I'm late," I apologize to Mason when I skid to a stop in front of him.

Mason looks up from his laptop looking mildly annoyed and slightly amused as he takes in my disheveled appearance. "I take it things went well with Rebel?"

I slide into the chair across from Mason and pull out my laptop, not bothering to hide my smile.

"We're dating, I guess?" I roll the word *boyfriend* around on my tongue, but it feels weird to say to someone other than Hendrix.

"Nice." Mason nods. "So, our game is finished; are you ready to talk marketing?"

I smile at Mason's awkward non-sequitur and quickly switch my mental settings from gossip to work.

It turns out Mason has done his research. He emails me a bulleted list with several articles attached that explain why the plan he's outlined is likely to be successful if properly executed.

"When did you have time to find all this?"

Mason shrugs and pushes his glasses up his nose. "I like to research stuff."

His tone is apologetic, like he expects I'm going to tease him. The ex of his must've really done a number on his self-esteem.

"That's really cool and extremely helpful. Thank you."

After a few hours, Mason and I have a solid plan in place to get ready for the launch of our game.

"I can't believe how well this is coming together." I shake my head and smile. There's a weightlessness in my chest. This might really work out.

"I don't want to count any chickens, but I have a good feeling about this."

"What do you say we have the guys meet us for lunch to celebrate?" I suggest.

Mason blushes and chews on his thumbnail. "Um...yeah, sure."

I pull out my phone and dial Hendrix.

"Hey, sexy," he answers. I can hear the sound of moans

in the background, and I smile. I don't know if I'll ever get over how cool it is that Hendrix is in the porn business.

"Hey, I don't know what your day looks like, but Mason and I were thinking it'd be cool to meet you and Heart for lunch."

"Oh, shoot, lunch won't work, but why don't you and Mason swing by my place this evening? I was going to have all the guys over and order pizza."

"Cool, see you then."

∽

MASON and I show up at Hendrix's place around seven. Mason looks like a nervous cat looking for somewhere to hide when we step into the living room filled with half a dozen gorgeous men.

"Hey, baby," Hendrix presses a quick kiss to my lips, and I can feel every set of eyes in the room on us.

"So, boyfriends finally, huh?" Pixie asks with a smile, his eyes flicking between the two of us.

"Uh...um...ah," I stammer.

Hendrix and I talked about it and agreed we *are* exclusive, and we *are* serious. That equals boyfriends, I get that. So why is it so damn awkward to say that out loud?

"What Troy is trying to say is 'why yes, we are dating exclusively, which many would call boyfriends. I am uncomfortable with the term myself, but am so lucky I have a sexy man like Rebel to call my own'," he supplies, putting his arm around my shoulders.

"Yeah, what he said," I mumble, hoping I don't look as stupid as I feel right now.

"Come help me grab drinks for everybody?"

I follow Hendrix to his kitchen where he pushes me up

against a counter and kisses me hard and dirty. My fingers curl into his hair, plastering him against me.

"I'm sorry if Pixie made you uncomfortable, or if I was off base with my response," he says when we come up for air.

"It's fine. I'm just getting used to the whole thing."

"Take all the time you need to adjust, just don't push me away," Hendrix tells me sternly, and I nod in agreement.

With one more quick kiss, he steps back and turns to the fridge to start handing me a few beers to take out to the living room.

Back with the group, Mason has made himself comfortable on the couch between Heart and Pixie, playing a videogame. Brewer and Campy are deep in a conversation about disease processes, of all things, and Bear is off to the side, stealing glances at Pixie that I'm sure he hopes no one notices.

"No Tank tonight?" I ask as I pass out the drinks I brought in.

"That antisocial asshole thinks he's too good to hang out with us," Brewer tells me. "Or I guess I should say, he thinks he's too good to hang out with me, because if I wasn't here, I guarantee he would be," Brewer explains with an edge to his tone.

"What's his issue with you?"

"He's a dickhead?" Brewer guesses. "I don't fucking know. He took one look at me and hated me on sight. Fuck him, I don't care."

Something about the way Brewer says it makes me think he does care, at least a little. But I'm not going to get in the middle of something I don't know anything about.

After the pizza arrives, we end up eating over a game of Cards Against Humanity and laughing until Pixie almost chokes on a bite of crust. Bear rubs and pats Pixie's back protectively afterward in a way that makes me wonder if something is going on there. Who knew hanging out with porn stars would be like a soap opera?

It isn't until midnight that everyone starts to leave, and I help Hendrix clean up.

"You'll stay the night, right?"

I hesitate for a second, out of habit more than anything, before I agree. And then we both strip down and fall into bed together in a tangle of limbs and a chorus of whimpers and moans.

∼

I STARTLE AWAKE with the feeling of a body lying half on top of me, and I scramble out from under it with my heart pounding against my ribcage.

"Don't go," Hendrix complains in a sleepy slur.

Some of my tension eases at the sound of his voice, but my pulse is still hammering, making it impossible for me to just lay back down. I ease out of bed and head toward the kitchen for a drink of water. Glass in hand, I walk over to the kitchen window and gaze out into the dark night, sipping my water and counting my heartbeats so I have something to focus on. I wish I was home so I could just pack a bowl to get back to sleep.

"Something wrong?"

Hendrix's voice startles me. "No, I always lurk naked in the dark kitchen in the middle of the night."

"Uh-huh," Hendrix says with a cocked eyebrow. His hair is pulled up in a messy bun, and he's got sleep lines on his left cheek.

I turn back to the window and sip my water. Hendrix's

strong arms wrap around me from behind, and his lips find my shoulder and then the side of my neck.

"Talk to me, baby," he asks, nuzzling his nose against the back of my neck.

I take a deep breath, steeling my nerves to admit something to Hendrix that I never thought I'd talk about with anyone. I didn't think I'd ever *need* to explain it to anyone, because I didn't anticipate ever having a man in my life I would choose to share a bed with on a regular basis. But I *want* to share a bed with Hendrix, which means he needs to understand why it's a struggle for me.

"I'm not good at sharing a bed, because growing up in the system, bouncing around to different houses with kids and foster parents I didn't know, my biggest fear was that I'd wake up with someone else in my bed, if you catch my drift."

Hendrix's arms tense around me, and his breath puffs between my shoulder blades, his forehead against the back of my neck. "Did anyone...?" he asks after a few seconds.

"No. There was one guy who was a little handsy but nothing more serious than some unwanted hugs or tickling. I heard stories, though, from other kids, and it's one of those unspoken things everyone knows you're supposed to look out for. So, when I wake up and I'm not alone in bed, sometimes I forget that I'm not a helpless thirteen-year-old in a foster home."

"I'm so sorry. I know I'm a pretty clingy sleeper; do you want me to try to give you more space? I could buy a bigger bed. I'll do anything to make sure I don't scare you when you're sleeping."

My throat tightens at the naked vulnerability in Hendrix's tone. I know he'll truly do anything to make sure I'm happy and comfortable.

"I fucking love you," I blurt, and as soon as the words are out, a relieved laugh follows them. *That wasn't so hard.*

Hendrix stills against me and is silent long enough I start to get nervous. But then his strong hands are on my hips, spinning me to face him. He takes the water from my hand, sets it on the counter, and then he grabs my face.

"I fucking love you back, banana boy."

Our mouths clash in a flurry of lips and tongues.

"Let's go back to bed," I suggest when Hendrix's hard cock presses against mine.

"Okay, but I have to warn you, I'm not going to fuck you; I'm going to make sweet love to you."

"Gross," I laugh and shove Hendrix's shoulder. "Race you," I suggest and then bolt toward the bedroom before he can respond.

Hendrix tackles me onto the bed, and we fall in a laughing, groping heap.

"Thank you for taking a chance on me," Hendrix whispers against my lips as our laughter fades.

"Thank you for giving me time to come around to the idea of someone being a stable presence in my life."

"I'll always give you anything you need as long as you don't run away."

"I'm not going anywhere, I promise."

Hendrix's arms tighten around me, and he pulls me against his chest. I take a deep breath, pulling his essence into my lungs and holding it there as long as I can. Hendrix won't leave me. Deep in my gut, I know he's here to stay.

And with that comforting thought, I drift back to sleep.

The next time I wake up, the sun is shining through the crack between the curtains, and Hendrix is once again draped half over me. I don't panic this time, but I'm sure there will be plenty more panicky nights before I get past this for good, eventually.

I run my fingers through Hendrix's hair, giving his scalp a little massage. The thought of him leaving me like everyone else has is like a punch in the gut. It's scary as hell to let someone have this much power over me. If he wants to, Hendrix could utterly destroy me. And even knowing he won't, it's still terrifying.

Maybe Hendrix was right. Maybe I need some closure.

"Morning, gorgeous," Hendrix mumbles, blinking awake with a smile.

"I think I need to find my parents."

Hendrix draws back, his eyebrows scrunched in confusion.

"Can we have coffee first?"

"Of course, doofus, I didn't mean today. I just meant that I think you're right; I need closure. Will you help me find them?"

"Anything for you. That's what you do when you love someone."

My stomach somersaults at his words. Last night wasn't a dream, I really told Hendrix I love him. And it felt so damn good.

"I love you." I test the words in the cold light of day, and Hendrix looks like sunshine is beaming from his very soul.

"*Gross,*" he mocks me before rolling on top of me and kissing me breathless.

34

REBEL

It takes the private detective I hired less than a day to find Troy's mother. All he needed was his mom's first and last name and date of birth, plus Troy's own date of birth. Jackie Butler lives only a hundred miles away from Troy, just northeast of San Diego. I don't know how Troy will take this news. What's worse is that she is indeed remarried and has new kids. Other kids, whatever the politically correct term is.

I'm happy that the PI actually calls me at work, so I have a little time to consider how I want to bring this up to Troy. There's no way I'm doing this over the phone. This is something he has to hear in person.

We agree to meet over Chinese takeout at my place, and when he rings the bell, I drag him inside for a thorough kiss. He barely manages to put down the food he picked up before my mouth is on his, and we spent a few minutes enjoying each other's taste, right there in the hallway.

"Hi," I say somewhat stupidly when I've finally had my fill.

"Hi," he says and sends me a goofy smile. I guess our

new relationship status takes some getting used to for both of us.

He puts the food on the table while I grab plates, silverware, and sodas. There's an easy familiarity in this process that makes me feel warm inside. I can see us doing things like this together for...for a long while. Maybe forever?

I smile. I'd better not tell Troy that. Might just give him a heart attack. He's come far, my banana boy, but words like forever are bound to send him into a hissy fit.

"How was work?" he asks after we're seated at the table, enjoying the delicious orange chicken.

"Good. We had interviews with five guys for possible new hires. Three were good fits, and I think they'll be great additions."

Troy grins. "You need three guys to replace you?"

"Dude, you know it," I laugh. Then my face gets serious. "Babe, the PI called."

Troy's hand stops halfway to his mouth, and he's frozen for a second or two, before putting his hand down. His eyes meet mine, and I know he doesn't have words. "He found your mom. She's alive and doing well, he says. She works as a full-time waitress at a diner."

He swallows. "Is she...healthy? I don't remember much of my parents, but I think they were drug addicts. I remember needles, somehow."

That little sliver of information makes me want to hug him and never let go. "Yeah, she is, as far as he could tell. She has a steady job, and..." I hesitate. How do I put this? I don't want him to get hurt. "She has a family, babe. A new husband and two girls, eight and six years old. She's doing well, it seems."

"He saw her?" Troy asks, speaking slowly.

"Yeah. She's close to San Diego."

"I have sisters?"

I nod. "Yeah. two. Half-sisters, though. She remarried."

"Did she divorce my father?"

And now comes the truly heartbreaking part. "No, babe. Your father passed away, years ago."

He swallows again, and his hands clench into fists. "Does he know the cause of death?"

"Drug overdose. He was found dead in a known drug house, according to the PI. No one claimed the body, so he was cremated by the city."

"Oh."

I wait for him to say more, but his eyes glaze over. I don't know if he's thinking and needs time or if he's unable to process. I wish I knew what to do. I want to make him feel better, somehow, but I have no idea how.

"Did I ever tell you about Elise?" Troy says suddenly.

I'm pretty sure it's a rhetorical question since we both know he's told me shit, but I answer him anyway. "No. Who was she?"

I have no idea what he's gonna say, but when he speaks, it's not the answer I was expecting. "She was the only mother I ever had."

This time, I know I'm not supposed to say anything, so I listen as he shares a heartbreaking tale of finding parental love, only to lose it just as quickly.

"After she died, I had two more foster families, and after that, it was group homes all the way till I aged out of the system. Nobody wanted me anymore. I was too old and had too much of a reputation for being difficult. Elise, she was the only one who ever loved me unconditionally."

I wipe away the tears on my cheeks, not embarrassed in the least that he sees how much his pain affects me. "And me," I add softly.

"And you," he repeats. He breathes in deeply, then exhales slowly. "Do you think she'd want to see me, my birth mother?"

"The question is do you want to see her. Do you want to hear from her what happened, why she gave you up?"

"What if she rejects me all over again?"

I want to reassure him that that's not gonna happen, but I can't. There are some seriously fucked up people in this world, and I have no idea if his mother is one of them. She already abandoned her son once. Who the fuck knows if she'll do it again?

"If she does, then at least you'll know. You'll never have to wonder 'what if' again. And no matter what happens, I'll be here."

He lifts those stunning golden eyes up to meet mine. "I know. I know you'll be there. It's scary as fuck, all of this, but let's do this. I wanna meet my mother."

∽

THE PI GAVE me a phone number, but Troy and I decide not to call her. He wants to just drive down and sort of confront her, and I'm on board with that. We have her home address and the diner where she works, and so a few days later, on a bright and sunny Saturday, we make the trip south.

Troy doesn't say much while I drive, but he does reach out every now and then to put his hand on my leg, so I know he's just trying to process it all. I get it. It's not every day you get to meet the woman who left you at a police station when you were six years old.

I've honestly tried to imagine myself in his shoes, but I can't. I can't even fathom my parents doing anything like that. God, they're crazy at times, but they love me with all they have—Marley, too. Until I met Troy, I never fully appreciated that, I think.

"Wanna try the diner first?" I ask Troy when we get close.

He nods. "Yeah. Seems safer than showing up at her house unannounced, especially with my...my sisters. They're young, and I don't want them to have to witness it if it goes badly."

He's such a softie underneath that cool, prickly exterior. "Okay, babe."

Ten minutes later, we pull up in the parking lot of an old-fashioned diner. It's just after two, so we've missed the lunch rush, and it looks like it's relatively quiet. We don't even know if she's working, but there's only one way to find out.

"You ready?" I ask.

"God, no, but let's go," Troy says, his face pale.

I wanna grab his hand as we walk to the entrance, but I hold back. He's always been reluctant with PDAs, and maybe he doesn't want the first thing his mother sees is that he's gay. For all we know, she could be a homophobic bitch. But right before I open the door, he reaches for my hand and laces his fingers through mine. I press a quick kiss to his cheek. "I'm here, no matter what."

"I know," he says, and his eyes show me that he means it. It fills me with joy that he's starting to believe I mean it when I say I love him.

Hand in hand, we walk inside where a young blonde approaches us right away. "Hi," she says with a friendly smile. "For two?"

I look at Troy, but his eyes are darting through the diner.

"We were wondering if Jackie is working?" I ask.

Blondie looks at us quizzically for a second but then nods. "Yeah. Hold on a sec, and I'll get her for you."

Troy's grip on my hand becomes rather painful, but I don't say a word. A few bruises seem like a small price to pay for being there for him.

Half a minute later, a forty-something woman walks toward us. Her face is friendly and open, but with deep and tired lines that show a hard life. She has dark blonde hair, tied back into a neat ponytail, and her pale blue uniform hangs loose around her slender frame. As soon as I see her eyes, I know who she is, because it's like looking at Troy's.

"Hi," she says with a friendly smile, looking at me first. "Dani said you were looking for me?"

Her eyes travel to Troy, and she freezes. She's maybe twenty feet away from us still, but she halts on the spot.

"Oh my god," she whispers.

It takes a her a few seconds to take three faltering steps in our direction, and all that time, Troy doesn't say a word. He merely stares at her, the same way she's staring at him.

Tears fill her eyes, those same golden eyes I love so much. Her voice breaks when she speaks.

"Troy?"

35

TROY

My mouth goes dry, and the only response I can offer is a slow nod.

Jackie's hand flies up to cover her mouth, and her shoulders start to shake, tears streaming down her face. I squeeze Hendrix's hand even tighter, and I catch him flinching out of the corner of my eye. I force myself to loosen my grip a fraction.

"Jackie, we were hoping you'd have a few minutes to talk? Or, if not now, maybe after your shift ends?" Hendrix asks in an even voice, and I swear I could kiss him.

"I can take a break," she manages to say once she gets herself under control. "Have a seat at that booth, and I'll bring us some coffee."

When she steps away, I release a breath I hadn't realized I was holding.

"How are you doing?" Hendrix asks, rubbing soothing circles on my back.

"Okay so far."

He steers me over to the table Jackie pointed us toward, and we sit down. She returns a few minutes later with a carafe of coffee, and it looks like she's gotten herself together a little better and dried her eyes.

"I can't believe you're here," she says.

"That makes two of us," I finally manage to croak out words. "I need to know why."

Jackie nods with a resigned expression. "I was a shitty mom, kid, no two ways about it. Frank knocked me up when we were only seventeen, not even out of high school. My parents flipped out, told me I had to get an abortion. When I refused, they kicked me out. I regret a lot of things in my life, but I don't regret that choice."

I swallow around a lump in my throat and nod. My leg bounces under the table, and Hendrix reaches under to put a hand on my knee.

"Why not just give me up right away, then? Why keep me until I was six and then dump me?" *Was I bad? Unlovable? Disposable?*

"I wanted to do right by you. And at first, everything seemed like it might be okay. We weren't going to be living the high life or anything, but Frank got a decent job, and we were a family. We used to take you on fun little outings every Sunday. We'd go to the zoo, the park, the arcade. Your little eyes just lit up when you saw all the colors and lights of all those games at the arcade."

"I don't remember any of that," I admit.

"No, I suppose you wouldn't. Well, in any event, things didn't stay like that forever, as I'm sure you well know. I didn't see the signs at first, but when we started coming up short for rent and groceries every month, I put the pieces together. I was so angry with Frank for getting mixed up in drugs, but when I confronted him, he made it sound kind of fun, like a nice little escape. I was a nineteen-year-old mother with no friends, a backbreaking job, and a husband who was rumored to be sleeping with half the girls on the block. A little reprieve sounded so nice."

"Meanwhile, your kid sat alone in his bedroom wondering if his parents were coming home, and if they did, what state they'd be in. I never knew if you'd remember to feed me or leave me sitting in my own piss for a day and a half."

Hendrix sucks in a surprised breath beside me, but Jackie doesn't look surprised by my outburst.

"That's why I had to do what I did. I was in too deep at that point. I kept telling myself I was going to get clean and do right by you, but every day that went by, I felt like more of a failure to you. I didn't plan it ahead of time. I woke up that morning particularly lucid and sick to my stomach when I walked into your bedroom and noticed how skinny and dirty I'd let you become. I decided I was going to take you to the grocery store and get whatever you wanted and that I would turn things around. I knew you needed better than what I was giving you.

"We were sitting at a stoplight when I noticed the police station up ahead. And suddenly, I knew it was the only right thing I could do. I knew there had to be a better family out there for you, someone who could do right by you."

I clear my throat and nod again. I try to surreptitiously wipe the moisture from the corner of my eyes, and if Hendrix and Jackie notice, they're polite enough not to say.

"When did you get clean?" I ask.

"I went into rehab that same week, but I relapsed a few times over the next eight years. When Frank died, that was just the wake-up call I needed. I'll be eleven years sober next month."

"That's a long time," I mumble, my leg starting to

bounce again under the table. "You know I never was adopted? I had some foster families and then lived in a group home until I aged out of the system."

"I didn't know." Jackie bows her head, and I hear her sniffle. "I'm so sorry. I wanted to look for you, but I was so sure you'd have been adopted by a wonderful family. And I was afraid you'd hate me. If I'm being honest, it was more the latter. I was selfish. I couldn't stand the thought of looking into your eyes and seeing nothing but hatred."

"I stopped hating you a long time ago," I admit. "Elise told me this Buddhist saying that holding on to anger is like drinking poison and expecting someone else to die."

Jackie doesn't ask who Elise was, and I don't bother to enlighten her.

"I know I don't deserve a second chance to be in your life, but I'd love the chance to get to know you."

I chew the inside of my cheek and jerk my head noncommittally.

Hendrix's breath tickles my cheek as he leans in. "If you need time to process, that's okay. We can leave and make plans to talk to her again in the future," he whispers in suggestion.

I glance over at Jackie to see her reaction to Hendrix's overt display. She doesn't seem fazed by it, so at least that's one point in her favor.

"You have a new husband and daughters now. I don't want to intrude."

"You wouldn't be. They know about you. I have your baby picture on my mantle, right next to my girls."

Those words break the dam, and the tears have no choice but to flow freely down my cheeks. I turn and bury my face in Hendrix's shoulder, allowing silent sobs to wrack my body. They both sit quietly until I pull myself back together.

"I'd like to exchange numbers and meet again," I manage to say after a few minutes.

Jackie pulls a pen out of her apron and writes her number on a napkin, then slides it across the table to me. "Can you just tell me, do you have a good life?"

I glance at Hendrix, and my heart swells to nearly bursting. I think of my new friends and my degree I'll soon be finished with. "Yeah, it's really good."

Jackie smiles and wipes her eyes. "Good, good. Now, I'd better get back to work. Call me any time. I can't wait for you to meet my girls."

"I'd like that," I agree before giving her a brief hug.

"What do you say to a hotel room for the night? I think a hot bath and a handjob are in order," Hendrix whispers as we head out of the diner toward his car.

"That sounds perfect, baby. Absolutely perfect."

36

REBEL

Six Months Later

I WAKE up with Troy in my arms, draped half over me, and I smile. He's come so far, my banana boy. He still panics every now and then when he wakes up in the middle of the night and feels me close to him, but it's becoming less and less frequent. Recently, he's started to seek my body when he's asleep. It used to be me finding him, but now he's craving the contact as much as I am.

God, he's so beautiful. Even with his eyes closed—they are, I think, my favorite part of him. Though I have to say his cock is pretty nice, too. And he damn well knows how to use it.

My guess is I top him maybe three out of four times, but every now and then, he gets in this aggressive mood and fucks the shit out of me. Yesterday, it was because he was celebrating, and he had all this energy he needed to get rid of. I happily volunteered as an object for his mood. Let's just say it was mutually satisfactory and leave it at that. My ass still smarts a little from his...enthusiasm.

I lean in and softly kiss his lips. He lets out a quiet little moan, and then those gorgeous eyes blink and open. A slow smile spreads across his face when he sees me. "Hey, baby," he says, his voice thick with sleep.

There's still a rush when he calls me that. I've had to work hard at getting my banana boy to trust me and open up to me, but it's been so worth it. "Good morning," I say and kiss him again, just because I want to.

"Is it time?" he asks.

"Nah. I woke you up a little early."

His smile widens. "You in the mood for some more celebrating?"

"Not if it involves your cock in my ass, babe. That was some serious pounding you did last night." He looks positively smug, and I grin. "Feeling good about ourselves, are we?"

His smile transforms into something else, something much deeper. "Yes, I am. I'm feeling really good. For the first time I can remember, I'm happy."

The look on his face makes me want to weep with gratitude. "You have no idea how happy that makes me, babe," I say.

We stare at each other with probably identical goofy smiles on our faces before he grabs my head and gives me a solid kiss. "Okay, enough with the sappy shit. How about a celebratory blowjob to wake me up?"

I reach for his cock, which is rock hard. "You look plenty awake to me."

He blinks his eyes, pouts. "Please? Because I'm super smart and awesome?"

He is, no doubt. He's graduating today, getting the degree he's worked so hard for. And I couldn't be prouder of him.

It hasn't been easy for him, this last year. Our relationship required him to do a lot of learning and confronting himself with baggage he never fully realized he had. And meeting Jackie and his sisters wasn't a walk in the park, either. They're not super close, yet, but they're in touch, and he's trying hard. That's all anyone can ask after what he went through, and I don't think Jackie was even expecting this much.

"You are super smart and awesome, but I'm not sure how that relates to getting a blowjob," I say.

"Dude, it's a blowjob. Work with me here."

We both laugh at those familiar words. My banana boy. I keep grinning until I take him in, because despite what some people think, you can't smile with a cock in your mouth. I dare you to try it.

I go for fast and dirty, and he's unloading down my throat in under three minutes. I haven't forgotten my skills, apparently.

"Mmmm," he sighs. "You're so damn good at that."

He pulls me up and gives me a sloppy kiss, licking out my mouth for the last remnants of his cum. When he's done, he cups my cheek. "I love you."

My heart jumps, as it always does when he says those words. They're still rare, and thus so precious to me. "I love you, too."

He looks at me as if he's waiting for something, and I scrunch my nose.

"Are you gonna ask, or were you planning on waiting till tonight?" he says with a mysterious smile.

"Ask what?"

He smiles. "Ask me to move in with you."

My mouth drops open. "How did you...?"

He gently shakes his head. "Did you really think I wouldn't notice how sneaky you've been about encouraging me to bring over more clothes? My study books? Dude, you had me install my PlayStation here 'cause you told me your TV was so much bigger, and it would be more fun for me to play here. Pretty much all my stuff is here except for my furniture and kitchen shit—which I don't use anyway."

Oh, shit. Apparently, I haven't been as stealthy and subtle as I had hoped. I clear my throat. "How did you know I wanted to ask you today?"

"I spotted a bill from your insurance company. You added me to your renters insurance, starting today. You're so freaking good at shit like that, by the way. Underneath that wild porn star beats the heart of a dependable man, baby."

I sigh, admitting defeat. The good news is that Troy doesn't look mad. More like, expectant, really. As if he still wants me to say the actual words. And then I realize it. He does. He needs me to say the words because he won't believe it's real until he hears me say it.

I take a deep breath. "I love you, Troy. So much. And I would love for you to move in with me. I wanna go to sleep every night with you in my arms, knowing you'll be there tomorrow and the day after. I wanna spend every morning waking up like this. I want to love you the best I can, if you'll let me."

I run out of breath, and all this time, he's been looking at me with a soft expression. "Are you asking me to move in or are you asking me for more? 'Cause that sounded pretty romantic to me, a bit over the top for a moving in request, really. More like a proposal."

My heart stops. It just stops. He's not mad, and he's not

freaked out, but there's something in his eyes I've never seen before. Something soft and loving and...trusting. "I was asking you to move in with me?" I ask, my voice barely audible.

He kisses me softly on my lips.

"Yes."

KEEP AN EYE OUT FOR MORE BALLSY BOYS!

Will Tank and Brewer end up killing each other? Will Mason stick by his declaration not to mess around with a porn star? And what's up with Campy, Heart, and Pixie?

Don't miss the rest of the Ballsy Boys series:

- Tank
- Heart
- Campy
- Pixie

MORE ABOUT K.M. NEUHOLD

Author K.M.Neuhold is a complete romance junkie, a total sap in every way. She started her journey as an author in new adult, MF romance, but after a chance reading of an MM book she was completely hooked on everything about lovely- and sometimes damaged- men finding their Happily Ever After together.

She has a strong passion for writing characters with a lot of heart and soul, and a bit of humor as well. And she fully admits that her OCD tendencies of making sure every side character has a full backstory will likely always lead to every book having a spin-off or series.

When she's not writing she's a lion tamer, an astronaut, and a superhero...just kidding, she's likely watching Netflix and snuggling with her husky while her amazing husband brings her coffee.

Stalk Me
Website: www.authorkmneuhold.com
Email: kmneuhold@gmail.com
Instagram: @KMNeuhold

Twitter: @KMNeuhold

Bookbub: https://goo.gl/MV6UXp

Join my mailing list for special bonus scenes and teasers: https://landing.mailerlite.com/webforms/landing/m4p6v2

Facebook Reader Group Neuhold's Nerds: You want to be here, we have crazy amounts of fun: http://facebook.com/groups/kmneuhold

MORE ABOUT NORA PHOENIX

Would you like the long or the short version of my bio? The short? You got it.

I write steamy gay romance books and I love it. I also love reading books. Books are everything.

How was that? A little more detail? Gotcha.

I started writing my first stories when I was a teen...on a freaking typewriter. I still have these, and they're adorably romantic. And bad, haha. Fear of failing kept me from following my dream to become a romance author, so you can imagine how proud and ecstatic I am that I finally overcame my fears and self doubt and did it. I adore my genre because I love writing and reading about flawed, strong men who are just a tad broken..but find their happy ever after anyway.

My favorite books to read are pretty much all MM/gay romances as long as it has a happy end. Kink is a plus... Aside from that, I also read a lot of nonfiction and not just books on writing. Popular psychology is a favorite topic of mine and so are self help and sociology.

Hobbies? Ain't nobody got time for that. Just kidding. I

love traveling, spending time near the ocean, and hiking. But I love books more.

Come hang out with me in my Facebook Group Nora's Nook where I share previews, sneak peeks, freebies, fun stuff, and much more:
https://www.facebook.com/groups/norasnook/

Wanna get first dibs on freebies, updates, sales, and more? Sign up for my newsletter (no spamming your inbox full... promise!) here:
http://www.noraphoenix.com/newsletter/

You can also stalk me on Twitter:
https://twitter.com/NoraFromBHR
On Instagram:
https://www.instagram.com/nora.phoenix/
On Bookbub:
https://www.bookbub.com/profile/nora-phoenix

BOOKS BY K.M. NEUHOLD

Stand Alones
Change of Heart

Heathens Ink
Rescue Me
Going Commando
From Ashes
Shattered Pieces
Inked in Vegas
Flash Me

Inked (AKA Heathens Ink Spin-off stories)
Unraveled
Uncomplicated

Replay
Face the Music
Play it by Ear
Beat of Their Own Drum
Strike a Chord

Ballsy Boys
    Rebel
    Tank
    Heart
    Campy
    Pixie
    Don't Miss The Kinky Boys Coming Soon

Working Out The Kinks
    Stay
    Heel

Short Stand Alones
    That One Summer (YA)
    Always You
    Kiss and Run (Valentine's Inc Book 4)

BOOKS BY NORA PHOENIX

Perfect Hands Series

Raw, emotional, both sweet and sexy, with a solid dash of kink, that's the Perfect Hands series. All books can be read as standalones.

- **Firm Hand** (daddy care with a younger daddy and an older boy)
- **Gentle Hand** (sweet daddy care with age play)

No Shame Series

If you love steamy MM romance with a little twist, you'll love the No Shame series. Sexy, emotional, with a bit of suspense and all the feels. Make sure to read in order, as this is a series with a continuing storyline.

- **No Filter**
- **No Limits**
- **No Fear**
- **No Shame**

- **No Angel**

And for all the fun, grab the **No Shame box set** which includes all five books plus exclusive bonus chapters and deleted scenes.

Irresistible Omegas Series

An mpreg series with all the heat, epic world building, poly romances (the first two books are MMMM and the rest of the series is MMM), a bit of suspense, and characters that will stay with you for a long time. This is a continuing series, so read in order.

- **Alpha's Sacrifice**
- **Alpha's Submission**
- **Beta's Surrender**
- **Alpha's Pride**
- **Beta's Strength**
- **Omega's Protector**

Ballsy Boys Series

Sexy porn stars looking for real love! Expect plenty of steam, but all the feels as well. They can be read as standalones, but are more fun when read in order.

- **Ballsy** (free prequel available through my website)
- **Rebel**
- **Tank**
- **Heart**
- **Campy**

- Pixie

Ignite Series

An epic dystopian sci-fi trilogy (one book out, two more to follow) where three men have to not only escape a government that wants to jail them for being gay but aliens as well. Slow burn MMM romance.

- Ignite

Stand Alones

I also have a few stand alone, so check these out!

- **Kissing the Teacher** (sexy daddy kink)
- **The Time of My Life** (two men meet at a TV singing contest)
- **Shipping the Captain** (falling for the boss on a cruise ship)

Printed in Great Britain
by Amazon